Marry Me Please, Cowboy

Marry Me Please, Cowboy

A Coyote Cowboys of Montana Romance

Sinclair Jayne

Marry Me Please, Cowboy

Copyright© 2023 Sinclair Jayne
Tule Publishing First Printing, September 2023

The Tule Publishing, Inc.

ALL RIGHTS RESERVED

First Publication by Tule Publishing 2023

Cover design by Lee Hyat Designs

No part of this book may be used or reproduced in any manner whatsoever without written permission except in the case of brief quotations embodied in critical articles and reviews.

This is a work of fiction. Names, characters, places, and incidents are products of the author's imagination or are used fictitiously. Any resemblance to actual events, locales, organizations, or persons, living or dead, is entirely coincidental.

ISBN: 978-1-961544-19-2

Dear Reader,

Marry Me Please Cowboy is a project I've been looking forward to for a long time because it is part of Tule Publishing's Tenth Anniversary September 2023. Tule Publishing was founded by Jane Porter with a big boost from several friends and authors—CJ Carmichael, Megan Crane and Lillian Darcy. They brainstormed the Tule created town of Marietta, Montana and the 75th Copper Mountain Rodeo. To celebrate, Jane, Carla and Megan and I gathered in Canmore, Canada to brainstorm the 85th Copper Mountain Rodeo. What fun we had discussing an end of summer rodeo in the deep winter of an Alberta Canada—spectacular scenery and even more incredible creative friends. We used the same titles of the original multi-author series, adding only a "please," to all of them. The story I wrote is also part of my Montana Coyote Cowboys—book two, where five former Special Forces soldiers head to Marietta Montana to carry a task or an amend for a fallen friend and to find their way back to the land and ranches where they grew up

I'd like to dedicate *Marry Me Please Cowboy* to the team at Tule Publishing who always has my back. Also, and always Jane Porter who means more to me than I can articulate. And of course a out to Jane, Carla and Megan who listened when I shared my ideas and sparked even more.

Sinclair Jayne.

Prologue

SERIOUSLY?

Willow McBride glared at the white and pink plastic stick with the two bold pink lines. Not one. Two. And not even a pale second one so that she could pretend. Not that she'd ever lived one day of her life in denial. She hadn't had that luxury because her mom was fragile—a creative, prone to migraines, and inexplicable impulses to sage rooms, sprinkle sea salt, read strangers' auras or walk barefoot into the night to communicate with spirits or head to her studio to paint.

By the time Willow had been six, she knew how to wake herself up before dawn, dress, do laundry, make breakfast, complete her chores, and pack a lunch and snack for herself and brother and run a mile down the gravel drive to catch the school bus. By eight, she'd mastered the art of casseroles and Crock-Pot cooking.

She'd been a mom to her mom before puberty and had no wish to repeat the experience.

Willow allowed herself one stomp of her electric-blue custom Kelly Boots with the fringe and white stars before she exited the rodeo fairground bathrooms. She cracked the stick in half and tossed it in one of the large metal trash receptacles brimming with cups of mostly drunk soda, kettle corn, cold fries, congealed 'cheese' on broken nacho chips and half-eaten hot dogs oozing mustard, ketchup and relish.

She dredged up her fan smile, the champion barrel racer one, and sharked through the crowds to the backstage area. Little Belt Cowboys Rodeo was the first in Montana's pro rodeo summer circuit, and she was two weeks late.

Breathe.

She should have skipped the exhibition Glacier Country Rodeo that had kicked off the rodeo season. She didn't have anything to prove, and it would have given her another two weeks to do repairs on the front steps and porch of the homestead house on the dwindling McBride ranch. She hoped to live in the tiny house, which once belonged to her maternal grandparents and had been absorbed into the McBride spread once they'd died.

But she'd wanted to make a good impression on the sponsors, maybe grab a few new ones before the season was underway. She'd imagined investing in the homestead house over the next few years just as she'd rebuilt the old barn so she could use it to launch her own horse training program. For years during the off-season, she'd worked at the Wilder Dreams stables for Tucker Wilder, who'd been her mentor, boss and friend. She liked working for Tucker but had had such an uncertain childhood fraught with financial difficulties that she wanted to have control over her destiny.

She didn't want fate or her dumb hormones to dictate squat.

She waved to a few of her competitors—the other barrel racers—preparing their horses, while her mind spun with regret.

She'd had a fun couple months with Jake Reynolds last season, but when she'd headed home in September, they'd both said goodbye and, she thought, meant it. But he'd been there smiling when she'd exited the winner's circle for the first exhibition event of the season, prize money in hand, ready to take her to a country-western honkytonk to celebrate and schmooze with the sponsors. Jake, a bull rider, was a favorite with fans and sponsors and so easy to say yes to.

I should have said no.

Shoulda, coulda, woulda. The words drum beat in her brain. But no. After a short autumn, long winter and cold spring working, finishing the renovations on the old barn, and helping her dad on the flailing ranch, paying bills and ensuring her mom ate, Willow had been ready for fun. Jake was a good storyteller, a better dancer and generous in bed.

"Dumb fun," she muttered still seeing those dang cheery pink lines taunting her though she'd trashed the evidence.

Just when she finally felt in control of her life and out from under the constant specter of poverty and fear for her Special Forces brother's safety, because he'd announced he was coming home for good, Willow had been tossed into the dirt.

She swallowed her dismay and panic. She could handle this. She had to. And she needed to pull herself together. She had to be one hundred percent when she and Montana Wind entered the arena this afternoon. Focus. No doubt. And with a baby on the way, the money would be even more important.

How long could she ride? How long could she hide it from her unpredictable mother and taciturn father? Heck, what would the fans think? And the sponsors? Rodeos projected the image of family-friendly events with far more conservative fans than Willow imagined other sports had. She and Jake had never talked about a future beyond the next rodeo or dinner and dancing date.

She'd have to tell him.

And that soured her stomach.

Don't think about it now.

She didn't want to think about it ever.

The financial insecurity and daily instability that had colored her entire childhood roared back with a vengeance, and she stopped walking, closed her eyes, and let her fingers brush along the worn wood of the corrals housing the horses. She breathed in the familiar scent: horse, dirt, sawdust, popcorn and fried food.

Focus. Only the next ride mattered.

She breathed in and out. Confident she could strong-arm her worry back into the dark hole in her head like she'd done as a child. Her mom and dad and the failing ranch needed her and her income. Her baby would need her—if she kept it, but could she give her baby up for adoption?

The lid on the panic and questions wouldn't stay shut.

She'd been a fool. She knew better. Last season she'd been on top, and she'd relaxed a little, let herself succumb to the flirtations of bull rider and part-time model and actor wannabe Jake Reynolds. Their romance had been casual and good fun, but quite public. She hadn't liked the public part, but being on the arm of a fan favorite had increased her visibility. Jake was very easy on the eyes and could charm anyone, including stupid her. She'd never been comfortable with the social elements of her job, but Jake had made them easy.

She wanted to kick herself for letting her guard down. She'd only ever relied on herself. But now Jake would be in the mix. What would he think? What would he want to do? Willow shoved the questions aside. She'd find out soon enough.

Chapter One

THE SLIDE OF metal just before the chute opened was the best sound in the world. But, no lie, it was potentially the most ominous. Today the hard hit and clang of metal—like a dozen miners hitting a vein of iron ore—heralded potential disaster. Two thousand pounds of bull crashed into the chute gate as Blasphemous's horn hooked metal. The huge head dipped before rearing back in panic, forcing Huck Jones to angle nearly parallel along the thrashing bull's spine. The gasps, shouts and shrieks messed with his whole keep-calm-and-carry-on rodeo cowboy vibe because his next move could get him killed.

That would be an unpleasant irony—he'd spent nearly a decade slipping in and out of global hotspots as army Special Forces only to bite it on the back of a bull in front of a bunch of summer tourists.

Huck Jones hit the dirt, rolled and clamored to the top of the chute gate as the same angry and disoriented two thousand pounds spun around to charge back into the chute. Huck hopped to the other side of the chute and dropped down to safety, not even breathing hard.

Not the best debut on the Montana circuit at the

Northwest Montana Fair & Rodeo in Kalispell, but since he was still vertical and breathing with nothing broken, not the worst.

He thought of the colorful blue words his brothers in arms would have shouted seeing that disastrous rollout but swallowed them. He shook with the flood of adrenaline and slapped his hat against his thigh—no helmet for him—he'd had to wear one for too many years in Special Forces. It felt too good to wear the black Resistol Cody Johnson that his foster granddad had kept safe for him through his multiple deployments. He did wear a mouth guard because Jim Austin, the old-school rancher outside of Cody, Wyoming, who'd taken him in at thirteen, had forked out eight grand for his first ever dental work and braces.

He'd also taught him how to read, do the ranch's books and study before giving him his first taste of public school when he enrolled him in his freshman year of high school after a year of intensive work to 'get him up to speed.' Jim had also taught him how to be a steward of the land and animals, finish what he started and to treat himself and others with respect, and how to pray, which is probably what he should be doing right about now.

"That sure was something to see." Jim, stood—still looking fit at seventy-five—on top of the chute and stared down at him, subtly checking for injuries.

Huck tongued out his mouth guard so he could speak. "Happy to amuse you."

"I ain't amused. Buckin' broncs don't got horns and after what you've been through, I'd hoped you'd lost your taste for danger."

Huck didn't have a taste for danger. He'd just wanted to pit his skills against a bull's. He'd been practicing this summer and had accrued enough points to try it at this rodeo, and he hated that he wouldn't get a score.

"You still intent on showing off?"

"Pretty sure that was an epic fail." He tried to keep the disappointment out of his voice. Sure, he'd ridden bulls and broncs as a teen, but this summer, his first out of the service, he and Jim had spent most weekends on the Wyoming rodeo circuit—kind of a bucket list for both of them. He'd had quite a bit of success steer wrestling and saddle-bronc riding, but bull riding had been tapping his shoulder. The purse was bigger and the points on the bull combined with the other events would guarantee his entry into the Copper Mountain Rodeo in Marietta, Montana, next weekend.

"Not necessarily," Jim drawled. "Bull's disqualified," he said laconically. "You going to give it another go?"

His thigh hurt where a hoof had caught him. His hip and ribs hurt from hitting the dirt, and he'd twisted his right wrist in the grip when he'd kicked out. Maybe he should stick to saddle broncs, but he'd been practicing on bulls during the Cody Nite Rodeo series all August and was getting a taste for it that he probably shouldn't.

"Heck yes, sir."

Jim gave a slight nod to the judging panel, and Huck heard his name announced and the crowd's cheers as another bull was led through the chute—not the one he'd ride, another cowboy was already queued up. But he'd get another shot today, and that was all a cowboy, and his mentor, who was also checking off another dream, could ask for.

He gave a final look at Jim, toothpick in his mouth—no longer the disgusting chew, finally, after his first dance with cancer three years ago. Turning away, Huck jammed his hat back on his head and walked toward his duffel to rewrap his thumb that felt like it had pulled out of the socket again. The ribbing from the other cowboys, who were regulars on the Montana circuit, which he certainly was not, was all part of the experience. He allowed the teasing to roll off him and mouthed off a few one-liners of his own.

Spending the summer honing his skills at the local weekend rodeos in Dubois or Cody when not competing on the Wyoming rodeo circuit had been something he and Jim could do together while they each faced a major life decision. Huck—what he was going to do after nearly ten years in the army and Jim—was he going to hand over full control of his cattle ranch to his great-nephews, both of whom had finished college and graduate school—one in ranch management and the other in agriculture. They'd come to work for Jim a couple of years ago.

Summer was easing into fall. Huck had been sent home on a forced medical leave by a team of doctors and army psychiatrists after a mission had gone deeply south resulting in his team leader's death. Huck had been offered the chance to muster out early with ten years being served, but he was no closer to a decision about his future.

He'd hoped to work alongside Jim on his ranch, but Huck suspected Jim had had another health scare he wouldn't discuss and was easing out of running his ranch with an iron fist. The great-nephews were smart, good men. Wyoming born and bred and blood family. They had a right to the legacy. He wasn't and didn't. After a week 'home,' seeing Jim visibly aged and suspecting the cancer might be back, Huck had let go of the Wyoming ranch dream. Still he'd signed his papers to muster out, determined to help Jim with whatever he needed or wanted.

Jim had been there for him.

But they were in Montana for this weekend through next because Huck had a promise to keep to his brothers from his unit—the Coyote Cowboys—and the brother they'd lost, Jace McBride. Jace had left a list of amends and Huck was determined to do whatever it took to settle that score for Jace.

"Perfection." Willow held the apple slice on her palm and her beautiful Arabian, Montana Wind, pressed against her, blowing out air first and nuzzling her neck. "Yes you."

She scratched her beloved horse's ears, who shuffled closer and leaned in for more love.

In June, the rodeo season too had kicked off with heavenly perfection. Willow had shoved her pregnancy to the back of her mind after telling Jake. She'd been rather stunned when he'd immediately suggested marriage. He'd been adamant. His dad had walked out on his mom and him, and he had no intention of being a 'deadbeat dad.'

Willow hadn't said yes immediately. Marriage was a big deal. Her own parents were still married, but she wouldn't describe it as happy, exactly. It was a lot of silence and distance. Still Jake was persuasive, even having her look at rings online. She didn't want the expense or the fuss of a wedding, but marrying Jake made financial sense. They'd have two incomes. She wasn't sure if he'd keep competing and trying to cadge modeling and a few acting gigs. That didn't seem a very practical lifestyle with a baby, but just as she didn't want him to stomp on her dreams and ways of doing things, she needed to afford him the same respect.

So after a few weeks, she'd agreed. They'd decided to marry before the Copper Mountain Rodeo so her parents could be with them and her brother would be home from the service. Willow still brooded about her decision and the unexpected pregnancy, but Jake was sunny side up and still pushing for a bit more of a splashy wedding—for publicity, she suspected.

She told him to keep their baby news under wraps because everyone would start treating her differently. She didn't want to lose her edge or any potential sponsors or have anyone speculate that she might leave the circuit.

"Will you stop racing?" Jake had been astonished at that idea.

She hadn't had an answer. She wanted to be present for her child in a way she hadn't felt her mother or father had been for her. But traveling every weekend with a baby in a horse trailer with tiny living quarters didn't sound ideal. That's when Jake had speculated about abortion, and Willow's soul-punched reaction told her that that had never been an option for her.

"So we're getting married." Jake had kissed her dizzy and June had unfolded like a dream.

But on the Fourth of July weekend when Willow had scored her best race ever, her life had flamed in the fires of hell.

Jace, within weeks of coming home, had been killed on a mission the army remained close-lipped about. His body had been shipped home, but before it had even arrived, her father had driven onto a parcel of land he'd recently sold to a neighbor—five hundred acres that included the house Willow had grown up in and several barns and other outbuildings—and under the indifferent gaze of a harvest moon, shot himself.

Her mother, never particularly strong, had with her doctor's encouragement, checked herself into the local Maybell rehabilitation facility for a 'rest.' Her aunt Barb, who'd recently taken an early retirement from teaching, had come to Marietta for the funeral and agreed to stay on with her sister. The new owner of their former land, local rancher, Taryn Telford, had suggested they stay in the house, rent-free, as he only needed the land. But her mom insisted they leave. She didn't want the memories, and she and her sister preferred to return to their ancestral home that was adjacent to the former McBride land. Willow's aunt had arranged the move into their original homestead with all the organized efficiency that her sister lacked.

Numb and shattered, Willow had, for the first time in her life, clung to a man. Jake acted the part of fiancé and coach—dragging her back on the pro rodeo circuit, with the encouragement that 'competing will get your mind off things.' He'd pushed her to excel and stay atop the leaderboard. Driving herself and winning were so engrained in Willow that she just turned off her brain, shut down her heart, let Jake take over and won. Over and over.

Jake too was having a good season, even though he often left for modeling assignments and auditions and parts as an extra on a few western-themed TV shows. He often insisted she attend sponsor events with him, introducing her as his fiancée and ensuring that they were often photographed and interviewed together though he did most of the talking.

For the first time in her life, Willow had felt safe and cared for, yet the irony was, the closer the Copper Mountain

Rodeo loomed on the calendar, the more she questioned the marriage.

Her professional life had never been better—even with the subtle changes in her body she'd started noticing this month, she'd never felt stronger, more in tune with Montana Wind and Big Sky Blue, more clear-headed. She continued to win, raking in prize money and endorsements. But she felt like she was perched on an unexploded bomb. Her baby. Her future. The ranch. Her mother. Jake.

She'd let him take charge those first couple months, and he was really good at it—too good. But Willow had an independent streak as big as Montana, and she was starting to chafe with Jake's demands and expectations.

She knew her dominance in barrel racing couldn't last. She regularly checked in with her OB, and the baby was healthy, but she couldn't picture herself taking an infant out on the circuit next summer—pulling off to the side of the road to nurse the baby. And who would watch the baby when she practiced and competed? She tried to picture Jake with a baby in one of those front-pack carriers and failed. But the press would love it—the cowboy daddy. He'd eat that up, but she suspected he'd get someone else to do the actual caretaking when the baby kicked up a fuss as babies had a tendency to do.

She rolled her eyes and pressed her face into Montana Wind's neck, absorbing her warmth, her strength, her scent and her certainty, because Willow was full of doubt. She called home several times a week. Her mother was home from her 'rest' at the Maybell, and so excited about the wedding—far more excited than Willow. During their last conversation, her mom had burbled about a garden wedding like she'd had and dropped that Jake thought that idea was 'charming and perfect.' Probably because he hadn't seen the dead grasses choking the homestead garden.

He'd been talking up the wedding more and more because he'd heard about a film documentary about the origin of America's rodeos, and the Copper Mountain Rodeo was one of the four or five rodeos featured.

"Picture it, babe," he'd said one night when she'd been brushing her teeth, hoping for an early night, but he'd been dressed to go out and meet up with a couple of friends at the bar. "Beautiful champion barrel racer—that's you." He'd smiled. "Handsome, attentive bull rider marrying on a legacy ranch shortly before the eighty-fifth Copper Mountain Rodeo. Your brother died while serving our country. The next generation is on the way to honor him. The name Jace works for a boy or a girl. Garden wedding. Whole town there."

He'd even used his hands as he spoke like he was framing a shot.

"The crew won't be able to resist. I can use some of the footage for my portfolio."

Willow had gagged on the toothpaste and Jake had called his agent before leaving for a few hours, although, she reminded herself, he always asked her to come with him. It was just that the smell of alcohol, fried food and so many sweaty bodies gagged her now.

Willow shook off the memory. She needed to stay present. This was the week she went home and married. She felt chilled even though the early September sun beat down on her. She didn't want a film crew to meet her mom or see the pitiful remainder of a once-thriving ranch. And what exactly was Jake expecting? She hadn't really thought about what he would make of her dreamy, unfiltered, often checked-out mother or her blunt, unsmiling aunt. Did he imagine the McBride ranch was some thriving enterprise straight out of a *Yellowstone* script?

She shuddered.

She never talked about her family. She never talked about home. Jake had been on a casting call during the funeral, and she'd been relieved.

Her phone buzzed. Willow pulled the phone out of her pocket. Her mother. Her heart leapt both with trepidation and hope. Willow never knew which version of her mom she'd get, but the past couple of months—since she'd shared Jake's proposal, if not his impending fatherhood, her mom had been making more of an effort. She took her medicine. Attended a weekly grief-support group at St. James church and had even traveled to Kalispell to help her twin sister to finalize the sale of her home and move back to Marietta.

"Hey, Mom." Willow shook off her worries and infused

her voice with sunshine.

"Hi, sweetie. What do you think about geraniums?"

"I've never thought about them."

"I don't think sweet peas or roses match your vibe."

She nearly gave the last word three syllables.

"And daisies seem too sweet. And black-eyed Susans, well you know what they say about yellow, although it's more of a goldenrod."

Her mother's voice was animated in a way Willow hadn't heard it since childhood, and even then, her mom's connections had been hit and miss.

"Why are we discussing flowers?" Willow asked cautiously, not wanting to prick the balloon of her mother's good mood.

"Your wedding, silly. I've been talking to Risa at Sweet Pea Floral about a bouquet for you."

Willow winced. She didn't want the fuss or expense. She was paying for everything and wanted to keep it simple and low-cost—not like there'd be anyone at the courthouse except her and Jake and her mom and aunt.

"And the dress Jake picked out for you is so beautiful, but risqué for a wedding dress. Something about a mermaid. I didn't quite catch it, but it looks like something one of those Hollywood A-listers—that's what Jake said—would wear on the red carpet. He said, you'd look like a princess?" Even her mom doubted her ability to pull that off.

"Jake what? A dress?" Willow pressed the heel of her

palm on her forehead as a headache begin its first pulse. Beside her, Montana Wind stomped once and stirred restlessly, not liking her rising tension or losing Willow's full attention.

Instinctively she scratched under Montana Wind's chin and forced herself to breathe. OK so she didn't have any dresses in the cedar-lined chest where she'd packed up the few clothes she kept at home. But she hadn't been planning to wear jeans for her wedding. She'd wanted to, but she knew Jake wanted the whole makeup, long hair curled and down, and dress look.

"Mom, I already bought a dress online." It had been an off-the-shoulder pale blue, midi sweater dress. She'd loved the color, simplicity and the fact that it had been clearance from last year, and she could wear it again—if she ever needed a dress, which she would not.

"Jake wanted you to look like a princess on your big day, and I have to say you certainly will make an entrance if you can walk."

Willow stared at her phone wondering what that meant.

"I hope none of the older ranchers have a heart attack."

"I'm not getting married at the rodeo, Mom, and I haven't invited any guests." Willow stomped on her temper. "And Jake has no say on my dress. He isn't wearing it."

Another, more important thought hit. "It's not purchased yet, is it? Who paid for it and how much?"

"That is certainly not my place to ask," her mother said

with dignity. "He ordered it with help from Lisa, who owns Married in Marietta. The fitting is this evening. The universe provides."

The universe most definitely did not provide—not for the McBrides.

"I just…" She stopped trying to think how to phrase all the worries that clashed in her brain.

"You worry too much," her mom stated.

Because her mom worried too little. She bit back the caustic words.

"I'm watching expenses."

Money had been tight as long as she could remember, and even with Jace's death benefits and the sale of the land paying off back taxes and providing a financial cushion for once, Willow still watched every dollar she spent and planned for the future. She hadn't yet met with the lawyer or a CPA to learn if there might be a large tax burden on the horizon with two family deaths so close together. And the to-do list to make the homestead house fully functional, safe and snug just kept unscrolling with every visit.

"It's a beautiful dress," her mother whispered. "You deserve to be a beautiful bride. You are my only child still living."

Willow winced at her mother's words, but was guilt strong enough for her to toss aside caution and her personality to wear some fantasy concoction of lace, satin, velvet or whatever? She'd never been one of those girls who'd stood outside and dreamed of floating around in one of the store's beautiful frothy confections for prom and definitely never for a wedding.

"Isn't that sweet?" her mom said. "He took time out of his busy schedule to find you a dress."

He better not be sticking me with the bill for a dress I don't want.

"Even though he's so busy Jake's weighed in on the flowers and the dress and he's set up a meeting with a film crew about a rodeo documentary or something like that," her mother said admiringly.

Not the film crew again—although that sounded disturbingly on brand. With the season winding down, Jake needed to focus, stick his rides and remain injury free. They would need the money with the baby coming. Acting was not a dependable source of income.

Neither is the rodeo.

But she'd been in the serious money all season and intended to stay that way.

Her mom chatted on about food. She and Barb were going to try the steak house in town to see if they liked the food and if they could cater the wedding lunch.

Wedding lunch? Catering? Flowers? Mermaid dress? This was turning into an over-the-top and expensive wedding spectacle.

She saw Jake duck out of her trailer, two large duffel bags slung over his shoulder.

"Mom, I gotta go," she said quickly. She had to get this wedding interference sorted before they arrived in Marietta this evening. "I'll treat you and Aunt Barb to dinner at Rosita's," she promised, keeping her gaze on Jake as he dodged around several trucks, his head uncharacteristically tucked down, and broad shoulders rounded as if he wanted for the first time in his life to be unnoticed.

"Love you, both," she said quickly and hung up, not taking the time to savor the fact that she could actually say the words.

"Jake." She sprinted after him. "Jake, hold up." The timbre of her voice was pitched low for a woman—she'd caught a lot of grief for it when she'd been a kid, but in her twenties, men had found her voice sexy. She sounded, according to more than one man and more than a few interviewers, 'like Dua Lipa'—if only she'd had access to a pinch of that kind of wealth, she could have saved a bigger portion of the McBride land.

"Jake!"

Bewilderingly it seemed like Jake picked up the pace. Willow was pissed. What was going on? And then a cowboy stepped into Jake's path and set his body. The cowboy was as dark as Jake was fair. And with the sun behind him, haloing him, he looked like something out of the pages of a western novel. The cowboy pointed at her.

Willow stopped running. It was embarrassing to have a stranger catch her fiancé, but more embarrassing that she'd been chasing him. Perhaps Jake had been wearing his new AirPods, that he'd ordered as a pre-wedding present for himself. She'd objected to the splurge but held her tongue. Jake was convinced being featured in the documentary—which wasn't at all a sure thing as far as she was concerned—was going to be the exposure that boosted him a rung or two up the acting ladder.

Jake turned around. His face split into a grin.

"Hey, baby, thought you were still in the sponsor tent."

"I finished early," she said, feeling a little breathless, but not from the sprint. The cowboy had yet to move away. He had an air of watchfulness that was a little intimidating. The sun was still behind him, and the black cowboy hat shadowed his features. And he was wearing chaps—black, fringe but no fancy detailing like most rodeo cowboys had.

Willow had seen plenty of men in chaps—Jake especially, so why was she staring? Guiltily she dragged her disturbingly fascinated gaze back to Jake.

"I thought we could get an earlier start and take my mom and aunt to dinner." She smiled and relaxed her shoulders that seemed stuck to her ears.

She waited for the cowboy to leave, but he didn't move. His stillness had an almost supernatural quality to it, like he was mythical.

No. I will not be weird like my mom.

Maybe the cowboy was overly protective, because even she couldn't deny the tension that snap, crackled and popped between her and Jake. She looked at his twin duffels. Those too looked new.

"Where are you going?" she asked, doing her best to keep any hint of demand out of her voice. Just as she didn't want to feel answerable to him, she wanted to respect Jake's independence, but they were marrying in a handful of days. Her parents hadn't had what she thought of as an ideal marriage, but even she knew they shouldn't be sneaking out on each other.

"Darlin'," Jake drawled even though she knew he was from outside Bakersfield, California. "We're not even married yet, and you're trying to tug on my chain."

"We're getting married on Thursday. That's four days from now." She briefly closed her eyes. He could count. "We need to talk about the wedding."

And how much it's suddenly costing.

"I have a callback and meeting with my agent."

"Today?" she squeaked. Clearing her voice, she grasped at calm. "Since when?"

Jake's smile tightened. "Babe, work comes first."

Hadn't that been the story of her life—the ranch, Jace, her mom's paintings and spirit guides had always come long before she ever had.

She stomped down the spurt of resentment. She was no longer a child. She owned her life. She felt rather than saw the cowboy's increased focus on Jake.

"Agreed," she said keeping her voice firm, but light and

her emotions locked tightly down. "But you were the one who wanted to get married," she reminded him, "and suggested we wait until the Copper Mountain Rodeo."

"And why wouldn't I, Willow? You are a beautiful champion, and it's your hometown." Jake's smile hit full wattage again, and she wondered what exact prize he thought he was getting with her and Marietta. He didn't seem any more equipped to be a dad than she felt to be a mom, and since she'd told him of her pregnancy, he'd been kind and sweet, but not nearly into sex like he'd been before, whereas Willow's appetite had increased to an embarrassing and almost desperate degree.

"That's why I asked my agent for a plane ticket and driver. I can do the callback, plus there's the possibility of another audition and a couple of meetings with casting directors on Monday. Then I'll head to your legacy ranch and hopefully meet with the documentary film crew on Monday night."

Willow felt the breath she'd apparently been holding on to leak out. Legacy ranch? Film crew? She didn't have enough spit to swallow. Surely she hadn't misled him. She rarely talked of home or her family.

"I'll be gone only one day, babe."

She looked at the two full duffel bags and couldn't let it go.

"Why do you need so much for a one-day trip?"

"Not sure what look the casting agents might want."

Again, he hit her with his beautiful, trademark, flirty grin, but it strained. "Why are you being possessive, babe?"

"I'm not being possessive," she denied. Was she? "You just didn't say anything about heading to LA, and the plan was…"

"Plans change," Jake said.

Willow's attention strayed to the cowboy who'd yet to move, but she could feel his dark gaze pin her to the dead grass of the fairgrounds parking lot.

"You mind, pal?" Jake glared over his shoulder. "This is private."

"You Willow McBride?" the cowboy asked. His voice grated a little like he didn't often use it.

"Yes." Her tension cranked.

"I'll stay then."

"What the hell?" Jake swung around and chest-bumped the cowboy, who didn't budge. Looking at his profile, Willow had the impression of the craggy peaks of Copper Mountain. He also had a scar that ran from the underside of his jutting jaw and angled down his throat along his trachea, visible through his casually buttoned black western-style shirt.

The scar looked newish, still pink against the deep tan of his skin.

"You really want to dance with me?" The cowboy asked softly as Jake continued to press into his space.

"Are you stalking my fiancée?"

"The fiancée you're scurrying away from like a city cockroach?"

"That's it." Jake dropped the duffel bags, his body puffing, and Willow stepped in, a frisson of alarm for Jake tingled in her chest.

"It's no big deal." She stepped close to Jake and took his arm, which quivered with tension. He shook her off.

Dang it.

"Careful of the lady," the cowboy said.

Lady. Willow nearly snorted like Montana Wind did when irritated. Willow had the impression that while Jake was gearing up for a bluff of *my testosterone meets your testosterone*, he wouldn't risk his good looks. But the cowboy didn't look like he postured or played games. He wore confidence as easily as his shirt, chaps and worn Wranglers. He held himself taut and still, ready for anything and reminded her a little of Jace during the few occasions he'd come home for any length of time.

Grief, anger and resentment that Jace had left, risked his life for twenty years, and was never again coming home, kicked her chest with the power of a hoof.

"Don't tell me what to do or how to treat my wife."

"Not your wife 'til Thursday," the cowboy reminded him. His voice was nearly a whisper, but it felt like a whip.

The cowboy was ballsy, but Willow wasn't in the mood.

"Jake, you don't want to be late for your pickup," she said and calmly reached for one of the duffel bag straps. And he definitely wouldn't want any bruises, but she kept that disloyal opinion to herself. "I just wish you'd told me you were leaving, that's all."

"It was last minute," he said sulkily, shooting her a look before pinning his attention back on the cowboy. "Besides, I don't have to check in with you about all my plans. We never had that kind of relationship before."

"No," she said, resentful that he made her sound like a nag. "We didn't. And we won't."

Jake's tension dissipated and his grin was more playful, mischievous.

"Course not, that's why I caught myself a cowgirl. Independent."

"Skilled with roping and training recalcitrant large animals," she said sweetly. "And independent means that I'll wear the wedding dress I chose. Have a good trip." She turned on her heel and strode back to her trailer to load up her horses and get on the road before she said something that she couldn't take back.

It took her a few moments to realize the cowboy was following her.

She spun around.

"I'm already pissed at one cowboy. You really want to make it a double?"

She could swear his inscrutable expression briefly exposed the promise of a smile that was quickly shut down.

"No, ma'am, but those amber eyes of yours sure catch

fire when you're mad, so it might be worth it."

"My eyes are brown."

"We'll just have to agree to disagree on that, ma'am. Amber and golden fire when you're riled."

"Ma'am," she dismissed. "You know my name." It was an invitation for him to get to the point.

"I know more than that."

"Really." Her voice cooled. She was at her trailer now with a stranger, who had not been intimidated by Jake's posturing. But she didn't feel threatened. Plenty of other rodeo cowboys and cowgirls were loading up on a sunny Sunday late afternoon, and the familiar sounds and smells soothed her temper and frayed nerves.

Montana Wind nuzzled the cowboy, and he spoke softly to the horse first in Spanish and then in English. He pulled a carrot out of the breast pocket of his shirt, and the horse gently took the offering. Montana Wind had never warmed to Jake, and she tried to not notice the difference.

She walked Montana Wind up the trailer ramp to join Big Sky Blue in the adjacent stall. While she checked the water, he added a flake of hay to the feeders and a scoop of oats without being asked.

"Okay, slightly intrigued." She hopped down and swung the doors shut on the trailer. "Who are you and why are you here?"

"Huck Jones." He stuck his hand out to shake, and without thinking, Willow slipped her hand into his warm, calloused one, shocked when a spark went all the way up to her shoulder. She stared into his black eyes. His pupils dilated and blended in with his dark irises, which made her feel like she was swimming in a midnight sky.

"And I care, why?" She tried to break the spell.

"I'm walking you down the aisle to give you away to that utterly unworthy prick."

Chapter Two

SHE JERKED HER hand away and swung around to slap him. She was fast, but he was faster.

He curled his fingers around her much smaller ones, two inches from his cheek.

He should have let her have the slap. He'd been out of line. But this was Jace's sister. Jace wouldn't have let that pretty but worthless cowboy duck out on his sister or flip her any attitude without returning fire.

But then the feel of her fingers flexing underneath his distracted him from his original intent.

Her beautiful amber eyes lightened to gold, and the dark flecks sparked, making him feel like he too was catching fire.

It was unlike him to be so imaginative. And unacceptable. Willow was Jace's sister. She was engaged. And ignorant that he was nearly as responsible for Jace's death as the sniper who'd gotten off the shots. Jace had slowly bled out in his arms despite Huck's battlefield wound training and almost mythical healing skills so that some of the men had taken to calling him doc. Jace had died choking on his own blood while forcing Huck to dig through his bloodied pants to find the list of amends Jace had written down for when he returned to Marietta. Huck had promised him that all his Coyote Cowboys would carry out his wishes.

Stay present.

"Now what?" he asked conversationally.

"You let go of my hand."

"And?"

"And?" One brow rose in cool inquiry, further stoking his inconvenient and unwanted attraction.

"You want an apology?"

"Not really an apology if I have to command it."

"Command? Interesting verb."

"I'm a thesaurus of action words," she stated. Her breathing was slightly elevated, and he shouldn't notice, but he did because her spectacular breasts strained at the snaps of her sparkling competition shirt.

"That so?" It was wrong to be enjoying himself. He'd have to unpack the hopelessness of that later.

"Release me." Something filtered through her gorgeous eyes—like a shaft of sunlight, and he wondered if he was having one-tenth of the impact on her as she was on him.

Unlikely.

She pulled away, pressing her palm against her thigh. They continued to stare at each other. He could practically hear the whir of her brain as she assessed him. She rocked back a little on her boot heels and tucked both hands in the back pockets of her dark denim blindingly blinged jeans. Yeah, he'd noticed her pockets with rhinestones in the shape of crosses worshipping her ass.

Amen.

"So, Huck Jones—" she said his name like she didn't believe it was real, and she wasn't exactly wrong there "—you don't like my fiancé, but you're walking me down the aisle," she prompted.

"I served with Jace." He forced the words out.

She staggered back. Her heel hit a divot in the fairgrounds parking lot grass, and even though she easily rebalanced herself, he'd instinctively stepped forward, both hands on her slim but taut arms to steady her.

"You're a soldier?" she whispered, sounding tortured. Confusion clouded her pretty features. No wonder. He looked like every other cowboy packing up their horses and rigs and heading home or to the next rodeo.

"Was," he said, not willing to tell her anything more. "Cowboy again now. Cowboy forever." One thing he was certain of.

She jerked a nod, then her gaze skittered away from him as if he was just too much to take in. She pressed her hands on her cheeks—they trembled—and then she wiped her palms down her face. He couldn't help himself, he took her hands in his, but this time they were ice cold.

"You knew my brother?" Her voice shook, and she sounded so young, so lost, that he had to fight the impulse to pull her into his arms. He had done this—destroyed her family.

"He was the best man I've ever met," he said honestly, although Jim, who'd taken him in as an angry, flailing, feral kid who'd already been tossed out of four group homes, also sat on top of his list. "Absolutely the best man."

He heard the crack of her palm against his cheek before he felt the sharp sting of pain.

"I'm sorry," she whispered, horror filling her like a pitcher of ice water on a summer day.

Twice she'd tried to slap a stranger. He'd let her succeed the second time. Her knees buckled with shame, yet her body felt cold and rigid as a block of ice. What was wrong with her? She was never out of control. Never. She wasn't her mother, a tumbleweed tossed into the maelstrom of her emotions.

She sagged onto the steps of the living quarters of her trailer.

"Lower your head." His voice was like melted caramel with nuts, interesting, yet soothing her, dragging her back from the brink of something.

"Breathe in through your nose on a count of four and hold for four, then release on four," he said softly.

Willow closed her eyes. She could listen to his voice forever.

"You should be a late-night radio DJ."

"I put people to sleep?"

There was a hint of amusement in his voice—not what she'd been expecting considering her shameful behavior.

"You should be angry with me," she told him.

"Breathe," he said, and Willow, who normally never let anyone boss her, except Jake the past crazy couple of months, complied.

Twice. And then again. Her lack of control scared her. So did her light-headedness and the way her vision had grayed at the edges. Was it her emotions? The baby? She drew in a deep, shuddering breath, even more worried and dismayed.

This was the first time she'd let herself think about the baby—its well-being. She was an athlete at the top of her game and always ate for fuel and health so other than adding a prenatal vitamin, she hadn't made many adjustments to accommodate the new life.

Other than agreeing to marry the baby daddy.

"I am sorry." She said the words slowly, meaning them. "I'm not usually so impulsive or emotional. You didn't deserve that. I don't think I've ever slapped anyone, not even at a sponsorship party when a cowboy got a little too handsy."

"You pack a wallop. Good to know." Huck smiled, and she loved the way his eyes creased, lending warmth to his angular, ethnically ambiguous features that looked a little like those stone idols on some far away island.

"Not exactly the family-friendly brand the rodeo sponsors want," she said almost holding her breath to see if he'd smile again.

"The first time I deserved. Second bucked me off the plot."

"Yeah, me too," she admitted, feeling an answering smile tug at her lips. "But Jake was acting weird and then when you mentioned…Jace." She looked away, hating the spurt of resentment that felt volcanic.

Couldn't she grieve her brother like normal people did—with buckets of tears and taking to her bed for weeks? Instead, she'd raced out onto the rodeo circuit days after she'd buried half her family.

His hand lightly shackled her wrist, and she liked his calloused warmth, the quiet strength. He must think she was as high-strung as an Arabian.

"Can I get you some water? You're still pale, and your breathing and heart rate are elevated."

"That's because…" She bit back her admission that it was his fault her body was on high alert. His heat and combined scent of leather and bergamot and the way his onyx eyes seemed to sear through her armor and touch her soul all combined to put her body on high sexual alert.

He was effortlessly potent.

What would happen if he tried?

She needed to cling to her control. She wasn't an animal, subject to her hormone surges or a man's pheromones.

"Of course you are," he said.

She pressed her fingertips against her lips. "Did I say that out loud?"

He nodded, and she saw a hint of a smile in his dark eyes. His eyes had a devastating power that seemed to sear right through her to her soul.

What's happening? It's like we've…no. I don't want to think weird thoughts like my mom.

Panic spiked.

"And so am I."

Wait. Did he feel this intense, inevitable pull too? Alarms clanged through her. This was impossible. She wasn't her mother. She was responsible. Not impulsive or reactive to 'feels' or whims of the universe. There was no magic fate. No outside destiny. She was in total control.

Never before had she felt both thrilled and terrified.

Pull yourself together.

"I've got a few hours' drive ahead of me." She cast a quick look at the sun. She wanted to make it home before dark, but she needed to do something routine and mundane before she climbed in her truck hauling her two precious horses.

"I'm going to make some tea. You want anything?"

Switching to tea from coffee had been the one concession she'd had to make since the baby. She hadn't been a big fan of alcohol since her father had climbed into a bottle and often stayed there. Sure, she could shoot whiskey socially if an occasion warranted, but usually it didn't.

"I'll take a coffee if you've got it. No worries if you don't."

"I do."

"What time Thursday?"

Willow stood, and he rose with her, their breath mingling, and for a moment she wondered what he would taste like. Feel like. He had such a contained energy, but she could still feel it tangle with her own and hum through her body.

She retreated into her trailer and turned on the electric kettle and warmed up the Keurig. She pulled two mugs down from the locked cabinets. The trailer quarters were tight, but she'd left the door open and caught a whiff of citrus, leather, bergamot and earth. It was viscerally appealing, and her mouth watered like she wanted to take a bite.

"Why do you think you're walking me down some mythical aisle?"

"Mythical?" He remained on the grass of the parking lot outside, but still radiated a presence. "You're not marrying in a church?"

His shock, which bordered on offense, should have been funny, but his reaction embarrassed her in some way. Jace and her aunt too had assumed she'd have a big wedding at St. James church, which she'd attended throughout her childhood.

To cover her discomfort, she pawed through her tea bags, and pulled out her collection of coffee pods.

"I wanted to keep it small, simple. The courthouse will do."

"Will do?" His voice was low and rough but held a tone that seemed to pluck something deep inside her body. Probably he was judging her. So many people did.

"You don't have a right to an opinion," she told him. "My mom and Jake are trying to turn my getting married into something more."

"Don't Jake and your mom have a say in the wedding? It's a big deal. Lifetime commitment."

Her heart jumped to her throat, choking her, and she willed the electric kettle to boil. "It's not your business."

"Jace planned to walk you down the aisle. So that's what I will do." He was back to looking like a stone idol again.

She should be irritated, but he was insanely hot and his directness and confidence was comforting in an unexpected way.

"What flavor?" She changed the subject and showed him the basket of Keurig pods.

"Barista's choice."

She popped in a pod and let the hiss of brewing coffee and hum of the machine speak for her for a moment while she gathered her thoughts.

"Why Jake?" Huck cut to the chase. "Pursuing acting is hardly a responsible career choice for a married man, especially in Montana."

His tone was low, his voice husky, cutting out in a couple of places, but she could feel his high-horse judgment just fine.

"Neither is a rodeo cowboy," she snarked. "But I'm not marrying Jake thinking he'll take care of me. I take care of myself."

Willow had been responsible for herself for as far back as she could remember. Her parents or big brother hadn't coddled or protected her.

"Been doing it for years, so you can ditch the cowboy-soldier side-eye."

"Marriage is a partnership."

"You married?"

He shook his head.

The coffee finished and she handed him the mug, certain he took it black, no sugar. There was no hint of sweetness in the intensity of his black eyes or in the hard edges of his face and hewn body.

"Go on," she invited. "You, a single man, a single soldier, a single cowboy were going to tell me what marriage is." She kept her advantage standing tall in the doorway of the trailer, while he stood outside, backlit.

"I'm not the one marrying," he said softly and took an appreciative sip.

Willow had to tear her fascinated gaze away from his strong, tanned throat, and that dangerous scar that snaked down and disappeared under fabric even though two snaps of his shirt were parted—so he felt no need to hide the scar.

It was also impossible to ignore the flex of muscle in his forearms with his sleeves rolled up to his elbows.

She turned her back on him to make her tea. What was she doing, flirting? Lusting? She was getting married in a few days. She was knocked up.

"You're right." She poured the hot water over the tea leaves, not letting it steep longer than ninety seconds. "I am the one taking the plunge into the unknown."

She tried to make it sound like a game. She'd committed to Jake. She was loyal. It was time to break the spell Huck seemed to be weaving between them. If she were her mother, she'd think he was a spirit guide coaxing her back on the correct path.

No. Wait. That thought stopped her. She was on the right path. Her hands shook a little as she prepared her tea. She didn't like her doubt. It was weakness, and she wasn't letting Jace's soldier friend best her.

"So, Huck, how did you get stuck with the archaic notion of giving away your dead comrade's sister's hand in marriage? Unlucky?"

I'M IN TROUBLE.

No doubt.

Her half-smile, when she handed him his coffee, nearly knocked him sideways. She reminded him then of Jace. Her sass in the face of her pain that felt like a shot to his solar plexus. She was cowgirl tough. And the way her eyes lightened—caught the light—as if the hints of yellow swirled around revealing a new emotion or facet felt like a pool of fire beckoning him to jump in and burn. Then there was the slight cleft in her chin—more of a divot than Jace's, and a hint of dimples that Jace had not had. Dimples had been a weakness he hadn't realized he had.

She was Jace's sister. Almost another man's wife.

Her fire and her flirt were as natural to her as breathing and were definitely going to be a test.

He looked up at the sky as if he'd see God laughing at him.

"Hey." She left the trailer and joined him on the grass. "I'm kidding." She blew on her pale-colored tea that smelled like lemon and something spicy—ginger maybe. "There's not going to be an aisle. And a man like you—getting anywhere near a bride will give you terminal heebie-jeebies."

"Not sure what those are."

She laughed and stuck out a slim, toned arm. Her royal-blue western shirt with silky black piping had the sleeves rolled up to her mid forearm. "It's when the hair stands up on your arm, and you feel quivery inside. Mine are hiding right now, but they're there."

"I'm pretty tough," he noted holding out his arm next to hers. Her skin tone was so creamy, flawless. He was such a contrast of dark to light, scarred to flawless.

"I was never one of those girls who dreamed about floating down a church aisle in an ice cream cone of a dress with an audience and pledging my fealty to a man. And the first father-daughter dance? Forget it." Her voice turned bitter.

She sipped her tea, lowering her lashes—heavily mascaraed black, whereas her eyebrows matched her strawberry-blonde thick hair that was slicked back in a low ponytail that he itched to touch.

"Then why marry?" Especially a jerk who'd walk out to take a bunch of dumb meetings, leaving her to drive several hours home alone.

She looked up and he caught the flash of vulnerability that he hadn't expected. She looked away across the parking lot. It was half-empty. He could see his truck and trailer parked two rows away. He'd already loaded his beautiful black quarter horse. He'd purchased the horse in Wyoming from Jim, who'd trained him. Jim, with no creative bones in his body, had called the majestic horse Midnight, and Huck had left it.

Jim was originally going to ride with him into Marietta, but he'd contacted an old friend—Ben Ballantyne—who'd shown up at this rodeo, and they'd hung out together all day and now Jim was riding shotgun with Ben and planning to stay the week at the Three Trees Ranch. Huck, who would be competing in two Copper Mountain Rodeo events next weekend, had the week free until Willow's wedding.

The silence stretched, and he thought she wouldn't answer.

"I have my reasons," Willow said.

"Good enough." He touched the brim of his hat to tell her he'd let it go for now, even though, for Jace's sake, he wasn't sure he should.

"You don't have to do this," she said. "I've been without Jace as a constant in my life since I was eight."

That rocked him. He'd always envied Jace his family. "I'd imagined y'all were tight-knit."

Her full lips, which he'd been trying not to think of as pillowy, tightened.

"You imagined wrong." She sipped her tea moodily. "I don't want to destroy any…memories or…feelings you cherish about Jace." She looked directly at him. "If you served with him. You probably knew him better than I did."

Her words lanced his core. Jace had talked so eloquently about his family, his ranch, joining them again on McBride land. Rebuilding the legacy. He'd invited all his brothers to join him. Make homes in Marietta. Create businesses together.

"I wasn't an oops baby," she continued. Her slightly husky voice that was low and sexy AF was having a definite impact on one rebellious part of his body he usually could control better.

"My mom and dad tried to have more kids after Jace. She lost quite a few, and it…" Willow broke off, and Huck thought he saw a wave of something rush over her face—

grief? Fear?

    He took a step forward, hand on her shoulder.

    "Willow?" He tried to see into her eyes.

    She spun away from him. "I never really thought about that." She sounded distressed. "Maybe that's why…" She broke off and shook her head as if the unpleasant realization could fall out.

    "Any assumptions you have about my parents, our family, the ranch are just that. Assumptions. Jace was ten when I was born. He joined the army after high school and most of our communication was video chats or texts. He didn't come home all that much, and when he did it was for visits that were invariably cut short by a super-secret mission he could never share."

    She looked across the emptying field as if some answer hid behind one of the few remaining rigs. "When he was home, he and my dad would be out on the ranch talking about the future that never was. My dad and Jace were close. Jace and my mom were his…everything."

    It was a long speech that revealed more than she likely wanted. It also sounded like the knell of doom for his dream to meet a happy family. He should have known—not like he hadn't wondered why Jace had planned to walk his sister down the aisle instead of his father. He wanted to ask but didn't. He was here for Jace. Not himself. Everything was need-to-know—just like many missions he'd run.

    If she'd poured out the beverages in to-go cups he could

have made an excuse and gotten in his truck and waited to follow her home, because he wasn't going to let her drive alone, even if she wouldn't appreciate what she'd no doubt think of as his unwanted cowboy chivalry.

"I'm getting married on Thursday." She stated the obvious and drained her tea.

Then she went into her trailer and washed out her cup before securing it in the locked cabinet. He finished his coffee, wanting to wash it out himself, but not wanting to crowd her in her space.

She smiled, probably at his dilemma, as she took his cup and washed it.

"I'm not conflicted about getting married," she said. "But I'm not happy that it's turning into a wedding extravaganza. I don't want the expense. I'm saving to start my own business."

She did seem goal-oriented. Certain. Huck's admiration continued to rise even as his confusion about something indefinable also mounted. She seemed shadowed as if hiding secrets. Huck's life was defined by secrets, and he could smell them.

"I know you want to honor Jace, but you don't need to be a part of whatever circus Jake or my mom are dreaming up. I think Jake is hoping for some publicity or something because there's a film crew working on a documentary about the history and evolution of rodeos in the west and Marietta's Copper Mountain Rodeo is one of the rodeos they're featuring. Jake likely thinks that because I'm a hometown girl I'll get fifteen seconds of fame, and he wants to be by my side."

"That's a little cynical."

She secured his cup as well.

"Not the blushing bride. Surprise, surprise." She hopped down beside him. Her expression smoothed as the sarcasm disappeared in the afternoon breeze that had kicked up.

She locked the trailer door and folded up the stairs, even as he moved to help.

"I don't mean to be unfriendly." She touched his arm, her expression rueful. "You're a friend of Jace's and that means you're welcome at our home, such as it is."

What the heck did that mean?

"My mom…she's…well, she's my mom and Jace's mom, and I guarantee she's not what you're expecting."

"Not expecting anything."

That got her attention.

The sun that had been playing peekaboo with the clouds lost its hiding place and bathed Willow in a golden light that turned her thick ponytail fiery, and he realized then that he'd been lying to himself and to her. He had been expecting something, hoping for something he couldn't name, but had never had.

"I can never decide if that's sad or not," she said softly. "To have expectations and be disappointed or to not have them."

He didn't have an answer for that, and he felt out of words. He'd never been much of a talker. That had been Jace or Ryder Lea, another of the Coyote Cowboy brothers.

"You never told me, why you?" she prompted. "Why did you get this absurd task?"

He didn't want to tell her the randomness of picking this 'amend' out of her brother's bloody helmet. The desperate last words. The cruelty of fate.

"You're right. I didn't."

She blinked. He tipped his hat and turned and walked to his truck.

"Seriously? Huck? Why you?" she called out behind him.

He didn't bother to turn around because she was already hard to walk away from. Jace's sister kicked up feelings he shouldn't have. Had never imagined he could have. And he wanted to think about that. Not. But he had to prepare himself.

"Why you?" Her repeated question floated up, and he lifted a hand in a goodbye.

"Yeah, Jace," he mused under his breath. "Why the hell, me?"

Chapter Three

WILLOW SANG THE final Miranda Lambert song on this playlist and gave up the fight to not stop and pee. Just one of the irritating reminders of being pregnant, which she kept trying to ignore.

She signaled at the next rest stop, and like a shadow, Huck too pulled over. She peed and did a few stretches. A local 4-H group was selling baked goods as a county fair fundraiser, and Willow bought a huge brownie with walnuts and chocolate chips that were slightly melty from the heat.

"Delish. Keep the change." She handed over a ten and smiled at the two girls, who stared at her transfixed. Likely they were rodeo fans.

"What animals do you show?"

"Mustangs," they both said. "We're part of a nonprofit that helps protect wild mustangs, and we raise money also for 4-H. If we raise enough, we can adopt one of our horses that we train for the year. That's why Jesse and I do extra fundraisers and work after school." Their words tumbled over each other, and they bounced on their toes enthusiastically.

Had she ever been that excited?

Willow's heart pinched. She knew all about working hard and working young and falling in love with a horse you couldn't have.

"I'll take another two brownies, One for my mom and one for my aunt," she said, feeling Huck approach rather than hearing him.

"You're shorting your dad?" Huck asked, pulling out a twenty and handing it to the two girls as they handed her two more brownies wrapped in plastic wrap.

Just like that her body went numb and everything sounded under water. Huck didn't know about Jace's dad. How could he? He'd been worlds away. This was not the time or place to tell him.

"No," she said, pulling her brownie in two and giving him the much bigger piece. "This is for you. I'll feel less guilty about the calories."

She hadn't planned to have more than a bite. Since the accusing pink lines, she'd severely limited all indulgences, wanting to keep her weight gain minimal until after the finals.

He looked at her body—and it felt more like a medical assessment than a man looking at an attractive woman, and she wanted to kick herself for noticing his appraisal at all. Sheeze. She shouldn't want him to notice her as a woman. But she did. Jake hadn't seemed all that interested in her body lately, even though she hadn't changed much physically except that her breasts were fuller and more sensitive.

Even thinking about her breasts with Huck this close felt sinful and as decadent as the brownie she held.

Huck took a bite of the brownie and chewed thoughtfully like he was a food judge.

"You've got some baking skills," he said quietly to the two girls. "You barrel racers?"

"We want to be." They bounced up on their toes again. "We get to practice sometimes at the stables where we work extra on the weekends."

They answered him but looked at Willow.

"That's how I started getting my practice time—working in a stable for time on a horse."

"Can we take a selfie?"

The girls whipped out their phones from their back pockets so quickly Willow laughed. "It's like the new fast draw in a western."

They posed together doing some serious and some goofy ones, and Huck took a picture of all of them with Willow's phone. He purchased two more brownies with another twenty before they headed back to their rigs.

"You're a ke—" She broke off before she said the revealing word. "Polite, Huck Jones. Your mama raised you right," she teased, lifting her leg behind her and angling to kick him lightly in the butt.

She'd almost called him a keeper. Why was she becoming the flirtiest huss in Montana?

"My mother didn't stick around long enough to warn me

about anything."

He stopped walking. So did she.

"Forget I said that."

It was an impossible thing to unhear.

"Oh, Huck." Without thinking she stepped into him, one hand splayed on his forearm. She could feel the tension and strength vibrate in his body, and yet he looked so fluid and Zen.

"I'm so self-centered. I've been feeling sorry for myself and unsettled about going back home, but I had a mom and dad growing up even if they weren't ideal. And a home even though money was tight." She nibbled on her lip, shamed at her selfishness. "And until Jace left home he was a good big brother. Helped me when he could. I hated that he left and I dwelled more on his absence than the time we had together."

Why had she wasted so much time on the negative? She kept her gaze steady on Huck so that he'd see her sincerity. He was also disturbingly easy on the eyes, but she needed to remember this epiphany. Let it guide her as she raised her own child. She wanted her baby's childhood to be so different from hers.

He stared back and Willow could pinpoint the exact moment looking into his black gaze changed for her and for him. His eyes lit, heated, intensified so that she felt like she was being touched. She yearned to step close to his body, feel his heat and strength and shape. Did it fit with hers? Her nipples pebbled in her lacy bra—no way he wouldn't notice that through her tank top as she hadn't rebuttoned her shirt.

The late afternoon breeze kicked up warm and playful, ruffling his hair so that a lock fell across his flat, wide forehead. She reached up to brush it aside, but he caught her hand.

"Don't," he said.

She felt the blush wash over her cheeks and down her neck to her collarbone. She was flirting. She was wanton. And she didn't even really care. She was standing on a metaphorical precipice, but instead of feeling like she was about to fall, she felt like she could finally fly.

"Just testing your gentleman skills," she said lightly.

He was still holding her arm, one thumb on her inner wrist, and she internally begged him to stroke her, do something to prove she wasn't the only one affected by this energy that hummed and surged between them.

"Not sure I have too many where you're concerned, Willow McBride."

She thought he was joking, but there wasn't a hint of fun in the hard, stern planes of his face. Nor was there emotion, and it was as intriguing as it was unsettling. What would it take for this man to laugh, to smile, to relax, to love?

"But I am following you to your home. And I am walking you down the aisle."

"To marry another man," she prompted herself as much as him.

"Definitely."

There was no give in his voice and, really, did she want there to be? She was conflicted enough about the concept of marriage. Her parents had left nothing to idolize. Jake had felt easy. Safe. So now why was she courting impossible and dangerous?

Jake was fun. Kind. He wouldn't be taciturn and distant. He was health-conscious. Goal-oriented, even if they didn't share the same goals. He wouldn't drink himself unconscious night after night. Jake was simple, social. He wouldn't disappear for hours 'painting.'

She was making the right choice.

"Just wedding nerves," she tried to joke, but couldn't quite force a smile. "You know."

"Can't ever see myself marrying," Huck finished the brownie. "Wouldn't know the first thing about a relationship." He truly looked puzzled. "What woman would want a man like me?"

"Like you?" she echoed. They were standing in a rest area parking lot facing each other like they had all the time in the world to catch up when she knew she had to get on the road and get her horses settled and somehow sort out her wedding plans with her mom. And she'd need to let her know about the baby at some point. Maybe after the finals.

What in the world did Huck think would deter women from him? He was hot. Protective. Respectful. He listened. She'd seen him check on his horse before they'd driven off. That horse was loved and cared for. Not much else to say.

"Willow," Huck said after a pause that should have been awkward but wasn't. "Not that I object. I don't. I'm here and willing, but why was Jace planning to walk you down the aisle, not your dad?"

There was not enough time to explain that, but she couldn't refuse the pull in those onyx eyes. They sucked her in like a black hole.

"Our father drank. Jace probably wasn't sure he'd be sober enough to do it."

"Drank?" She heard the alert pick up.

She closed her eyes as if that would stave off the memory of the sheriff's visit. His closed-off expression, knowing he was a harbinger of doom on a family already shattered. "He killed himself when we learned the news about Jace."

"Willow."

The pain of his voice snapped her eyes open. Huck hadn't even known her dad, yet he was staggered by the news, whereas she just kept trudging through life, head up, gaze forward. Don't think. Don't remember.

"The bullet just beat the alcohol," she said, feeling numb. "But really my dad had checked out years ago when Jace left and stayed away."

"But Jace had all these plans." Huck looked pale. "He was coming home. He talked about you and your family all the time. He was so proud of your career and your goals of training cutting horses and barrel racing. He wanted to work the ranch with his dad again. Bring it back to financial health. He had this list of amends and things he planned to accomplish."

She thought about the tragedy inherent in Huck's words.

It sounded like Jace was trying to rewind the past, and for the first time in her life Willow wondered if perhaps Jace had been running away to the service rather than running toward something.

And yet Jace had had a successful career. Promotions. Medals. He'd been a leader, someone a man like Huck had respected to the point he was willing to complete a task for.

"You showing up here to walk me down the aisle sounds like something out of a movie." She struggled not to think about her brother, so far away and hurting, planning to come home yet being cut down before he could do it. If she started to cry, she'd never stop.

"But my life has no resemblance to a movie. Not one piece of it. You should turn around, Huck Jones. There's no need to keep a promise to a dead man. I told Jace in early June I was getting married, but never made him promise to walk me down the aisle."

She'd never imagined that would be a possibility even if she'd wanted him to. And then he'd died a few weeks later.

"I'm the man making the promise." His tone was a vow, and he looked like a Paleolithic god as he uttered the words.

"Fine." She shrugged a shoulder, not wanting him to see how much his words, his demeanor, her brother's almost delusional intentions were having an impact on her. But she knew that her resistance was also unfair to Huck. Just as Jace's wishes and his death had thrust Huck into the middle of her drama, her desire to just get the legal part of the marriage over with at the courthouse was keeping him there.

"We all got something to make amends for."

HUCK FOLLOWED THE skillfully driven horse trailer toward Marietta with his mind in turmoil. A task that should have been easy—although nothing about marriage sounded easy to him—now had complicated stamped all over it.

The warm, welcoming family he'd expected to find steeped in grief, but pulling together for the joy of a wedding, now sounded as if they hadn't existed long before Jace's death. And the radiant bride definitely gave the sun a run for its money in shine, but she didn't seem happy. And the toe of his boots itched to kick the groom permanently into California. Actor, his ass. Absurd. The groom was playing at being a cowboy biding his time to become an actor who would then likely pretend to be a cowboy.

Huck tapped the beat to the ridiculously catchy 'Old Town Road' on his steering wheel as he followed Willow down the steep mountain pass. The song was weird and a dirge-like quality in places—a touch of grim he could relate to. He wished he could sing, but even before his injury he couldn't carry a tune. Jace had sung all the time.

The song suited his mood.

It was a good thing he'd been following because Willow's truck blew a tire about fifty miles out of town, and though she'd capably kept the truck and trailer under control, Huck about had a heart attack.

He popped out of his truck, grabbed his tool kit from under the driver's seat and stalked over, his heart still painfully pounding. He'd been cooler under sniper fire, and he rubbed his knuckles along his sternum as if that would settle the frightened beast down.

Willow pulled her own tool kit from behind her driver seat, but he brandished his, which was bigger. "I got it."

"Why?" She held her tool kit against her chest. "Because you're the man?"

"No, because I got it, and Jace would kick my you know what if I didn't help his sister change a tire on her truck."

"Who do you think taught me to change tires while on leave?" she asked sweetly.

"Thought you might want to check on your horses after the blowout." If he thought that would have her yielding, he was wrong.

"I will. I'll have to unhitch to jack up the truck."

So they'd worked together, and Huck who was used to controlling his emotions, shelved the attraction, except when he would catch her scent or they'd accidentally touch; but the companionship was harder to ignore. He'd missed that since leaving the military. Sure, it was possible to find it on the rodeo circuit, but he didn't like hitting the bars. And after ten years in the service, he didn't fit in anymore. Besides, he'd told himself, he was rodeoing to spend time with Jim.

"What was one of the things you liked the most about my brother?" Willow asked as she twisted on the first lug nut.

"Just one?" He handed her the second lug nut.

She paused and looked at him. Her smile was filled with sadness, and her amber eyes darkened.

"That's sweet," she said. "Really? More than one thing?"

"So many." His voice broke, and he had to clear his throat. "Jace always saw the good in people. He saw their potential. He had patience. He didn't have to assert his will or get in anyone's face or make them feel small to get his point across. He not only could listen, but he also wanted to listen."

For a moment, she looked as if his words had struck her. Tears filled her eyes, and she quickly turned back to the tire, speedily screwing on the second and then third lug nut.

More than a few tears traced down her cheeks that looked petal-soft, and he wondered what her tears would taste like, and how it would feel to have the right to wipe them away.

What was wrong with him? Willow didn't need him. And if she knew that he'd been responsible for Jace's death, she'd kick him to the other side of the county.

She finished twisting on the last lug nut, and then took a package of wipes out of her purse and handed him one.

"Thank you for helping," she said softly.

"Was nothing," he said, feeling troubled as he watched her meticulously clean her hands. "Did I make you sad talking about your brother?" he asked. Normally he didn't bother with much conversation, but this was Jace's sister, and he was a man now, a civvy, and he needed to learn how to deal with people better.

"It was something," Willow argued. "You are a kind man, Huck Jones."

He stirred uncomfortably. He'd never been good with compliments—not that he'd received a lot. He couldn't remember much of his childhood until he came to Jim's. Jim hadn't been much for words or praise, but he'd never hit him, locked him in a room, starved him or humiliated him in front of others to make an example of him. No. Jim had worked him hard. Treated him fair and set the best example he'd seen of how a man should behave.

"I was just wondering how Jake would describe me," she mused.

He stared at her. "He loves you." Even as he said it, he realized how dumb that was because that didn't describe Willow but Jake's feelings for her.

She made a funny sound and gracefully stood. He followed and their breath mingled. They both froze as if they'd hit a trip wire.

"Huck," she said. "Jace is dead. He won't know if you dog out, and in his heart, he wouldn't blame you. His ghost won't haunt you."

His ghost already did. "*I* will know."

She tilted her head a little, her gaze watchful. In the sun that was beginning to dip behind the mountain range to the west, she glowed gold like a candle, and again he marveled that her fiancé had let her get on the road in her rig alone days before their wedding. What idiot did that?

If she were mine…

But she wasn't. Never would be. And he knew there was no happy ever after waiting for him on a front porch in a swing, watching a sunset with his woman while their children played in the front yard.

"Stop trying to get rid of me," he said. "I'm a man who keeps his word. Your brother left a list of amends he wanted to make or things he planned to do. The men in our unit—my brothers—we all made a vow to Jace and to each other. We will all head to Marietta at some point in the coming year, to take care of business and then show our regards."

For a long moment she said nothing. The beginning of the evening breeze tugged on her ponytail and a few stray tendrils that had escaped danced around her face.

"Oh, Huck." Her voice was so gentle. "I'm sorry. I'm being selfish again. Losing my brother isn't just my loss. It's yours too. I see that now. I'm sure your brothers too are grieving."

"We were the Coyote Cowboys. It started out as a taunt to a few of the men in basic who'd grown up on a ranch and it stuck, and each of us who joined the unit over the years kept the moniker as a badge of pride."

Why was he telling her that?

"Yeah." She smiled sadly. "Well, you and any of the Coyote Cowboys are welcome at the ranch. If you need a place to board your horse, the one thing that's in top shape is our barn. Your horse can have its own stall. There's plenty of bedding, feed and an arena, and what's left of the property for exercise. The homestead house is pretty small and run-down and my aunt and mom now live there, but there's a full bathroom in the barn, and eventually I'll have an apartment built in the loft area. I already have a new truss and supports for the weight. But you can hook up your trailer to water and power. I got that installed."

"Appreciate it." He dipped his head in thanks. "My foster granddad is visiting with friends outside Marietta. If I can park my rig on your property until the rodeo, I'm happy to pay by doing chores."

"Careful, you have no idea what you could be letting yourself into with that promise, Cowboy," she said.

He was pleased to see the beginnings of a smile lit her eyes.

"So walking me down the aisle is all you got going this week?"

"I'm signed up for a couple of events at the Copper

Mountain Rodeo. I was…sprung…" He broke off, not ready to share that. "And while I had some healing to do, Jim and I thought it would be fun to spend some of the summer on the Wyoming rodeo circuit—our own bucket list."

He kept his voice neutral but saw her gaze stray to his scar. Normally he didn't care, but he wondered if she was putting two and two together and coming up with four— that he'd been injured along with Jace, only he'd made it home where no one was waiting for him, but her brother hadn't.

"What events?"

"Steer wrestling and saddle bronc." Not a bull rider, top of the rodeo food chain, although he was definitely understanding the thrill of it now that he'd tried it.

"Jace mentioned that he and his team designed a crest and y'all got tatted." Her smile grew. "Wonder if I'll catch a glimpse of that artwork on display at the rodeo."

"You thinking I can't stick my ride?" he drawled, enjoying her teasing more than he should.

"Time will tell, Cowboy. Try to keep up now."

She strode away, ponytail saucily bouncing. And he wondered if she'd been insinuating that he'd tatted his ass. A handful of playful words should not jerk him to half-mast.

Willow climbed in her truck and slammed the door. It took him a moment to adjust himself well enough to follow.

Chapter Four

WILLOW HATED THIS part of the drive. The last ten miles on Highway 89. Then ten more miles on country roads toward what was once the McBride ranch—not that it had been a grand spread in her lifetime. It hadn't. The McBrides had started having bad luck and losing ground for a couple of generations. And now she was bringing one more generation on board.

She turned on the radio to the opening chords of a Chris Stapleton ballad. Even the music wouldn't cooperate to boost her mood. She would have liked one of his upbeat songs with his trademark raspy wail urging her to get back into the fight. But no. She got "Broken Halos."

Willow balled her fist on the steering wheel.

She would not accept defeat. She would not bring her child into a broken life. She was going to be whole. Happy. Willow McBride was an optimist and winner.

Giving up on the radio, she told her phone to play Chris's "Starting Over."

"Take that," she told fate.

Twenty minutes later she really had to pee again and was relieved to make the last turn and bump slowly along the pitted gravel road that looked and felt like it had been attacked by a meteor shower more than once.

Smoothing out the drive was far down on her list.

The cattle guards were still in place though no longer needed, and the fences here were beyond broken—resembling the last few drunks at the bar at closing time. Even without cattle, she needed to fix the fences or else she could lose more land to cattle straying, and if she weren't responsible, she could find herself embroiled in court over a land dispute.

She didn't have the money or time for that. But if she were going to come home to raise her child, she'd need to have income, and no one would want to board, take barrel-racing lessons or have her train their horses, if what they saw of the property looked like a ghost town and the drive in bruised their kidneys.

The familiar heaviness of homecoming settled over her like a wet blanket. What would Jake think? She feared he was somehow expecting a spread right out of *Yellowstone*.

She shoved off her nerves and dread that centered more on which version of her mom she'd get today. Her mom had sounded focused on the phone. Maybe the stay at the hospital had helped her to pull her out of the worst of her grief spiral. Willow needed to count her blessings. She still had a home, a mom, an aunt. Poor Huck seemed to have nothing but himself to start over with.

She told her phone to play Harry Styles's perky "As It

Was." She rolled down her window all the way, sang and pounded out the rhythm on the side of her truck. She was home for the week. She was going to win first at the Copper Mountain Rodeo. And this was going to be a shiny new beginning.

She swept past the homestead house with its faded, peeling white paint, problematic roof and sagging front porch and was surprised her mom or aunt weren't out front. Anyone could hear visitors a mile off on their two miles of bad road.

She pulled up close to the barn, turned off her engine and dashed in to use the small, no frills but fully functional bathroom.

As she washed her hands, she heard voices.

Willow hurried out of the barn, digging deep for a smile, and bracing herself for…maybe not the worst, but with her mother, it could be anything.

HUCK DROVE PAST a house that looked like it had started to fade during the Great Depression and had never again been spruced up. He angled next to Willow's truck just in time to see her bolt for the barn. Weird, she struck him as a woman who put her animals first judging by how spotless her trailer, though clearly well used, had been. He got out of his truck and headed toward the barn.

"Oh, dear boy, hello, hello, hello."

Huck turned around and saw two slim women walking toward him over uneven ground. One must be Willow's mom. One of the women looked like a typical ranching matriarch—crisp jeans, western shirt, sleeves rolled to the elbows, wide leather belt, sandy-blonde hair lightly threaded with gray, pulled back in a low bun, and she wore battered cowboy boots. She had her arm linked through another woman's, who looked like she'd walked out of a Gothic novel. Her red hair blew wildly around her, and she wore a white…nightgown? It blew around her legs in the breeze and had puffed sleeves and small purple flowers. She wore pink slippers. Was she ill?

"Oh, hello. I've been expecting you for some time." She continued to approach him, walking cautiously almost as if she were stepping on stones spaced out in a creek. "Is that your mother? She looks exhausted."

Chills raised the hairs on the back of his neck.

"Um…ma'am?"

She frowned. "I can't understand her. I don't speak that language. Do you?"

"Ma'am?" Confused Huck reverted to manners that Jim had instilled. He looked at the other woman, who looked as normal as her companion looked ethereal. He was afraid to shake her hand in case he bruised her.

"She's been so worried about you," she said conversationally.

"Mandy, let him settle in and be introduced before you start in with your spirit world."

Huck blinked. He felt like he'd arrived to see a family drama show, but instead had wandered into an episode of *Ghost Adventures*.

"It's okay, not everyone can see them," Mandy said, smiling off to his left. "Willow will take good care of him. She's marvelously practical and loyal bone-deep. And you'll take care of her," Mandy said complacently to Huck after a long moment of visual perusal that felt like a touch. "Willow's far more vulnerable than she lets on. My fault. Well ours. But mostly mine. Girls need their mothers."

Huck felt like his head had been plucked off and thrown in the overgrown dead grass, and his skin felt like it wanted to crawl off his back. He couldn't help looking over his shoulder at nothing but too-long browned grass waving eerily in the late afternoon breeze. Even so, the back of his neck prickled with cold.

"Mandy, stop. We discussed this."

"You never did want to learn the language of the spirits, Barb," Mandy said.

"Too many people alive who need someone to talk to."

"Well, now that you're retired, perhaps?"

"Unlikely." She turned to Huck. "I'm Barbara Boylen." She stepped forward and shook his hand firmly. "This is my sister, Amanda, Willow's mother. Welcome to our home, Jake."

"Oh." He shook her hand and then dropped it like she'd burned him and wished Willow would reappear. This was all kinds of awkward. "I'm not Jake."

"Of course he's not Jake," Mandy said at the same time. "I've spoken to him several times on the phone, and yes he's alive," she said to her sister, and Huck had an urge to laugh that he turned into a cough. "This young man has a totally different energy. And then there's his poor mother. Such a tragedy. Yes, I am so sorry. I have lost many babies too, and now my son, but we will take care of your dear boy. Hardly a baby now."

Huck hadn't realized he'd taken two steps back until he took another and nearly fell on his butt when he briefly touched something icy cold.

"What's going on?" he demanded. Was this some kind of joke Willow and her mom were pulling. Was that why she'd disappeared? Was Willow orchestrating this or just in the barn laughing?

"I had thought perhaps Jace would arrive with you? You were the one with him in my dream, but I couldn't understand what you were saying." Amanda touched her throat.

"Ma'am." Huck drew back his shoulders and tried not to look at his truck. What had happened on that mission was top secret. The team had not officially been there. "I'm Huck Jones. I served with your son Jace. He was a good man and a fine leader. A friend. The best. I am so very, very sorry your loss." He spoke the formal words, emphasizing the last ones.

"Thank you," Barbara said.

"When I woke up this morning, I thought that's when Jace would be arriving to help us prepare for Willow's wedding. I'm sure he's anxious to check out Jake."

Mandy didn't seem like she was trying to punk him, and Huck, who'd dealt with a lot of soldiers suffering PTSD, wondered if perhaps Willow's mom couldn't deal with her son and husband's deaths one on top of the other. Maybe her sister was her caretaker, and he had to man up and not be freaked out.

"Jace has passed on," Huck said, stating the obvious.

"She means his spirit should have made it home by now," Barb said like she was letting him know that dinner would be served in five minutes.

"Exactly. You always knew how to phrase things so clearly, Barb."

Huck barely swallowed his snort at that statement.

"Nice to meet you both." He didn't bother with explaining why he was there. Willow could do that after they had a talk. "Excuse me, I need to see to the horses."

"Of course, but not Huck Jones. Your name is all wrong." Amanda McBride crinkled her nose, looking over his shoulder again. "What's his given name?"

Huck went rigid, chilled to his bones. A casual Google search wouldn't turn that up. "It is Huck Jones, ma'am. I served with your son."

What was she playing at?

"Huck Jones," he repeated. "All legal." He had the government paperwork in a safety deposit box in Cody, Wyoming, to prove it.

"Huck." Barbara put a restraining arm on her frowning sister. "Any friend of Jace's is of course welcome here."

"Did you come to help with the goats? Barb has had a brilliant idea. Quite therapeutic, and we can earn a little money. And the flowers and herbs will be beautiful and fragrant. Do you like cheese, Huck?"

He felt dizzy from all the twists in the conversation.

"On a burger nothing like it." He rallied, just as he heard the barn door slide open and Willow ran out, her ponytail streaming like a banner behind her catching the sun.

She was fire.

"Mom."

"My baby, the bride." Amanda McBride pulled away from her sister, but tripped over her slippers and stumbled. Huck caught her and tried to get the pink fuzzy slippers back on her feet, but she kicked out of them again and met her daughter midway in the too-long grasses.

Willow enveloped her mom in a hug. "You're going to hurt the soles of your feet being outside without slippers."

Her mom hugged her back. "No, I have wings to fly. Your father made sure of that."

Willow's eyes tightly closed, and a fierce emotion seized her features, and Huck's confusion and creeped-out thoughts settled. Something was wrong here. He shouldn't be privy to this personal moment, but Willow needed him. Jace's family had needed Jace too, but they were getting Huck instead, and he would not let Jace or his family down.

"Darling, I can't breathe." Willow's mom pulled away a little. "You look so beautiful. You're glowing, and your young man is so handsome—and so in need of a home."

Willow startled. "Mom, Jake's not arrived yet. He had an appointment…" She broke off as her mom waved one arm in the air.

"Not Jake. Huck is your prince. He even tried to help me put my slippers back on. That's a sign. Princely behavior."

Willow looked at Huck, trying to gauge his take on this homecoming. How much conversation had she missed? He looked…not rattled. He had his usual stone idol look, so maybe her mom had been less in la-la land than usual. "Maybe Huck is *your* prince," she teased.

She was bone-tired and still needed to put Montana Wind and Blue away.

"We were discussing the goats. Not as masculine as cattle or bison, but he likes cheese on burgers."

Willow looked around the yard, then at her aunt, who stood a little away from them, arms crossed, her expression wary.

"Goats?" She heard the alarm in her voice. "Mom." She moistened her lips. "Goats are destructive grazers, and our fences, well…I know I need to repair them, but I need to keep the barn and arena and corrals functional. I'll work on the fences…" She broke off. Fences were hard work to keep up in any season and needed at least two people—a crew would be expensive. But in winter fences would be beyond challenging to fix, and she wasn't sure about Jake's ranching skills. But she'd have her baby by early spring.

And then she'd have to decide…

"Yes, I know." Her mom patted her arm, interrupting her racing thoughts. "You've done your best, Willow. And horses will bring in more money, but goats are an idea Barb and I had. A hobby farm, but also a way to make money. And if we sell the infused cheese at the farmer's market in the spring and summer in town, I can also do tarot readings. People like that. Barb thinks it will be good for me to get out of the house and off the property. What do you think, Willow?"

Willow shot her aunt a look. She'd barely moved in, and she already had ideas that were going to require money and time and expose her mom to ridicule. But Willow knew she was not being fair. Her mom and aunt were still relatively young. Her aunt had retired, closed up her life and moved in with her sister—and not into a comfortable, pretty home, not yet anyway. The homestead was ramshackle and isolated.

"Goats," she repeated, trying to sound casual, not cutting. Her aunt shrugged her shoulders like it didn't matter, but Willow could tell it did. Her aunt had never had her own children. She'd been a teacher. She'd lived in a town.

"We can bring back the garden, like our grandparents used to have it. Do you remember, Barb? So magical. I could hear the flowers singing at night." Her mom continued to talk, sweeping her arms wide like she was a game show host model, and Willow lost the plot.

The garden boxes of the original homestead were so dilapidated and choked with weeds, you couldn't tell there had once been several raised beds.

"It will give us something to do and care for and also bring in money. We can sell bouquets in our booth." Mandy smiled at her sister. "Barb has her pension, but we don't want to be a burden on you and Huck."

"Mom, I'm marrying Jake," she said carefully, not daring to look at Huck.

"A garden wedding." Her mom sounded decided, startling Willow as the conversation took another impossible turn. "Just like mine. Do you remember, Barb, the flower crowns we made?"

"Mom," Willow said carefully, hating that she always had to be the killjoy. "We don't have a garden."

"We will. Oh. I need to get dressed. We have the fitting at five. Lisa is keeping the store open late for us. And then we can have dinner in town. Rosita's, you said, right?"

"A fitting?"

"I told you about the dress."

"But I don't want…"

"Willow, honey, you can't get married in your jeans and boots and a T-shirt, even if you are filling it out even better than you used to."

"Mom!"

"I'm sure your groom has noticed, right?" She winked at Huck.

Poor Huck. They were all staring at him now implying that he'd noticed her bigger cup size. Her mom had, of course. Willow hoped she didn't guess why or ramble about baby souls flying around her body like those Egyptian ba spirits that had so terrified her as a child when her mom would tell her bedtime stories about her lost angels flying around the ranch, never getting to be born.

"You have a beautiful daughter, ma'am." Huck finally spoke and tipped his hat rather than deny his groom status. Five minutes with her mom, and he'd learned reality was so flexible that it could do the splits, and sometimes it was best to pretend not to notice. Willow tried to grab her earlier can-do attitude a la Harry Styles, but it was gone.

"I'll help Willow settle her horses and mine, and then we'll all head into town to see this beautiful dress and have dinner. My treat," he said firmly, and quickly strode toward his trailer.

Chapter Five

"Oooooooh, beautiful." Mandy McBride took a sip of champagne and stared at Willow as if she were a holy relic. "You look like an angel, baby."

Angelic was the last thing Willow felt. She was seething and wanting to rip herself out of the tight, sexy gown that appeared to be sheer with strategically placed flower lace appliqués. The dress was strapless and pushed her now cup-size-bigger breasts up so that Willow felt like she was offering them on a plate. And the dress hugged her body all the way to her knees before flaring out to form a train.

Jake picked this dress? What the heck? It was not her at all, and she was too afraid to even ask about the cost. And why did Jake have an opinion? Surely a wedding dress should be her choice.

All the white blinded her along with the conflicting messages of glamorous, sexy and sweet. The dress screamed touch/don't touch.

Well, she'd been touched by one cowboy and the proof was going to soon show. If she'd seen the dress in a magazine, she would have flipped the page. Beautiful but wildly impractical. She might not be tall, but she had a cowgirl's quick, get-stuff-done stride.

And then there was the money, but her mom was staring at her so enraptured in a way Willow had always longed for. Even her aunt was smiling and enjoying the champagne. For a moment, she felt like she had a normal family. Happy. Whole. It was a seductive lure.

"How can you possibly frown in such a beautiful dress?" her mother asked—looking at her empty champagne glass in confusion as if wondering where all the bubbly had gone.

"It is a beautiful dress." Willow realized she had to say something as her mother and aunt stood beside her beaming.

Lisa, the owner of Married in Marietta Boutique, had given them a moment of privacy before bustling back in with a small charcuterie board.

Her aunt happily started picking at the food, but Willow had read that she wasn't supposed to eat those types of meats. And she couldn't start indulging in carbs or she'd be out of her jeans in days. The olives and pickles looked tasty, and her stomach loudly rumbled. Lisa returned, and eyed the dress like Willow would a horse, and she nearly laughed at her own thought.

"You are a vision," Lisa said. "The fit is spectacular. I thought we'd have to take the bust in from your mother's measurements, but it's perfect." She walked around Willow, examining the fit of the dress. "It's quite lovely. You look like a movie star."

"That's my fiancé's dream, not mine," she said wryly.

"Then he'll love it. So glamorous and classic—like out of those black-and-white films that played on Turner Classic Movies. I loved watching those as a kid," Lisa said. "With you wearing that dress, I bet that film crew in town working on a documentary about rodeos wouldn't be able to resist a romantic rodeo wedding. Handsome cowboy." She indicated where Huck was standing somewhere behind the curtain. "Champion hometown barrel racer."

"That's an idea." Her aunt unfolded her arms. "We could re-create the garden wedding just like you had, Mandy," her aunt said. She spread some goat cheese on two crackers and handed one to her sister. "If we could get the film crew to come, they might have a budget for scenery to get us started. I can clear out the weeds with an excavator, but we've talked about building a trellis, adding a path of pavers and putting some whiskey barrels on casters for flowers, building some boxes for vegetables and a back patio would be nice. Maybe they could help with a bit of that. We'd have the beginnings of an English-style garden for next spring, right, Mandy?"

The hope in her aunt's voice felt like a punch, especially when her mom perked up even more.

"Oh, that would be lovely, Barb. I know you volunteered at a botanical garden on weekends. You must miss it. What do you think, Willow?"

Both her mom and aunt looked at her like golden retriever puppies behind bars at a rescue shelter. She tried to take a deep breath—impossible in this dress.

"I'm getting married on Thursday mid-morning," Willow reminded them, carefully, feeling like a villain. Why did she always have to be the reality check? "A documentary crew isn't going to build you an English garden in three days."

Her mom looked crushed, then she perked up. "But you can, Willow. You are so determined. Even as a toddler you wanted to do everything yourself, following Jace around, not me. So independent and fierce."

Willow didn't remember herself like that at all.

"I want you to have the wedding you deserve—a beautiful day, a thriving garden on the original homestead, married to your soul mate."

In the mirror, she saw her expression scrunch. The dress. The daunting task of creating a garden out of a patch of dirt in three days. She bit back her response, not wanting to be mean. Her mom had lost so much. Her aunt had left everything to move back in with her sister. And she was bringing them all another mouth to feed. Two more with Jake, whom she was beginning to suspect might be off at auditions more than helping on the ranch. They hadn't sorted out their married life plans yet.

Her mother indulged in a second glass of bubbles with her sister, while Lisa poured Willow more sparkling water with fresh blueberries and raspberries.

This was the most engaged she'd seen her mom in years and a miracle compared to how her mother had behaved after Jace's death. But creating a garden in a few days? Huck had said he was here through the week and would help with anything she needed, but this seemed too big of an ask.

But if she didn't ask, she wouldn't know.

"Huck," she called out. He was outside of the dressing room probably irritated to find himself standing around in a bridal shop.

"Dear, it's bad luck for the groom to see the wedding dress before the wedding." Her mom sipped her champagne with a smile.

"Huck's not my groom, Mom," she reminded her and took a fortifying sip of her sparkling water so she could ask the price of the dress. "I'm marrying Jake." She gulped more of the cool liquid.

Her mother smiled brightly as if Willow was the deluded one. "You're marrying Huck after the end of the rodeo."

Willow choked on the bubbles and had no choice but to spew out the liquid, which splattered on the full-length mirror. Hoping to avoid nailing the dress, she hopped backward off the little platform just as Huck swished open one of the cream dressing room curtains with a classic WTF expression on his face, crumpling as she crashed into him.

IN THE BRIDAL shop, Huck had felt like he was crawling out of his skin. He had always been, by nature, a man of action, not self-reflection, but this situation with Willow that had seemed so easy at the outset—okay, not easy, because every time he imagined walking Willow in flowing white down the aisle, he expected a giant lightning bolt to be hurled at him because it should be Jace here. If only he hadn't done something so dumb and uncommon as to lose his footing on rocks, he wouldn't have exposed their position. Jace wouldn't have felt the need to protect him. He wouldn't have been hit. And if Huck had been more skilled, quicker with the pressure bandages, faster with the frenetic extraction, somehow, he could have saved him.

But no.

He was here, not Jace. And he had to ensure that this wedding went off without a hitch in four days.

He blew out a breath and raked his hand through his hair. Rows of bridal dresses surrounded him like accusing ghosts.

He could hear the women talking, but not what they were saying exactly, though he did hear the word 'champagne' and giggles. He could handle that especially when he heard Willow call his name.

Grabbing the bottle of bubbles, he stalked over to the dressing room with the frothy, feminine curtains draped from the ceiling.

"Coming in," he warned softly and swished open the curtain just as he heard his name again, but this time linked with Willow's and marriage.

Confusion and shock weakened his knees, and when he

met her startled gaze in the bank of gilt mirrors, Willow spit out a spray of water and then jumped backward straight into him. He hadn't been prepared, but he'd spent years honing his body into a weapon, and the months on bucking broncs and bulls had his balance on a knife's edge.

He held on to the champagne and instinctively wrapped his arm around Willow's waist to keep them both upright.

"Wow." He could barely breathe looking at her in the mirror and feeling the soft, warm curves of her body pressed intimately against him.

He tried to shut down his visceral response. The last thing either of them needed was for that part of him to wake up and interrupt the conversation in a bridal shop with the bride—not his—and her mom and aunt and the store owner.

Too late—the feel of her body combined with the spectacular visual was a wicked punch of lust, and he tried to shift so she wouldn't feel his growing erection. Willow moved at the same time, and he bit back a groan.

"This is the dress, huh? Spectacular," he said, desperate to distract himself from the lust boiling low in his body.

He was utterly stunned at how beautiful she was.

Her hair was out of the ponytail and flowed in waves past her shoulder blades. Her skin was pale cream and luminous, and her eyes were huge and shiny like new pennies. And the dress…the dress…he'd never seen anything like it. It seemed like something a mermaid would wear, rising up out of the ocean like Aphrodite in that famous painting he'd once seen online.

It fit her like skin and was so dang sexy that he felt it was utterly provocative. She looked naked in between the lacy florets.

"You look like a dream," he stammered feeling all kinds of awkward like he had as a teen when he'd crashed into the homecoming queen, Becky Lebac, while rushing down a high school hallway trying to not be late to class again.

Dredging deep for his faltering willpower, he released her and stepped back. He had to clear his voice before he could speak.

"You look beautiful," he practically growled before remembering why he was here. "Jace would have loved it. That's the dress. She'll take it."

"Wait. What? Huck no. It's too expensive, and too elegant and a whole lot of other too muches for me."

"You deserve this dress."

"Huck." Her eyes were luminous. "But it's just a courthouse…"

"Garden wedding." Mandy held her champagne glass up toward Huck with a pointed look at the bottle he strategically held down low.

"I'm thirsty, Cowboy," she said, a smile playing around her lips. Did she know the effect her daughter had on him? She should be offended, not amused. Huck poured Mandy and her sister another glass of champagne, silently cursing his misbehaving manhood.

"I'm buying you the dress," he said recklessly having no

idea how expensive bridal dresses were, but not caring because that dress had been made for Willow and she deserved to have a beautiful dress for her wedding, even if he thought her groom was an undeserving toad, which insulted toads everywhere. Jace would have bought her the dress, and he would have walked her down the aisle looking like a million dollars himself. Willow had been Jace's baby sister, his only sibling, and he would have done right by her.

"Wedding present," he told her flatly and pressed a finger over her parted lips, as she prepared to volley another argument at him.

Her eyes narrowed and sparked then widened. Her irises went gold, which kicked up his heat level, yet at the same time relaxed him. Instead of feeling awkward and guilty, he felt like he was doing the right thing. He was also beginning to see the humor in the strange situation. Who would have thought a five-year-old kid abandoned in a gas station mini mart in Cody, Wyoming, would buy a sexy but elegant wedding dress for a champion barrel racer, who looked like a warrior goddess but rode like a cowgirl demon?

"Huck, you're not…" She spoke as soon as he lifted his finger.

"You're welcome." He pressed his finger back on her pillowy lips.

She bit his finger a little harder than would be playful and dang if he didn't like that bite.

He turned to the shop owner and said something he'd never thought he'd have to say in his lifetime. "I need a suit."

Chapter Six

"I HAVEN'T BEEN here before." Her mom looked around the festive Rosita's with childlike delight. She'd even asked for the kids' menu and crayons and was now doing one of her quick sketches of Huck from several angles, which he was trying to man up and ignore.

Willow briefly wondered how Jake would handle her mother—probably he'd charm her by telling her stories of his recent auditions and star sightings.

"Do I like Mexican food?" her mom asked Huck.

"I don't know anyone who doesn't like chips, salsa and guacamole," Huck said, dipping a chip liberally into both dips and then handing it to her mom. "Go for it."

At least her mom hadn't yet busted out the tarot cards or discussed Huck's aura, and she hadn't randomly advised anyone in the restaurant about their future.

Willow's heart pinched. Her mother had never been normal—never been like the other moms volunteering at the book sale or packing her lunch or attending her sporting events or hosting birthday sleepovers or fussing in the kitchen while baking cookies or making a soup. She'd never once nagged her to do her homework or make it to the bus on time. If Willow wanted something to happen, she made it happen herself.

And she'd hated and resented that.

What kind of daughter was she?

What kind of mom will I be?

"Oh, you are correct, Huck. This is delicious." Mandy chomped down on the chip and smiled at Huck.

He dipped his own chip into the guac and popped it in his mouth, smiling back.

"This is fun. We should do this more often."

Willow smothered a sigh at her mother's delight. It should be fun. And she felt like the biggest buzzkill because her stomach was in knots of worry. How was she going to get the porch fixed so that it was safe? How could she create the semblance of a garden in a few days? How much would it cost to get the roof repaired before winter? Could she find a contractor who could do it?

Normally she'd buy supplies and clamber up on the roof and replace the worst of the damage and wear, but with the baby, she felt like she was already pushing it by barrel racing. Her OB hadn't loved the idea, but she hadn't been particularly worried as it was an activity Willow did often, so her body was accustomed to the exercise. Quite a few women competed into their second trimester, but as her body continued to change, her joints would loosen and her balance would shift, creating more potential risk of injury.

Willow still planned to make it to the finals next month

and then move home and help her mom and aunt with repairs to the house and work for Tucker Wilder at her stables at least until the baby came. But she realized sitting there, listening to her mom chat with Huck, that she hadn't asked Jake where he envisioned them living in the off-season.

Usually that's when he modeled and hit the audition circuit hard in California. She wasn't worried about a long-distance relationship, but would he want that? She didn't want to live in LA. Her life was here. Her mom and aunt needed her and her income and skills. But what about privacy? Dread balled in her tummy. The homestead house was tiny. Three small bedrooms and one small bathroom for four people and soon a baby.

Tomorrow problem.

The server arrived. Willow hadn't even looked at the menu.

"What would you suggest, Huck?" her mom asked brightly.

"Mom, it's the twenty-first century. Order for yourself." Her voice came out way harsher than she'd meant.

"There are a lot of choices," Huck said and discussed the different burritos and taco options with her mom while the server fumbled her pen and openly stared at him. When he looked up, she shot him a dynamite smile and asked what she could get him.

Probably a side of you.

Snark much? Willow resolved to not let her attitude and

worries ruin the rare evening out. Tomorrow when Jake arrived, they'd sort the wedding—and the future. She couldn't live in the day-by-day mode she'd hunkered down in since those two pink accusing lines.

It was her turn to order. She glared at the menu. Tacos were her go-to favorite food always, but she'd been dodging carbs for months, determined to provide the baby and herself with nutrition but no extras. She ordered a chicken fajita salad—hold the tortillas.

"Where's the fun in that?" Huck murmured in her ear, and she tried not to notice the heat his body gave off, and his fresh, earthy scent that had a hint of spice that made her mouth water a little like she was hungry.

"It's racing season." She primly used the standby that had helped her navigate the past few months when someone commented that she was no longer joining anyone for coffees or at the bar or heading into a local burger joint for grease and gossip.

Huck had ordered a beer and when it arrived, he clinked his bottle with everyone else's water glass.

"A toast to Willow and Jake," he said in a low voice. "To their many years of happiness and success."

"To happiness at last," her mom sang out.

Willow tried to get into the spirit of the evening. But the more her mom and Barb googled goats and discussed goat cheese recipes, the tenser she became. Would her mom take care of the goats? Unlikely. She'd head into her studio and lock the door and do whatever she did in there. Willow had yet to see a painting emerge.

"I think you're supposed to be having a good time," Huck said. "When's the ecstatic groom arriving? Am I supposed to take him out for drinks and a stern talking-to or get him drunk and buy him a lap dance?" he asked casually and took a deep swallow of beer.

How did he make drinking sexy? "I didn't know you danced."

He laughed. "I do, but not that kind."

"Two-step? Swing? Line dancing?" Her interest was piqued.

"He'd better," her mom said taking another chip and loading it up. "He's going to do the first dance with you in the garden."

"The groom and the bride get the first dance," Willow reminded her. "But we're not going to have a dance. Jake and I are marrying at the courthouse," she said firmly.

She didn't have time to fix the saggy front porch and create a garden in a few days, unless all the spirits her mom insisted surrounded them could become corporeal and pitch in.

"Oh, no, no, no." Her mom's eyes filled with tears. "Not the courthouse. We will need the memories. The pictures. The family around."

She opened her mouth to tell her mom that she and Aunt Barb would be there at the courthouse with her and

Jake, but she just couldn't say it.

Her aunt curved an arm protectively around her sister.

"Mandy, the wedding will be special. We've ordered the cake and contacted guests and rented the chairs and table. I've always enjoyed photography. Willow can order lots of flowers and buy some trees and plants from the nursery. We'll need to figure out the food and drinks, still but we'll make it work—joy and hope in the face of a double tragedy."

Willow stared at them in numbed horror, the numbers not only adding up in her head, but also the public spectacle of it all.

"The courthouse is practical," she said soothingly, trying to choke back the guilt. "And I have a dress. And we can have lunch at the Graff."

She'd pinch her pennies after her wedding.

"But what about all the guests? And the garden? You should be married where all the Boylens married. Where the spirits of the Boylens and McBrides mingle on the last of their shared legacy."

The McBrides should have taken better care of their land then.

But she kept the angry thought to herself.

Her school guidance counselor, Mr. Lane, had always encouraged his students to 'assume that others have the best intentions.' Willow had never done that with her family. Not once. And sitting there in Rosita's with her mom near tears and her aunt consoling her, Willow wanted to shout at the unfairness of it all. It was her wedding. But she also wanted to kick her behind. Frustration and self-loathing and sorrow were a potent, acidic brew, and gray spots danced in her vision.

"Hey, we got this." Huck's arm was around her, and he pulled her body tightly to his. "Breathe," he encouraged, one hand soothing down her spine. "Just breathe. In on four, hold, out on four."

She gulped in air.

"Again," his dark voice graveled against her cheek, and without meaning to, she splayed her hand on his thigh. "You're good. We're good. Better than."

"Mandy and Barb." Huck's voice easily carried over the rising din of the families settling in for a Sunday dinner out. Excitement was rife in the air as it was rodeo week in Marietta, one of the biggest events of the year, second only perhaps to the Christmas Stroll. "Neither of you are to worry. I have a bit of a green thumb. You'll both have a garden by Thursday morning for a beautiful wedding for your beautiful daughter and niece."

She stared at him, shocked but almost believing the conviction in his voice.

"Of course, Huck." Mandy reached for another chip, tears shimmering through her smile. "Barb and I never doubted *you*."

Of course they doubted her. They were right. She was the unwelcome reality-check guest popping in and out of her mother's life.

"Huck," she said urgently and held up one finger as she tried to dig up an argument imagining all the work and the expense, and tight time limit—three days. "Did you not see the state of the yard when we drove up?"

He caught her finger "Do you doubt me, Willow McBride?"

Before she could answer, Carol Bingley walked up.

"Willow McBride, finally home to help your poor mother," she said.

Willow swallowed her scowl. Of course Carol Bingley would be here and had likely overheard everything.

"And you barely out of your season of grieving." Her face was appropriately drawn with seriousness. "Not a day goes by I don't pray for y'all losing a loyal son as well as a husband and father in the space of a week."

Willow could barely swallow around the lump in her throat as Carol dramatically touched her sternum. "Jace was a bit of a wild one, but he was a good son and a hero," Carol said. "And now I hear you're getting married, Willow. Congratulations. Joy in a season of sorrow."

Her eyes were alive with curiosity.

"Yes, Carol, a garden wedding at our sweet homestead house. On the original Boylen property," Mandy said proudly. "Willow's marrying a cowboy of course. Saddle bronc and steer wrestling."

"I heard actor and bull rider," Carol said.

Oh. No. Willow's heart thudded to her boots. Now she'd be known as a cheat before she even had a ring on her finger.

Note to self. Buy Jake's wedding band tomorrow.

"Marrying a cowboy might sound romantic but hardly practical." Carol looked for a moment like she'd bitten into something sour. "Although I once might have seen the appeal."

For a moment Carol Bingley looked…distant, and sad. Willow stared at her. Mrs. Bingley was married to and worked with the town's pharmacist. She was active in the community, knew everyone and everything, and lived in a big, beautiful house on the Bramble Lane. Mr. Bingley didn't seem to have a cowboy bone in his body.

"I have always had a fondness for the rodeo," Carol stated.

She did? Willow remembered all the times she'd had to run into the pharmacy for medical tape or wraps or chemical ice packs. Carol had always had some arch comment about how Willow seemed to fall off her horse as much as she maintained her seat. And she'd been in the pharmacy a time or two over the years when a member of the town's legacy ranching families, the Sheenans, were in buying supplies, medicine or condoms, and Carol would often deliver a verbal zinger with a hard smile.

"And this is your handsome groom," Carol said, frowning at Willow likely because she didn't introduce him.

"Carol Bingley," she introduced herself while Willow squirmed, wishing she could conveniently poof out of the restaurant like one of her mother's imaginary spirit guides.

"Huck Jones, ma'am." Huck rose with impeccable manners and shook her hand. "I served with Jace and am honored to serve him once again by walking Willow down the aisle to her groom."

"Indeed." Carol's eyes flared with interest.

Of course she wouldn't have missed how Willow had been squashed up against Huck, with his hand on her back while he helped her to calm down. And no, she wouldn't be fooled by Willow's baby arriving a few months early either.

Screw it.

Willow reached for a chip and crunched down hard.

"We do hope you and Frank will join us, Carol," Mandy said politely. "Thursday morning at eleven."

"Odd time," Carol said sweetly, "but with the rodeo a weekend wedding wouldn't do, I suppose. Frank and I wouldn't miss it."

Of course not.

THEY HIT BIG Z's twenty minutes before it closed. While he and Willow looked in the garden center at equipment they could rent—tools, various planting containers and other hardscape materials—Mandy and Barb wandered out to the nursery to look at plants.

"For small town this is a big store," Huck said feeling his nervous energy settle into something cool and organized.

Tackling unwieldy projects and creating order out of chaos was what he did—much easier than stewing over his attraction to Jace's sister and his worry that he should stop her from walking down that aisle. From what he could see, she hadn't once received a call or text from her fiancé—not that he had any idea how couples normally interacted.

"Grab one of the flat carts."

"Huck, you don't have to build my mom and aunt a garden in three days."

"Jace would."

"Well, he's not here," she shot back and then paled. "I'm doing it again."

"You've got a lot on your plate. Let me help, and if you'll work with me instead of against me, we can have a garden by Thursday morning. Let's move."

He barked orders, more to himself than Willow, but after making a couple of stabs at an apology, she rolled her cart right alongside his, gathering gardening supplies, a composter, landscape refuse bags, lumber and fastenings to create the boxes for the raised beds. There were even some metal pieces, which according to the picture, they could form into an arch over the planter boxes.

"I know you're a force of nature, but even you can't make plants grow to cover an arch in three days." Willow blocked him from stacking a handful of metal pieces onto his crowded cart.

"You marrying that guy or not?"

She stared at him, looking more riled and confused by the question than she should be.

Say no.

That out-of-nowhere thought irritated him. He was fulfilling his vow to Jace. He wasn't personally involved, but it sure was feeling like it.

"Never mind. I'm building a garden for your mom and aunt and helping out with any repairs that are needed on the house before I head out of town."

"You'll be living in your trailer in the barn until next summer then," Willow grumped.

"Then that's what I'll do."

"Why are you being so relentless?"

"Why are you giving up so easily?"

She took a step back, her eyes wide. The silence was telling, but of what, Huck didn't know. He'd never bothered with nuance or delving into anyone's psyche. For the last ten years, he'd followed orders. Achieved goals. Did what needed to be done. Something was holding Willow back. Was it his responsibility to figure that out? Would Jace have minded his own business? Unlikely.

"The house is over a hundred years old and hasn't been lived in for decades," Willow said. "And if you hadn't noticed my dad wasn't much on upkeep and repair over the past…" She spread out her arms. "I don't know. Maybe I'm not being fair." She sat on the edge of her cart, elbows on her thighs, head resting on the knuckles of both of her hands. "The ranch was heading downhill before my father inherited, but he could never seem to get it back to profitability. There were always things going wrong. The water table dropped. The spring dried up."

She was bothered about more than the house. Huck stared at the top of her shining hair, wishing he knew more about women than how to two-step and give them orgasms.

The owner of Big Z's, Paul Zabrinski, arrived before Huck could ask any more questions. He introduced himself and walked with them around the store. As Huck began to define the project, Paul made notes on a tablet and gave advice, and never tried to upsell them. He also had some design ideas that would 'fill out the area and add color' for the wedding.

Paul did a quick sketch on a legal pad and added some notes on the side.

"My wife Bailey's the artist, not me, but I've learned a few things over the years. My mom's a master gardener. Gardens are living works of art. This type of design will give you two a start, and then you can add onto it each season."

Beside him, Willow stirred, opened her mouth and then closed it. Huck didn't bother to correct Paul either.

"What do you think?" Paul asked.

"Great."

"It sounds expensive," Willow spoke over him.

Paul's face took on a professional mask as if he'd heard many customer arguments over the years and knew when to keep quiet and step away.

"I'll let you two discuss things."

"Willow." Huck had hit the end of his patience. "You are getting married Thursday morning in your garden."

"Which doesn't exist."

"It will. Your wedding is special. Your mother needs a good memory and so do you. Jace can't be here. I'm here for Jace." He slapped his chest. "Right here. Help me or get out of my way because I am doing right by my brother. He saved my life, and I…" He sucked in a deep breath and barely held back his shame and anguish. "And I couldn't do him the same honor, but I will make sure that his sister's wedding is beautiful, special and goes off without a hitch."

Even if the groom was bewilderingly absent.

And even if he could barely keep his hungry gaze off the bride.

She stared up at him and Huck felt like he'd just pulled his heart out of his chest and handed it to her—'hey, look at this'—with the store owner as witness.

For an uncomfortably long moment no one spoke. Then Paul Zabrinski and Willow drew breath at the same time. Paul indicated for Willow to speak first, but she shook her head and did a cute, graceful little twist of her hand.

"Do you have a greenhouse?" Paul asked.

"No." Willow looked down at the floor, but not before

Huck thought he caught a glitter of tears.

Dang. She was not a soldier. He needed to soften his approach, but he'd met more than a few cowgirl barrel racers this summer as he'd competed who were as tough as some of the men he'd served with, but likely they weren't dealing with twin the devils of grief hulking over them as they'd flirted and sassed all the cowboys tossing their sorry and used-up lines their way.

"Barn could work if you have a light source or a sunroom off your back porch," he added hopefully.

"What are you thinking?" Huck bottom-lined him.

"If you ordered livestock tanks, you could put casters on them, plant whatever you wanted—maybe some annuals or hardy foliage, and arrange them to create a garden effect, and then roll them into the barn for next spring."

He saw the flash of interest in Willow's expression.

"Or you could talk to Shane Knight, the bartender over at the Graff. She had Colt Wilder build something called a living wall for her garden—she uses it for all the potions or whatever she makes, but that too would add greenery height and texture and be mobile."

Huck opened his mouth to order the livestock tanks and head over to the Graff, wherever that was, to figure out what in the heck a living wall was, but he paused. He'd railroaded Willow a lot.

"What do you think?" he asked instead.

"Oh, now you're asking me?"

"Yep." She was pissed. Too bad. He had a job to do.

Willow looked at her smartwatch and nibbled her lip. An array of emotions chased across her features—likely arguments pro and con. He saw the capitulation and the stirring of interest before she opened her mouth.

"How many people are coming?" Huck asked, thinking that would depend on the dimensions of the garden and how many tanks they'd need to square off a garden space.

Sod or pavers or a mix?

He laughed aloud at the domestic thought just as a hint of a rueful smile teased Willow's delectable lips. Her eyes warmed with a hint of gold in all that heated amber.

"I haven't invited anyone except Jake, but this wedding doesn't seem to be about me. My mom and aunt are on a roll along with you so carry on, Huck."

"And you'll keep calm."

She made a face at him. "You are not that funny, Cowboy."

He took that to be as much permission as he was going to get.

"Twelve galvanized livestock tanks," he decided. And then ordered rolls of sod, broken slate to create a patio, sand, and then lumber to rebuild the front porch. "We need a trellis too," he remembered. "And some of those silk thingies or ribbons to weave around it."

"Have you been dreaming of your own big day and scouring bridal magazines since childhood? Got a Pinterest board started?" she teased.

"Daily. I'm thinking peach will be my accent color," he deadpanned.

"I can see that." Willow's assessment of him heated him to his toes. "I'll make sure to remember to order you a peach boutonniere for my wedding," Willow promised.

"Please forget," Huck said. "Let's grab the rest of what we need tonight so Paul can get home, and I can get to work."

HUCK GOT THE tractor working—no small feat—and he'd scooped out a rather daunting area of dead lawn while Willow set out all the lanterns she could find in the house and barn—good thing she'd thought to buy batteries—because if Huck was going to try to turn this dead lunar scape into a garden, she was going to have to stop obstructing him.

Why am I?

She wasn't ready to answer that.

"More doing, less thinking," she muttered and stomped off into the barn to check on the horses for the night. They were restless. Not surprising with a new occupant in the barn and the growl of machinery as night closed in.

Willow walked over to Midnight's stall. Not the most creative name, but the horse was as dark and broody as Huck was. Midnight eyed her with suspicion, not coming over to investigate her or nuzzle her for a treat.

"Fine, be that way," Willow spoke softly. "I will win you over."

Unlike Huck. She had no idea what he thought of her. Probably that she was selfish, conflicted, cold and controlling. She made a face, liking none of those adjectives.

Her mom and aunt seemed so excited about the wedding. Huck was driven to make their vision happen. Why wasn't she on board?

"Too tired. Too practical," she answered her own question. Even in high school she hadn't wanted to go to any of the dances or spend her hard-earned money from working at Tucker and Tanner's ranch and stables on a dress. And boys? She hadn't wanted to waste her time. Willow had felt let down by men.

And she still felt that way. She hated to admit it, but she was hurt that Jake had taken off for an audition and meetings instead of coming home with her. But what was worse, she was worried about what he'd think about her mom, the overly rustic homestead house, the reduced ranch.

She pressed her lips together, suddenly thinking that she should have planned this better—found Jake a place to stay in town, and them a hotel room for their wedding night. Jake liked his comfort, and the small childhood twin tarnished brass bed that she'd set up in the smallest bedroom of the homestead house would hardly accommodate them both—and on their wedding night?

That was begging for their marriage to get off on the wrong foot.

"Dumb, Willow." She knew that avoiding reality didn't even slow it down. She'd been so focused on the practical, she hadn't given romance or Jake a thought, she realized guiltily.

Wasn't there a B & B in town? Probably a lot of them by now—but she'd always fantasized about getting to go inside the Bramble House. Without giving herself time to talk, she googled the number and called.

It rang for a weirdly long time then was finally answered by someone she'd never met named Amy. The Bramble House was booked solid for the rodeo week. Of course it was. OK. She could fix this. There was the Graff. She winced thinking about the expense. And other places in town. She'd look online as soon as she convinced Huck to stop working for the night. It was embarrassing that he was working so hard for the wedding and to build something beautiful on what was left of the ranch while she was brooding.

The ranch should be a legacy that she fought to protect for her child.

But it just seemed like another thing to drag them both down.

Briefly her hand strayed over her abdomen—something she rarely did. But the child was real and coming, and she had to be ready.

Willow walked out into the yard that was bathed in moonlight and the glow of the lanterns. She remembered the party lights that Huck had bought strings and strings of. Maybe she should set some up around the barn and the one tree that had survived decades alone, standing sentinel over the homestead.

She stared at the droopy-looking house with the saggy front porch and roof that looked to be listing slightly. The tall oak dwarfed it.

Party lights would be a Band-Aid for the yard, but they'd be a start. Light in the dark. And she'd do it tonight. She clenched her fists in determination.

"What's wrong?"

She nearly dropped her phone. Silence reigned in the yard, and Huck stood before her, shadowed, his expression even more searching yet more enigmatic than usual.

"Nothing." She tucked her phone in her back pocket. "Everything. But nothing really. I just thought about…well…" She waved her arm to encompass the backyard of the house. "You've done so much."

"I'm a helper," he drawled. "Is this a big enough cleared area for the new sod, with a patio closer to the house?"

Willow couldn't really absorb his question. He was just so much…so much cowboy—so much determination and power and all the things she shouldn't be craving. She'd always done everything on her own and was proud of her independence. Now she was linking her life with Jake, but no way would Jake be working in the dark after competing and a long drive on a project for someone else.

She knew it was disloyal to compare the two men. She'd made her choice. She was stuck with it.

No, not stuck. She wiped at the sweat on her forehead with the back of her gloved hand. She must be really tired, to be thinking like that. "I just realized I should have booked something…you know for our wedding night—not that I'd been thinking of it as a wedding," she rushed to defend herself.

He looked at her carefully, really seeing her, she felt, and she wished his opinion didn't matter so much. She needed to think of him more as her dead brother's devoted friend instead of a man with a rockin' body, enigmatic drill of a stare that seemed to spark something wildly inappropriate in both her tummy and deeper—her soul, if she were inclined that way.

Which I am not.

"Why?"

"We don't have enough time for me to answer that question."

Had he just stepped closer? She hadn't seen him move or heard him, but he seemed close enough to touch.

"Willow, you don't have to marry Jake if you don't want to."

"I know." She dragged in a breath of the warm night and warmer man. "Sorry. I'm being a self-absorbed brat. This is the happiest I've seen my mom in a long time. She's had a lot of sorrow and trouble in her life, and I'm begrudging her a party, a morning of joy and society. Our property is isolated."

"Still not a reason to marry unless you…" He broke off, his expression sliding into confusion.

"Can't think of a reason you'd ever marry?" she challenged.

"No."

So stark. "How about love?" she invited. "Have you ever been in love?"

"Never," he admitted, and it was the saddest word in the saddest tone she'd ever heard.

In the moonlight she could see the scar angling low along his jaw and down his throat. She wondered if the injury had damaged his voice or had it always been so gravelly? The scar didn't yet look part of his skin. Had it happened more recently? Had it happened on the mission with Jace? She lacked the nerve to ask. But she felt like it was a talisman of his survival.

"Have you?"

Such a simple question. Expected. Except her throat choked off.

"I was thinking of hanging party lights up," she dodged, "because we are going to be pulling some late nights if we're going to get a garden and a patio ready in three days and three nights. That sounds biblical, but no that was seven and the world." She was babbling now. She turned to retrieve a few of the boxes of lights—screw the electricity bill this month. Look at her getting on board and going all in on the wedding.

"Willow." He caught her hand as she turned to flee. He looked so ancient and part of the land, like one of the stately rock formations on Copper Mountain.

The evening breeze kicked up, ruffling his inky hair—the only thing on him that moved.

"Are you in love with Jake?"

Was she? She had no idea what love would feel like. She didn't have a lot of experience. Jake had been her longest relationship, and that had been framed with frequent absences. But Jake was kind. Fun. Future-oriented. The father of her child. And though she hadn't wanted to get pregnant or have a baby and still didn't know how she was going to manage, she was going to love her child. She was going to put her child first and ensure that they felt seen, heard, important, cherished. And her baby should get a shot at having a daddy in his or her life.

She nodded, not able to break away from him even though his hands no longer held her in place on her arms.

"Say it," he whispered.

His eyes glittered, black obsidian grabbing hold of the shaft of moonlight and scattering it back at her like stars.

She thought of her brother dying so far away even as she harbored a new McBride in her body. Her father taking the easy way out. Her mother escaping into a different world in the middle of her family.

"I am in love," she promised.

"Then you will have a beautiful wedding with friends and family and maybe even a few ghosts watching."

He'd probably said the last bit to make her smile. To her horror, a tear slipped down her cheek, followed by another traitor.

But she couldn't brush them away. She couldn't even turn and retrieve the party lights. It was like her body needed permission to break this tangible hold he had on her.

He cupped her cheeks, his thumbs brushing the stream of tears. His hands were warm and rough and so comforting that it took all her willpower to not allow herself to melt into his body.

Where I belong.

But she didn't.

She didn't know what would happen next or what should happen. Instead, she felt like she was holding her breath and standing on the edge of something.

He leaned forward and kissed the corner of her left eye drenched in tears.

"That's my promise to you," he murmured.

Chapter Seven

HUCK SLEPT IN his trailer and was up ahead of the sunrise. He'd fed the horses, let them loose in the large corral after checking the fence line—the barn, arena and corral seemed like the only things not on the verge of falling apart. He'd mucked out the stalls and was raking in fresh sawdust as Willow approached with two steaming mugs of coffee.

"I slept in," she said, sounding both surprised and apologetic.

Gone were the jeans with the bling on her butt and the tight, embroidered western shirt, along with the artful makeup from yesterday that had contoured her cheeks and exaggerated her already stunning eyes. In place was a fresh-faced, youthful, girl-next-door beauty who sported a high ponytail. Her plain jeans hugged her lean legs, and she wore a rust-colored T-shirt, soft from many washes, and a green and white checked flannel shirt was tied around her waist.

The spit dried in his mouth, so he took the caffeine offering and kept his admiration to himself. This version of Willow was impossibly more appealing than yesterday's. She crackled with energy, and her fresh-from-the-shower scent of oranges and cinnamon mingled with the coffee. Life felt perfect at the moment. He had a purpose and the company of a beautiful woman—as long as he didn't remind himself that she wasn't his, nor was this dilapidated ranch and home his to pour in his time, heart and money.

He, just like this glimpse of a life of purpose and belonging, was on loan. Only fair since he'd been responsible for Jace being six feet under at the town cemetery.

"I think we should make a list of tasks," Willow said. "See what's reasonable and set a budget."

She frowned. Yeah, she was still smarting from him picking up the cost of the dress.

He didn't think he'd get away with paying for the whole garden project. He had plenty of money saved from his ten years of work, but he'd spent a chunk on the truck and the trailer and Midnight so that he and Jim could travel around this summer, and he could compete in local rodeos. He didn't have a more permanent job set up yet and would need one soon.

"I have a suggestion." He spoke quietly braced for her rejection. When it didn't come, he continued. "I have buddy in town who mustered out a few weeks ago. Another one of Jace's brothers."

Willow's gaze felt intimate, like a touch.

"What's his task?" Willow paused, the rim of her coffee cup resting on her lips, and he just about groaned wishing he were that cup. Why had he kissed her last night? It had been a reckless impulse, and he'd barely switched to kissing near her eye instead of her softly parted lips.

"Don't know. We weren't supposed to share any information until the task is complete."

"So, Thursday morning, you walk me down the aisle, give me away like an elephant gift, dust off your hands, tip your hat and walk out of the frame again?"

Her voice was light, but the words hit him like spattered gravel. He had three days, and then she'd want him to leave. His task would be complete, leaving him footloose again. Did she want that?

Of course. He was being stupid. Willow would be married Thursday.

"I'll move Midnight and my rig to the fairgrounds, on Thursday." He tried to keep the defensive note out of his voice. "I'm competing in two events."

No bull riding for him this round.

"And then?"

Huck was staring into an abyss, and he knew that was dangerous.

"Couple more rodeos, then season's over. Got no plans after."

That was when soldiers could get in trouble. Jace had worried about that. Jace had talked to them all, urged them to come to Marietta. He had land. Opportunities. They'd have each other as support. Find work or start businesses. But Jace wasn't here. None of them would have a support pillar.

"You have a family, Huck?" She blew on her coffee and sipped, her gaze steady, kind.

"No. Not really. I got Jim. He fostered me when I was a teen. I'll stay close to him if he needs me."

She sipped her coffee. He sipped his. He hadn't met many women who let silence breathe. But he only met women in bars, hooked up and was out the door so he hadn't given any of them much of a chance.

"Is there something you thought about doing after you were done soldiering? A dream or a place you wanted to visit if you had a chance?"

He had no answer for that. Emptiness filled his soul.

"I'll text my buddy Cross before I head to Big Z's to pick up the soil compactor we rented. See if he can stop by today and give us some advice. He's a ranch hand but also doing some construction work. He might be able to help."

He pushed off the corral fence, intending to get into his truck and gain some distance and perspective because Willow's casual question didn't feel so casual.

"Look who's running away this time." She followed him. "I spilled about love last night. Surely you have at least one dream you can share." She blocked his path. "Or are they all too…kinky?"

"Funny." If she only knew the thoughts that had kept him awake last night. Her. Jace dying. She wouldn't be asking.

"You remind me of Jace. He was all-out persistent, insisting that we make future plans. He wanted the Coyote Cowboys to muster out together. Live close. Build new lives. Start businesses."

"He cared about you."

"Why does that make you sad?"

"It doesn't." She sipped her coffee and looked around the barren yard that looked even worse now that a fairly large section was dug up. "But maybe it does a little—not that I'm proud of that. I'm happy my brother had friends, a family."

She sighed. "I just wish we'd been more in his thoughts."

"You were." Huck took a quick step and reached out, barely pulling back in time before he touched her.

"I think that's one of Jake's appeals. He's so cheerful and present. What you see is what you get."

That hardly sounded like a passionate declaration of love, and Jake wasn't present, but Huck kept his mouth shut and got in his truck. What did he know about love?

WILLOW WAS ON her second load of dumping weeds and dirt in a back side of the pasture that should probably be reseeded but was so far down her list she couldn't see it. Her aunt helped. Her mother walked around the backyard, pausing, turning and then looking up at the sky and around different directions of the property. The yard and property were neglected, but the view was spectacular.

"Was she always so spacey?"

"Yes, but no," Barb said and hefted another bag of dirt and yard waste out of the truck bed to spread in the dirt. "I was five years older and treated her more like a doll—doing so much for her. She was such an unusually beautiful child that it made it harder for her than me in some ways."

Willow huffed her disagreement.

"It's true. Everyone fussed over her. Did things for her. She was creative and imaginative, and we just let her dwell in her imagination more and more."

Willow dumped out the last of the dirt and she and her aunt went to work with their rakes so that the piles of dirt and debris would be somewhat smoothed and not blowing around.

"In high school she had trouble with mean girls who were envious of her looks and attention from boys so they worked to rip down her confidence. Our home life was a little rough, isolated. Our dad was gone a lot, and our mom took her anger and hurt out on Amanda once I'd gone to college on a scholarship. She escaped into books and her art and the drama club where she got to be other people."

Barb shrugged, philosophically. "Maybe I should have stayed or come home. Our dad left for good my freshman year, and our mom spiraled, dated a lot of men, some of whom were more interested in Mandy. I think that's what drew her to Jason McBride. He was an escape. They weren't suited, but his dad snapped up our land at a bargain."

Her aunt stopped raking. "I shouldn't gossip."

"It's not gossip when it's your family," Willow said, feeling deflated. She'd never met her maternal grandparents. Her mom had never spoken of them. Maybe that was why. "Sounds like Mom was part of a land deal."

She was sort of kidding, but Barb's tightening frown didn't ease her mind. "She wasn't suited for a rancher's wife. She's too creative, too dreamy, and she was really damaged by all the miscarriages after Jace. You were her miracle." Her aunt's features softened. "I escaped my homelife my way. Mandy escaped hers by getting pregnant and marrying right after high school."

They walked back to Willow's truck. "I wasn't there when Mandy needed me when she was a teenager dealing with a lot of crap, but I'm here now. I got my pension. Social Security will kick in in a few years. If we have a small income from goat cheese and teas and tarot reading or painting or whatever Mandy wants to do, we'll be fine. Everyone needs a purpose, Willow."

She nodded, worrying her lip, and swung herself into the truck. Her aunt waited outside, looking at her through the open door. "But I don't know, Aunt Barb, if Mom will really help you with the goats. They're stinkin' cute, but work."

"I'm used to hard work. I'll go crazy if I don't have something to do and somewhere to go. I'm going to the shelter in town after the wedding. Ranch needs a dog."

Willow nodded. Dogs were protection. And with goats, a dog or two was practical. But more bothered her. "Mom's…better now?"

"I think the depression of losing Jace and your dad has less of a grip. And now that I'm here, I'll make sure she takes her medicine for her bipolar."

Willow sucked in a sharp breath. It was the first time she'd heard a diagnosis. She should have known. She should have taken her mom to a mental health specialist instead of resenting her fits of dreamy creativity, days of hiding away and piled-up projects that she started and stopped.

Willow should have been home more to help—except her rodeo earnings had been bankrolling what was left of the ranch, if barely.

"But if you're asking if your mom really does see spirits or auras or whatever? Who knows? I was in an abnormal psych class as a freshman in college, and I remember the professor talking about the connection between the eyes and the brain. Something about cones and rods—so the eye can perceive more than what gets translated to the brain—like cats can perceive more light than we do, and I thought ahhhhh. Maybe Mandy's like a cat."

Barb firmly shut the truck door as if that explanation was all she needed, and the thud resounded in Willow's chest and bounced around like an echo.

"I'll walk back," her aunt said.

It wasn't far and rather than argue, Willow drove slowly

across the pasture, not wanting to kick up dust.

She felt humbled and more than a little ashamed because she'd imagined herself in charge of the two women, when it seemed that even as she'd been making plans, they had too. And what right did she have to dictate their hobbies or business enterprises? Willow parked her truck close to the barn. Huck's truck was filled with flagstone and bags of pea gravel. Willow had the landscaping tarp ready to nail down once they sketched an outline for the patio.

"Looks like we're really doing this garden and patio thing," she greeted, determined to stop complaining and stop obstructing.

"Looks like."

"I didn't thank you last night." She shifted onto her toes and then back again. "I'm sorry." She gulped in a breath. Why was apologizing so difficult? "I'm so used to doing everything on my own and being in control and now you've jumped into my crazy—spent an insane amount of money and…"

"Careful, Cowgirl." She saw the humor in his eyes and more than a hint of a smile on his lips. "Take a breath. Keep the seat on your horse or you might start giving me ideas that I can take over somehow."

"Like you haven't?" Why was it so hard to breathe? He smelled so fresh and good—pine, grass, bergamot and a hint of dirt. Delicious. If she didn't pull herself together, she was going to sway into him like some flirty buckle bunny.

"How I roll." The light in his eyes glimmered bright.

"Me too so shut down your insurrectionist ideas."

"That's better." He spoke softly, and he reached out as if he were going to touch her, but then stayed his hand. "There's the sparkle I was missing."

She had a sparkle? Jake had never said that. He'd not even texted his arrival time yet.

She stared at Huck. His eyes were so beautiful. His thoughts and emotions unfathomable. She could see the scar rip down his throat, and she wanted to touch it, soothe it, spread some ointment on it that would speed healing.

"Does it still hurt?" Her heart clutched thinking about how close Huck had come to possibly dying, perhaps alongside Jace.

He stepped away from her, and she felt as if the sun ducked behind a cloud. "I'm about as good as I'm going to get. Fit enough to walk you down the aisle," he said. "Let me get the earth compacted, and then we'll figure out what you want for the patio. I've been googling designs online."

"Said no soldier ever."

"Cowboy now, ma'am." He tipped his hat, and Willow stole it from him and plopped it on her own head. Things had been getting too weirdly maudlin, and she wanted him to smile. Heck, she wanted to feel happy.

"Prove it," she sassed then struck a pose and sashayed like what she imagined models did, but instead of a runway, she strutted across dirt.

She wasn't even halfway to the barn when Huck snaked an arm around her waist and lifted her up. She laughed and wiggled to get free.

"A cowboy's hat is sacred, Willow. I can get my lasso if you need further proof." His voice tickled her ear, and it felt so good to laugh, to be silly for once.

Then as if a blanket of reality spread over them, three things happened at once. Her aunt trudged back into the yard, two white trucks appeared over the rise of the property and drove toward them with purpose, and her mom banged out of the back door of the house and stood on the top step holding a baking dish.

"C'mon and get it," she sang out. "Breakfast burritos. Barb, I sound like I'm in a Wild West movie. Willow, we need a cowbell."

Huck released her, his eyes tracking her mom's progress down the rickety steps while Willow looked at the approaching trucks. Neither was Jake's. Her stomach churned uneasily. Who was coming?

Huck's stance changed slightly. It was more of a feeling of intensity than anything he physically did, but he was completely alert, facing the truck, and reminded her of a hunting dog about to go off lead.

The trucks pulled up and parked side by side—a logo in black scrolled on the side was familiar and, relaxing, Willow snagged a burrito, handed it to Huck and then took one for herself.

"Mom, this is good," Willow said surprised after the first bite. She'd usually done the cooking and had often pleaded with her ethereal mother to eat, wondering if perhaps she did exist on air and dreams.

"I imagined everyone would be hungry," she said complacently as Colt Wilder, one of Tucker's brothers-in-law Willow had only seen in passing at Tucker's expansive stables climbed out. Another man she didn't know closely followed.

"Huck—you beautiful bastard." The stranger pulled Huck, almost violently, into an embrace. "No call. No warning. Just a late-night text like a drunken ex."

He released Huck and then the two men crashed together again in a loud thump of a chest bump that devolved into a ritual of an extreme bro series of hand slaps, fist pumps and a shoulder bump and ended with both of them hugging and tipping back their heads and howling at the sky.

Willow watched the display of way too much testosterone in wonder. She was used to rodeo cowboys. This was more. She remembered sometimes getting glimpses of mountain goats headbutting rivals during matting season.

Maybe the dumb doc crew should be filming this.

She'd thought Huck had size. His friend had at least four or five inches on him. This was another man who'd served with and respected Jace enough to come to his hometown and do something for him.

What was it?

Did she inspire that dedication in anyone?

No.

Her wonder and curiosity about her brother grew. She'd been so angry at Jace for staying so far away for so long—leaving her to deal with their parents and the ranch. But he'd been doing good in the world. She'd barely known her brother, but Huck and this stranger could tell her things.

It's too late.

But maybe it wasn't.

Colt's shuttered gaze lingered on the reunion. He rounded his truck, clearly giving the men their space.

"This is Colt Wilder," the stranger said. "Funny story for later over a beer or two. He's one of us. Green Beret. One of my bosses at the Wilder Dreams ranch. He's brought a crew to help with the project you got rockin'."

The two men in the other truck were talking softly, ignoring the emotional reunion, and likely waiting for directions.

"You made it," the stranger said and eyed Huck as if trying to pull more information out of him through a mind meld. Then his silver-gray eyes met hers. "Is this Jace's sister?"

"Willow McBride," she introduced herself. "Are you going to pee on each other next? In which case I'll keep my distance."

"Good decision. Remington Cross. I served with your brother. An awesome leader. A better man," he said and shook her hand.

"Thank you." Willow was shocked to find herself tearing up. Colt approached, practically blocking the sun.

"Colt Wilder." He too shook her hand. "Seen you with Tucker. You've got a gift with horses."

"Thank you." The praise was unexpected. Colt had always intimidated her.

"Heard about the project and timeline and brought a sample of a living wall I built for Shane. It's an easy build and you can plant pretty much anything in it to create the feel of a full garden quick and cheap."

"That's me, quick and cheap," she said without thinking.

Huck gave her a look.

"Let's leave the two pups to reacquaint, and you can show me what we're dealing with on the house."

She shook her head. "I'm not sure…"

"Doesn't look safe, and if you and your mom and aunt are living in it, I need to check the structural integrity."

Willow imagined few people argued with him, especially when he used that tone.

"Cross and I will get you started today, and this second crew can work Tuesday and Wednesday to finish up as I'm booked solid through October, but family first."

"Family?"

Willow felt like if he kept talking, she was going to have to wire her jaw shut so she wouldn't be permanently slack-jawed.

Everything was happening so fast, and she could practically hear her money draining away.

"Maybe I should get Huck. He's been helping me as a favor to Jace, my brother."

"Sympathies for your loss, ma'am. That's why I'm here too, but let Huck and Cross have a moment. Cross needs it too. It's tough the first few months. Hell, it's just tough."

If possible, his expression went more stone and his gray eyes more silver, a little like Huck's friend, now that she was watching them more closely.

"Did you know my brother?"

"Wasn't in his unit. But we ran a few joint missions back in the day. I've been out five years. Huck will need space, but not too much. Patience. Care. Time. Give me your phone, I'll put my contact info in it. I have a support group helping vets reintegrate and get help with services, employment. Your man will need…"

Willow nearly jumped out of her boots. "Huck's not mine," she squeaked.

"Thought you needed a garden for a wedding."

"I do." Her mouth was so dry she could barely choke out those two syllables, and the irony of them should have been humorous, but instead dread spilled through her.

"Huck is standing in for my brother. I'm getting married to…" She paused, wondering if Jake would qualify himself more as an actor now or a bull rider. His modeling and acting had always seemed like more of a casual side hustle than a career, but Jake didn't seem so casual about it now.

"To a bull rider."

"Huh." He stared at her, and Willow wondered why he found that…disappointing?

"Show me your front porch, before we start unloading. I have a sketch I did last night after looking at Google Maps. Your mom called Tucker yesterday evening about your wedding, and Tucker roasted my nuts to get out here first thing, but I built the sample of the living wall before I came."

"Burrito?" Her mom smiled up at Colt as if he didn't radiate a magnetic intensity that raised the hair on her arms. Of course he'd be Tucker's brother-in-law. The whole Wilder clan by birth or marriage seemed larger than life, and supremely perfect physical specimens that Willow always had felt small and average working at the stables.

"Thank you, ma'am."

"I've brewed lots of coffee and sun tea for when you get thirsty." Her mom patted Colt's muscular and heavily tatted arm. "You boys are such a comfort to Jace. He's happy you've come to help."

Willow winced.

"Happy to do it," Colt said as if this were normal. "Anything for a brother."

Her mom nodded. "I'm Mandy. Jace's mom."

"Pleased to meet you. Mandy, you're going to want to wear sturdy shoes for the next week. I run a clean site, but with the construction there's always the risk of debris or nails."

Of course her mom was barefoot. Willow had asked her about it when she'd been a kid, and her mom had said she wanted to feel the pulse of the earth. Willow had lain down on the grass in her bathing suit and had felt nothing but warm grass ticking along with briers poking her and a few stinging nettles.

"Let's move." Colt took a bite of burrito and his long strides ate up the distance, and she practically had to run to catch up. He eyed the sagging porch and the roofline.

She shoved down her personal to-do list—book a hotel room for her wedding night, contact Tucker about getting her old job back because after the wedding and home repair expenses, her savings would be drained.

"You need new supports, and…" He eyed the roof, briefly walked to the other side of the small structure and then back again. "Probably a new roof beam and new joists before you reroof. And if you're going that route, you could raise the ceilings, for more space and light—the costs on raising the ceiling would be negligible."

"That doesn't sound negligible."

"How old's the house."

"My great-grandparents built it. And my grandparents raised my mom and aunt in it, but my brother and I grew up in a farmhouse near the northern end of the McBride ranch with a…" She broke off thinking of the beautiful view she'd had out her bedroom window of Copper Mountain and so much more. "My mom and dad were neighbors," she explained softly. "Their ranches adjoined, although the Boylen ranch was much smaller."

Though still intact.

"When did you get your last inspection?"

Willow blew out a breath. "No idea. Maybe never. McBrides have always done our own work, good or bad."

"Want me to take a look—I'm not a licensed inspector, but I can eyeball it, give you an idea of what you're dealing with?"

"Sure," she decided. It would have to be done at some point, she acknowledged. She needed a safe place for her mom and aunt to live, and she might be moving in here too with her baby in the early spring—with Jake.

Her mom joined them on the porch wearing a pair of hot pink cowboy boots that had a lot of bling on them.

"Haven't worn these in a while." She stuck her foot out. "Your brother's very intense," she said looking at Huck and Remy still talking.

"Remy's not my brother, ma'am. We've not fully sorted out what he is, but he's kin, and we're keeping him."

She smiled and cocked her head. "Your aura is a dazzling whir of dark and shiny silver and teal with a hint of pink."

"My wife's expecting our first girl. Maybe that's it."

Willow nearly fell off the porch step, hearing Colt's calm reply.

"And no ghosts are tagging behind you. None are trying

to talk to me."

"I keep them in here, safe and heard, ma'am." He tapped his head. "Mrs. McBride, is it okay if I enter your home to check for structural integrity?" He handed her a business card, which she didn't read, but pressed to her chest. Willow's aunt opened the door wider. She palmed a mug of coffee, her gaze worried.

"Please enter our home," she said soberly.

"Yes, please," her mom said a little breathlessly.

"Cross," Colt called out. "Need you for this. We got a job to do and are on the clock."

He ducked inside. After a last look at Huck, Willow—filled with trepidation about the costs and the future, but knowing the two were about to collide—could only follow.

Chapter Eight

HUCK DROVE.

It felt strange sitting in his truck, while she was waiting for a text from Jake that he had arrived in Bozeman. He said a buddy was bringing his truck to the airport and that he'd 'catch up with her later.'

She felt more unsettled than ever. She and Huck had spent all day Monday creating the patio out of flagstone and pea gravel while Colt's team had started framing a back deck for the house instead of the stacked cinder blocks that had replaced the rotted staircase years ago. Colt and Remy had worked on the structural integrity of the front of the house and had framed out a new porch.

As evening had closed in, she'd helped Huck build the living wall while her mom and aunt had returned to the nursery to pick up some herbs and other plants to fill in the small containers built into the wall. The sod for the new lawn had been delivered this morning, and the delivery team had rolled it out, watered it and said that even though it was late in the season, they had a chance it would survive if they didn't have an early winter.

"Everything in life's a chance." Huck had shrugged off

her worry, and this afternoon, to Willow's surprise, it actually looked like they would have a garden—if she and Huck were successful with this next errand. Huck took everything in stride, showing no doubt, and Willow felt ashamed that she seemed to seethe with doubt about everything—marriage to Jake, becoming a mother, giving up her racing career, starting her own business or staying with the safer option of working for Tucker. And then there was the whole 'where are we going to live' worry.

"I've never been to a barn sale," she said, looking out the window instead of obsessing about Huck's tanned hands on the steering wheel. She'd always had a thing for men's hands. They had the power to deeply turn her on, and Huck had sexy hands—strong, long fingers, but not too thin, slightly blunt, with clipped, rounded nails and half-moons showing under his cuticles. They were hands that had seen work but weren't battered.

She should be thinking about Jake's hands right now. His hands had, after all, been generous with orgasms. She was feeling contrary—irritated with him for not rushing to her side, and yet, not really wanting him here trying to persuade a film documentary crew to take an interest in their small country wedding.

"I've never decorated anything really," she added giving in to the nerves that kept cranking tighter.

Sitting with Huck in his truck felt intimate in a way that it shouldn't. They were on their way to a barn sale for goodness' sake—not a bar for whiskey and line dancing.

"So this afternoon it's the blind leading the blind," Huck said softly.

"This feels strange. I'm sorry you got roped into it."

"It does seem like something you'd do with your mom."

Willow laughed, through a choked-back sob.

"If she were a normal mom," she said and immediately felt ashamed. "Although she's been more focused on the garden and wedding than I thought she would."

She blew out her breath. She needed to let go of the past. Stay present. Work toward a happy, satisfying future. And tell her mom about the baby.

"She marches to her own drum," Huck said. "I'll admit she was not what I was expecting."

"Am I?" She couldn't help the question.

Huck took longer to answer than she was expecting, and she inwardly winced.

"Sorry. I put you on the spot. I was just wondering…" Gosh, how to say this? "I thought since you knew Jace probably better than I did that he had said…something about me."

Could I sound any more like a pathetic lost girl?

Huck seemed very focused on driving considering that the country road was empty of traffic, straight and flat.

"Jace talked a lot about home and his family. He was a warm man, responsible. He kept tabs on all of us—no matter how hard a mission, no matter how we got divided up and sent different places, he'd check in on us. He was a good leader and a better man."

Willow willed him to say more even as she chided herself. What could Jace have said about her that would have made any difference? He'd barely known her. She'd been a kid. She'd spent a handful of days with him as an adult.

Huck seemed to have trouble swallowing, and she stared fascinated and shamed. "I'm sorry." She touched his arm. "I'm making this hard on you, asking for something that you may not feel ready or able to give."

She sat back and willed a huge BARN SALE sign to appear so she could get out of the truck and not notice Huck's hands, the cut of his jaw, the scar that she'd actually had a fantasy about licking.

She'd always hated when women blamed their feelings on their hormones, but she had read that pregnancy hormones could make an expecting mom feel increasingly sexual. What was the evolutionary point of that? To keep the mate from straying? Hadn't kept Jake at her side.

She nibbled on her thumbnail.

"I don't even know what I'm looking for from you," she said, mocking her interest. "Jace was ten years older than me. He and my dad were so close. He had the chores that were farther from the house, required more skill and strength. But he was fun. He taught me to ride, but really, he was a teenager when I was a little kid. Then he was a text, a voice on the phone or a face on a screen. He'd come home for a few weeks at a time, and then disappear again, leaving everything…" She broke off, not sure what word she wanted. "Empty." She played with her ponytail.

"He loved you." Huck's voice sounded like gravel. "He made the ranch, Marietta, his parents, his sister, sound like a shining ideal. He wanted us all to move to Marietta. He made it sound possible for us all to be washed clean. Absolved. Free to start over."

"Do you want to start over?"

"Don't have much choice," he finally said after she thought he wasn't going to answer. "But like one of your mom's spirits, my past life will walk beside me, likely interrupting a lot."

She smiled. "At least you're taking her…her weirdness in stride."

"Can only walk in my own boots."

"Truer words haven't been spoken," Willow said softly.

Needing the connection, wanting Huck to know that he was helping her so much more than physically getting the house ready for the wedding, she reached out to touch his hand nearest to her.

He stiffened and she pulled back, tucking her hands between her thighs.

She felt the flush in her cheeks, and the back of her neck felt hot, and in between her breasts.

"Thank you." She kept her voice flat. "I'm realizing that I still view my childhood like I'm a kid, but I'm an adult, and need to let things go and focus on what I do have. You've helped me to see that."

"Me?" He sounded astonished, finally looking at her.

"Pain is part of life," Willow said. "You can't have the sweet without the bitter."

"Your brother taught me that." Huck's eyes were back on the road. "Not to dwell on mistakes or hard times but to learn from them. Also, not to be an island. He loved the military because he was part of a team. He belonged and had value but being part of a team meant that you had to accept everyone, their strengths and struggles, and help to shore up the weaknesses. The team was more important than the individual, but everyone had value."

She stared out the front window, listening to each word.

She had cut herself off. She realized that now. Pulled back physically and emotionally and mentally.

"I was a loner when I met Jace. He dragged me to the center." Huck's voice was a harsh whisper of words.

"Jace was a good man." Willow felt her throat choke up, and her eyes burned with tears she didn't want to shed. But maybe she should. Maybe if she finally cried, she could let go of all her anger. "I'm happy he had such good friends and that he was a good friend to all the Coyote Cowboys. It seems he learned a lot during his short life."

"And he unstintingly shared his knowledge and heart."

Unlike her. But she could be different. She could change. Her hands, tucked between her thighs, placed her wrists directly below her womb. She wanted to be present in her child's life. She wanted to love unconditionally and teach her child how to love and be loved. Help them to be resilient.

"I've been so resentful that I didn't have a normal functioning family," she said just as she saw the large BARN SALE in red spray paint on a battered plywood sign propped up against a tree. "And that Jace was gone for so many years. I've hated watching the ranch diminish through poor management, drought, the economy, taxes and back taxes, and yet, I'm healthy. Smart. Strong. I have family."

"You are a force of nature, Willow McBride. I've never doubted you. You may feel you've lost your way at times, but you are true north."

"Maybe Jace sent you to teach me something," she mused, realizing that it sounded a little like something her mother would say. But it resonated.

"Huck." She touched his arm, despite not meaning to, because he'd made it clear she made him uncomfortable, but she'd always been physical and had craved touch. "I don't know what your future plans are after walking me down the aisle and watching me win the buckle and prize money for barrel racing this weekend."

He laughed. "There's the cowgirl confidence I've been missing."

"But I intend to also watch you win steer wrestling or saddle bronc."

"Or? Make that both." His smile blasted and Willow,

even though seated, felt a little dizzy as the truck rolled to a stop in front of a huge red barn.

"But if you need a place to stay…a home base…" She began feeling reckless, but certain she had to say the words because she definitely meant them. Huck had meant something to Jace, and he meant something to her already after only two days.

"Willow you're marrying another man. You can't make promises."

"But I…"

"And I won't make a promise I can't keep."

She knew he was right, and she hated it. Something deep inside her shouted its disagreement, and they stared at each other as if daring something to happen. And then it did.

Willow felt the change. The attraction she'd been trying to ignore stirred, billowed up and floated free. The truck's windows were cracked, and the air scented with grass and dirt ruffled his hair, and the morning sun slanted across his hard-cut features. She could barely breathe as the frisson of awareness slid through her blood, heating it, making her effervescent, raising goose bumps on her skin.

I've been here before.

The voice made no sense. But it rang true, and she could see the awareness in his eyes, the desire, the wrestling for control, and she wanted to break his control and hers. She had a mad impulse to slip the leash of convention and do something that she admitted now that she'd always wanted to do. Kiss him.

He shocked her when he reached out and barely brushed his fingertips along her cheek and under her chin that she'd been teased jutted out too much and was too pointy when she'd been a kid.

"If I'd met you first, Willow…" He spoke with a quiet finality that chilled.

Huck hopped out of the truck like it was on fire.

What had just happened? What had she done? Mortification flooded her. She'd never been a faithless person. She'd always kept her word. She may not be in love with Jake how she'd imagined love would feel, and he might not be treating her like she thought an expectant father and fiancé should be treating her, but she'd never be disloyal.

She jumped out of the truck, jogging to catch up with him. She had to apologize. Explain. Though she had no idea what had just happened. She felt like she was trying to stop the rain.

"I'm sorry." She grabbed a hold of his arm. It felt like a steel beam. "I'm sorry. I don't know what just happened. I'm not like that." At least she'd never thought she was.

"It won't happen again," she vowed still holding him in place but coming around in front of him to see that she meant it. "I'm not a tease."

His expression startled her. He looked like he was in pain.

"Huck," she whispered, reaching for his face to soothe

the stark lines.

He caught her hand.

"This is hard enough," he gritted out. "I made a vow to Jace, to my brothers."

She pulled back. Her heart pounded. This was about Jace. Not her. Of course not. Her feelings crowded in, and she couldn't sort through them, but she knew with a sense of crushing despair that she wasn't entitled to any of them.

But she was not a little girl, and she didn't run away.

"Taking me out of the equation," she said firmly pressing her hands against her chest as if that would hold the pieces of her heart in place. "You were a good friend to Jace. You said that he imagined all of his brothers settling in Marietta, being a part of each other's lives. Your friend Cross is here. You said others would be coming. I want you to feel safe and welcome. Marietta, Montana, can be a home for you, Huck. You can belong here. Build a home. I won't interfere. Bother you. I can be a friend to you and all of Jace's brothers."

He didn't respond but her words seemed to cause him pain when she'd meant to comfort him.

"I want to be someone you can rely on. Nothing more. I promise."

Even as she said it, she knew she was lying, but anything else was impossible.

"I've always been on my own, Willow. I'm good keeping it that way."

"WHAT'S GOT YOU all hangdog?" Cross asked as he helped unload the truck of the purchases Willow had insisted on making, although he had bought a few more things she knew nothing about. He'd pick them up later today as a surprise secret project for her and Jake. The idea made him feel too big for his skin, but it was a test and would prove that his dislike of Jake had nothing to do with Willow. Selfless. Be a nice gesture, right?

"You and Willow fight?"

"Fight?" It was so far from reality, he was embarrassed. "She's Jace's sister. What could we fight about?"

"She's a fine-looking woman about to marry a man we know nothing about. That's plenty to fight about."

Huck looked at Cross, settling a little. "That's bothering me too," he admitted.

Nothing else.

"You met him?"

Unerringly Cross seemed to be taking on Jace's role of confidant.

"Briefly. He was sneaking out on Willow. He didn't like me. Didn't like him."

"Why?"

It was one of the first times he and Cross had had time to talk since they were working on different areas of the McBride construction project.

"Do you see him here?" Huck slashed a hand in the air. "What kind of man takes off a couple of days before his wedding to go on *acting* auditions?" He gave the word the full flavor of his feelings. "Is he a bull rider or an actor wannabe?"

Cross scowled. "He a good man?"

"Seems high on himself."

"He can back it up? Be a good husband and take care of Willow?"

Cross's last question slightly lightened Huck's mood. "I don't think Willow's looking for anyone to take care of her."

"Independent cowgirl." Cross seemed pleased. "Still."

They kept working as they spoke, and Huck paused and really looked at Cross. He seemed lighter somehow. His expression less shuttered. His eyes glittered with various emotions—humor being the one that surprised Huck the most. They'd yet to talk about his task for Jace, but Huck had picked up enough to understand that a kid was involved. And a woman. Maybe she was responsible for the more relaxed angle of his shoulders.

"Two days," he surprised himself by saying. "And I will have completed my duty."

"Then?"

"Signed up for two events in Copper Mountain Rodeo," Huck said slowly wondering why he'd opened his big mouth, but he must want someone else to weigh in on the empty road ahead. "I have a couple more Wyoming rodeos."

Cross had been placing ceramic pots on raised platforms with casters in groupings alongside the patio. He paused. "Then?"

Huck kept working.

"That's the question isn't it?" He kept his voice neutral, but the minute he uttered the dismissive words, he knew Cross saw through him like a window.

Cross's focus felt laser-sharp and hot. He'd brought this on himself. He wasn't ready to run any ideas by Cross but wished he were. Huck hadn't expected Jim to be so ready to hand over the ranch to his nephews, but he understood. He wasn't family. Jim had a right to retire. Huck could make his own way.

"Let's just hope that Hollywood Cowboy sticks his most important role and shows up at the altar," Cross said, giving Huck a look he tried to ignore. "Or you might find yourself standing in as the groom."

Chapter Nine

WILLOW PARKED HER truck—Main Street was busier than usual—no surprise with the rodeo only a few days away. She entered the Java Café, which was one of her favorite places in town. She loved their creative espresso orders and also their smoothies but hadn't allowed herself to indulge since discovering she was pregnant. High nutrition, low sugar and carb counts only. She didn't want the extra twenty pounds or more she'd read about hanging on after the baby's birth. Her career required fitness and every extra pound was a pound Montana Wind also had to carry.

Last night she'd ordered the brunch-type food from the Java that her mom and Aunt Barb had chosen using the online portal, but her mom insisted she check the order in person. Normally she would have blown off that request, but she wanted the excuse to smell the roasted coffee beans. And since she was feeling a little anxious about meeting Jake, she treated herself to a berry smoothie with protein.

While she waited, she endured congratulations and demands to see her ring, which she didn't have. She hadn't asked Jake for one, but since the barista and cashier looked so shocked and disappointed, Willow wondered if she'd failed a test. Or had Jake?

She wandered down Main Street, enjoying the window displays celebrating the rodeo. Some of the stores had adorable rodeo-themed scarecrows outside with signs urging patrons to vote. She smiled. Marietta was definitely growing—booming even, but it still maintained its small-town charm and connection to its roots, even as new traditions were introduced.

"There you are." Jake skewed his shiny red truck to the curb. "Hop in. I don't want to be late."

"Late?" she questioned, the straw poised between her lips. She stared at his handsome face through the half-rolled-down window.

Hello to you too.

"Late for what?"

She'd planned to show him the town and then take him to meet her mom and Aunt Barb. She still hadn't found accommodation for them on their wedding night, but it wasn't as if they hadn't squeezed in her trailer before.

"Get in."

Willow balked, not sure why. She wasn't the type of woman who expected a man to open doors for her or pull out a chair, but she couldn't help the traitorous memory poke of Huck doing just that again and again.

"I thought we could walk around the town," she said. "I was going to get my mom and aunt some of the chocolate boots that Sage Carrigan makes at her Copper Mountain

Chocolate Shop. It's tradition."

"We can get those later," Jake said. "Besides, I thought you'd given up sweets."

It was one thing for her to count her calories. Quite another if Jake thought he could weigh in. She opened her mouth to remind him it was her body, but he beat her.

"Not that you aren't looking mighty fine, but we got a meeting, babe."

She stared at him. This reunion wasn't going at all like she'd planned—not that she'd had a specific plan. "A what?"

"You losing brain cells with junior, darlin'? Hop in." He hit her with his smile, and for the first time her tummy didn't turn over. He leaned across the cab and swung the door open.

Willow looked around, and realizing she was near the pharmacy and not wanting to give Carol Bingley any ammunition, she climbed into the truck. Jake took off before she had herself buckled in.

"Is that a smoothie? Those have a ton of sugar."

Willow wondered if Jake would like to go to his meeting with pink smoothie all over his shirt. But the drink was too delicious to waste.

"Hello to you too." She buckled up and took a deep sip. "How was LA?"

Jake smiled and regaled her with a couple of stories about some meetings he'd had and a bar he'd gone to on La Cienega Boulevard. "Like in the Kenny Chesney song." His eyes shone with wonder. "Although obviously I wasn't writing I love you to some random woman on a bathroom mirror."

He laughed.

Willow continued to sip her smoothie, not wanting to speak impulsively. He'd never said he'd loved her. She'd never said it to him. Had anyone said it to her growing up?

Dismay filtered in. What if something was wrong with her or her family? What if she didn't know how to love?

"Do you really think we should get married?" she asked.

His window was down, the breeze ruffled his dirty-blond hair that fell so appealingly across his brow, and his skin glimmered almost as if it had been kissed with bronze. His blue eyes glowed with enthusiasm.

"That's what we're doing. We got junior on the way, and I don't want to be like my jerk of a bio dad who never made an appearance." For a moment something skittered across his face. She'd never seen this side of Jake. Vulnerable. It was good that he was opening up, right?

He glanced at her stomach. "Glad you're not showing yet. That's going to be weird." He laughed nervously and ran his hand through his hair and settled both hands back on the steering wheel. "Freaky to think that you're growing a human, but in a few months you'll be back to being you."

He frowned. "Right?"

"I don't know how long it takes," Willow said, more than a little nervous about it. Her mom had always been slim—to the point of looking ethereal, but Willow had reminded her to eat. She never had a problem with her own appetite.

"I met a producer in LA. She'd had a kid like three weeks ago, and she was back with her team, taking meetings, skinny as a stray cat, but there was a totally weird moment. She left the meeting to pump milk like some superstar dairy cow. She was gone for like twenty minutes. And then she rejoined the meeting like nothing had ever happened. Her nanny had the baby so maybe there was like a breast milk hand-off."

He looked at her breasts. "The girls are totally different," he noted. "Can't complain about that, but the idea of milk in there is all kinds of weird. That producer liked my audition. You'll be like her. Pop out the kid and be back in the saddle and back at work."

Willow clutched her smoothie, daunted by his too vivid picture of motherhood. Handing off breast milk? To who?

"You're leaving the kid with your mom next season, right? I mean we're not going to deal with it on the circuit; although I might be cast in a show by then, and we'll be in LA and you can stay home and take care of the kid."

Willow's tummy bottomed out.

"I haven't really thought that far ahead...I'm still adjusting to being pregnant. Actually, Jake, I haven't told my mom yet about the baby."

He turned onto Bramble Lane. How did he know where

he was going? The nav system wasn't on.

"Conservative huh?" He barked a laugh. "Montana. Church and all. She's in for a surprise. You, like, told me in June. Maybe we should have married straight away like I suggested. You're not going to be able to pass junior off as a couple weeks early."

"I'll tell her," Willow said.

Jake shrugged. "Your circus. I can keep my mouth shut. Not like we're living here after the wedding or anything."

Here it was, the opening to talk about next steps, and Willow found herself shriveling away from the conversation. She'd been so focused on getting the garden ready for her mom and Aunt Barb and trying not to freak out about how it was becoming a wedding extravaganza that she'd been doing a darn good job of shutting down future worries.

"About next season." She forced herself to plod into what could become a conversational mud pit. The more she thought about LA, the more it turned her stomach. Even if she wasn't competing, she wanted to work with horses. Live a ranch life. Be available to help her mom and aunt.

"We're here," Jake said, stopping in front of Bramble House.

"You booked us a room?" Pleasure soared. Jake wasn't as thoughtless as he'd seemed in the truck. They would have space and time to talk. Privacy. And she wouldn't be hip to shoulder with Huck, trying to ignore the electrical current that tugged and pulsed between them.

"Hardly," he said.

"Then why are we here?" She tried and failed to keep the disappointment out of her voice as her hungry gaze took in the beautiful historical house. She'd always been envious of this property—of the entire street, really. When she'd been in middle school and high school and she'd had a rare moment in town, she'd walked in the courthouse park and then along Bramble Street imagining herself living in a house that had what her friend Ginny Lane had called curb appeal. She'd imagined herself inside the house practicing piano, doing homework, laying the table for supper while her mom cooked and she helped, and her father would come home from work and hug them all and talk about his day.

Talk about a stupid TV-like fantasy family.

"I always wanted to go inside," she confessed mentally kicking herself for sharing that.

Jake was already out of the truck, his expression eager as he took in the house.

"I called to see if I could get you a room here because…well…" She felt herself flush. "My mom and aunt had to move into the old homestead house after the last sale of a parcel of land to pay off back taxes, and to provide some seed money for…" She broke off, humiliated to have to share their financial troubles. And Jake was staring at the house, not necessarily listening.

"But I thought for our wedding night we should…you know…" She wished he'd jump in with something, but instead his back was to her, and he was texting someone.

She got out of the truck, wishing she'd changed before coming into town. This was Bramble House. It had history—good history.

"Did you book something in town?" The Graff too had been full but maybe he'd thought ahead. He certainly managed to navigate life and get himself to LA often for other auditions, modeling assignments and callbacks.

"I tried." He grinned at her. "I tried to get a room here last night, but struck out, but then I met the film crew over at Grey's as well as some cowboys they were talking to and we got to talking…"

"Wait," she interrupted. "Last night? You were in town last night?"

"Yeah, got an earlier flight—on a private plane with Jack Flynn. He's one of the most in-demand stunt doubles on the sets of some of the top western shows. He's going to get me an interview when shooting starts up on his show next week, so I offered him a drink and a ride into town to meet up with his cousin Lucy—one of the producers on the rodeo documentary I told you about."

His blue eyes shone with enthusiasm.

"It's a prime opportunity, Willow. They are shooting in your town. Jack used to ride on the Montana circuit and his cousin Lucy is one of the producers on this documentary, so he introduced me, and we got talking—not flirting. I'm almost a married man so none of that. I told her about the wedding."

He sounded like an overzealous Boy Scout. Why was he acting like she would be jealous if he talked to another woman? They'd never had that kind of a dynamic.

"Why didn't you text me you were here? Why didn't you come to the house?"

He smiled and lightly took her hand. "I'm not always good at keeping in touch. Besides I met you today."

Did he want a prize or something?

"We got talking, played some pool, darts, and I got a line on a studio apartment—real nice—owned by another filmmaker—Ghost Quest—Calum Quest and his wife. Remember that guy? Wild that he lives in this tiny town, but Lucy loves it. She's been scouting shots this morning. Arranging interviews. I've been helping. Learning the ropes behind the scenes. Just as fascinating behind the camera. Maybe I'll go into directing and then producing. That's where the money is. Can you imagine—us with a house in the Hollywood Hills, our kid in private school? Summers at the spread you've got in Montana? Living the dream."

He looked puppy-like hopeful, and for a moment, she let herself dream. It would be okay. Jake had ambition—not the same as her, but lots of couples took different paths, and he did mention keeping a foot in Montana, although the McBride ranch was no longer what anyone in Montana would term a spread and hadn't been for a couple of decades or more. Everything had started to go south as her grandpa was handing over the reins to her father.

"You seem happy," she noted.

"I am. You'll love the crew. They'll love you. They wanted to see us together for chemistry and hear our story to see if they want to shoot some excerpts for the film. I wish you'd worn makeup." He frowned even though she only wore makeup when she was competing or attending a sponsor event.

"Lucy wanted to hear about what we got planned for our shotgun wedding and if it would work for the film."

"You didn't tell them it's a shotgun wedding?" Willow was aghast.

He laughed. "I don't kiss and tell even after a couple of beers. But I did talk it up and how your hero brother just died. People want a story." He frowned. "And I want more than a background millisecond in the documentary. Copper Mountain isn't the only rodeo they're featuring so we need to pop for the camera. They'll be thinking rodeo queen and the bull rider. That's why I wanted your strawberry hair tumbling down and catching the sun just so."

"Barrel racer," she reminded him. "Hair blowing everywhere rounding the barrels is begging for a disaster."

"That's right." He tugged her ponytail. "They'll love your authentic look." His gaze critically skimmed her body. "We make a good couple," he approved.

He kissed her cheek and started walking up to the house. Willow noticed the flowers that needed to be dead-headed and the plants that should be mulched soon to avoid being damaged by a potentially early frost. She'd heard the property had recently sold, but still the staff should be taking better care of it. She'd never seen it look less than magazine beautiful, and she knew Carol Bingley lived nearby and couldn't imagine the woman not knocking on the door several times a day to complain about the weeds and drooping flowers on the porch.

"Smile," Jake reminded her.

Right. She had to fake something to be authentic.

The new owner answered the door, introducing herself as Amy. She was young, pretty and flustered.

Jake introduced himself and stated their purpose.

"Yes, of course, I'll let them know you're waiting."

"Nice to meet you. I've always loved Bramble House," Willow said eagerly. "Any chance I could get a quick tour?"

"Maybe another day," she said vaguely. Amy was slim, but she blocked the door. "Right now why don't you make yourself comfortable on the front porch, and I'll let Lucy, Graham and Rick know you're here."

She smiled apologetically but firmly shut the door.

"Don't worry about it," Jake said. "Your homestead house probably has just as much faded history."

Faded being an understatement.

A few people exited the house—a slim woman with a blonde bob, pretty, polished features and a tailored trouser suit with a soft, pink T-shirt underneath that said something about riding cowboys.

"Relax." Jake paused and brushed a few tendrils of her hair that had escaped her ponytail out of her face. His expression was so sweetly tender that she blinked up at him feeling a bit stunned. "I missed you." His voice was low and warm and like heated maple syrup. "It's been too long."

Only three days, but he could have seen her yesterday.

"Just one more day to wait." He touched her cheek and then smiling turned them back toward their audience.

Only her excellent balance and athletic skills kept her from tripping as Jake slid his arm around her and moved them forward as if they were about to Texas two-step at Grey's, which she realized he quite likely had done last night all in the name of networking.

Was this real or was Jake acting?

"This is my soon-to-be bride Willow McBride, champion barrel racer, hometown girl, and her family has a spread out of town, deep roots in the rodeo community. Willow, this is the film producer, Lucy Wilson."

Willow shook Lucy's hand. "I feel like I'm auditioning for something," she joked, but it wasn't funny when Lucy scrutinized her like Willow did to horses at auctions.

"The camera will love you two as a couple. Your skin and eyes are luminous, and your hair has a copper sheen in the sun," Lucy noted. "Your brother died in service to our country, and he was a teen rodeo star, right? Your family's like fourth-generation rodeo?"

Someone'd done their homework.

"This is Graham North. He's the one doing all the interviews and the scripting with me when needed. Rick Johnson is our videographer. He's the eyes. Let's do some practice setups here at the B & B as we're going to run some interviews here for a historic look. Then the crew and I will drive out to your ranch, look at the site for the wedding. We're doing some exterior shots of a few local ranches today and tomorrow before shifting to town and the fairgrounds this weekend."

Lucy looked young, but she sounded all business. If Willow had been interested in appearing in a documentary about rodeos, she would have been impressed. Thinking about the local ranches they'd likely be visiting intimidated her, even though it wasn't a competition. The McBrides had lost so much, whereas the Telfords, Sheenans, Carrigans, Wilders, Wyatts and Ballantynes had grown and thrived.

Still, Jace had been coming home intending to fight and not only hold on to what was left but to build and add back to the legacy. She too was a fighter. She didn't want to let her brother down.

"Where's the wedding? Is it a grand house?" Lucy asked.

"The wedding plans have changed last minute to be in the…garden of my mom and aunt's original homestead. She wanted me to marry in the garden where she had her own wedding."

"Sentimental. I love it," Lucy said.

"We're still...ah...sprucing up the homestead and garden. My mom and aunt have moved there after my brother and father's recent deaths."

"Backyard wedding in rural Montana is supposed to be quaint. I'm imagining an explosion of blousy roses rioting all over a faded fence, waving grasses, mountains in the background, a few sentry oaks," Lucy said.

Her crew nodded. Willow swallowed. She and Huck had built a patio, laid fresh sod, and found a couple of rusted metal trellises and had plants in livestock feeders and a few living walls with various herbs.

"It's picture-perfect and has so much McBride history—weddings, picnics, celebrations," Jake promised. "That's why we chose it."

Jake hadn't bothered to look at it. If he had, she wouldn't have to juggle managing everyone's expectations of a rural, western ideal.

"It's a work in progress," Willow said. "And a friend who served with my brother has been working flat out with me to get our backyard ready for our small, intimate morning wedding Thursday."

"Thursday makes sense," Lucy made a note. "Because you and Jake are both competing this weekend."

"Bull rider," Jake said. "What friend?" He turned to Willow. "Not that scowling idiot I met?"

"He's a decorated soldier and a buckin' bronc and bull-dogging rodeo cowboy on the Wyoming Circuit," Willow defended. "But he is competing at Copper Mountain, and he's been working hard to help prepare for our wedding to honor Jace, because my mom pictured me getting married in a garden like she did."

She couldn't keep the throb of emotion out of her voice. Her family had lost so much. Why was she even talking to this film crew? She didn't want to put her family's struggles and history on display.

"Cowboy soldier's last name?" Lucy whipped her phone out. "That too could be an angle," she said to her colleagues.

"Huck Jones," Willow shared reluctantly. She didn't imagine Huck would want a camera shoved in his face.

"Ummmmm," Lucy made a sound deep in her throat. "Yes, please and a side of pipin' hot fries." She held up Huck's picture from the Wyoming Pro Rodeo online site, and even Willow felt the narrowed, onyx glare curl her toes in her boots. "We can tie in the angle of a soldier coming home, honoring a fallen brother, the lure of heading back on the rodeo circuit. Too bad we're not covering a rodeo in Wyoming. Still, we could use stock shots or…" Lucy's attention returned to her phone.

"Actually." She looked up at Willow, her gaze piercing. "Let's head to your ranch now. We can scout, do the practice questions Graham's worked up, and I can see if that smokin' hot charisma Huck's rockin' will translate to the camera or if he'll be unbearably awkward. Hard to imagine, but not everyone shines as brightly as you do on screen." Lucy smiled at Jake, who'd seemed irked at the change of plans, but he brightened and hugged Willow tightly to his side.

"Yes, I'll show you the ranch and the homestead—rich with Willow's family's history. Follow us."

"Actually." Willow needed some space to think. "Follow me. My truck's in town, and I'll need it tonight."

"Babe," Jake began, voice warm. "I can take you back to town later. We've been apart two days."

"Waste of gas. And you don't know the way," she said sticky-sweet herself. "Because you were out dancing and charming a film crew last night instead of meeting my mother."

She tossed her ponytail and gave Lucy a 'men, am I right?' look.

Jake coughed as her ponytail slapped his mouth.

Feeling a little better, Willow spun around and strode back to Jake's truck, reveling in the fast click of her boots on the pavement.

AFTER CHECKING IN with Jim who was enjoying his visit with his friend—they'd been saddling up to go for a ride—Huck spent the morning working with Colt's construction crew, doing what they told him. He'd learned to do most anything that needed doing with Jim on his ranch and then later in the service. He enjoyed the physicality of the labor, but not the noise. Before Colt and Cross took off for another job, leaving the crew, which had made quick progress, Colt had asked him about his future plans. He'd wanted to shrug off the question. He kept his business to himself, but Colt wasn't a man to ignore, and it was clear Cross respected him. Cross had a job as a ranch hand and a place to live on the Wilders' ranch. In the winter Colt and his crew had a contract with the city of Portland, Oregon, to build tiny houses as a way to create several 'villages' of transitional housing for their increasingly unhoused population. Colt figured more cities would come on board.

It sounded like worthy work. But noisy. Huck craved the quiet openness and freedom of the land. But Ryder and Calhoun would be arriving in Marietta at some point to complete their task for Jace. He didn't know their plans beyond that much more than he knew his. Still, Huck didn't say no. He was going to need work.

"I don't know my plans," he'd admitted to Colt as Colt packed up to head to another job. "Don't really have family. Got a couple more rodeos I'm signed up for before the season ends and nothing beyond that."

Not even Jim, maybe.

"You got friends here," Colt said, his unusual gray eyes that were a little like Cross's bored deep. "Cross says a few more are on the way in the next handful of months. Maybe that's another way to honor Jace. Learn to stay. Build a life."

But could he stay in a town where he'd see Willow happily on Jake's arm, Huck wondered as he watched Colt drive off.

"Learning to stay." He tasted the alien words several times as he worked throughout the morning.

What would that feel like?

He looked across the valley at the dead-on view of Copper Mountain. He didn't think anyone could tire of earth's geologic majesty—the slightly rolling hills leading up to stands of alpine forests, a shimmering lake he could see when the sun hit just right and then the impressive, arrogant, snow-capped peak standing tall next to the surrounding mountains.

But Marietta wasn't his hometown, yet Cross told him he was staying. He'd shared that his task for Jace had, like some Protean tale, morphed into applying to become a foster dad to a young teen girl. And he had a woman…or was working on it.

Maybe I could…

Mentally he kicked himself. Dumb. He was here to honor Jace and then have a hard talk with Jim about the future—convince him he had one. Get him to visit a doctor and see if the cancer was back. Then fight it. Maybe Marietta was a good place to do that. There was a hospital here. And Bozeman—the biggest town in the state—was thirty-five miles away.

What he was not here to do was moon over a woman who was as out of reach as the actual moon.

"Here you go, Huck." Mandy padded barefoot out on the back deck, holding a plate of two PBJ sandwiches, an apple and several cookies that smelled fragrantly warm.

"I thought it was time for you to take a break."

"Thank you, ma'am."

He remained standing, peeled off his gloves and rinsed his hands in the outdoor sink he'd installed. She sat down cross-legged on one of the Trex composite steps that he'd just finished. A frown skittered across her face.

"I don't like manufactured materials," she said, shuffling some large cards in her hands, her expression thoughtful, but her gaze seemed turned inward.

"Yes, ma'am," he agreed. "But Colt's right. The Trex materials will last longer in this climate. You won't need to maintain it like wood, and he had some left over from several jobs so…"

Or so Colt had said.

"Yes, so Colt said. He manages to say so much without actually speaking. Did you notice that?"

Dang, she was insightful. Huck took a bite of his sandwich.

"I could do a reading for you."

"Much obliged, ma'am, but no thank you," he mumbled once he'd chewed enough to swallow. Alarm pooled in his stomach though he wasn't quite sure why.

"Colt didn't want me to read his cards, either," Mandy said.

Huck looked at the large cards she shuffled rather abstractly. He didn't know what they were exactly—maybe a party game or something he'd seen at a fair once. He couldn't imagine Colt sitting down for anything like that, and he too wasn't keen.

"I prefer to let the future unfold and take care of itself," he stated even as he acknowledged that that wasn't his attitude at all. He prepared and overprepared for all the damage the future could herald—even as he knew the future would win.

"A tarot card reading is more of an opportunity for you to work on issues that are crowding you," she said. "It's not spooky in the way some people fear—more of a tool to better understand yourself so that you can choose a path, not blindly stumble forward as you have been doing."

Huck paused mid-bite of his apple. "Ma'am?" He choked on the syllable.

He saw Willow's truck bouncing up the road, faster than usual, followed by a bright red truck at a safter distance and then a dark SUV. The vehicles kicked up clouds of dust—irritating since both doors of the house were open so Colt's crew could easily work.

Mandy stood up. "Tell Willow I have a headache and am lying down. And Huck…" She looked at him over her shoulder. "We're about to be family so stop ma'aming me."

She left the plate and the apples and disappeared into the house. Willow's aunt joined him on the back deck, putting on her gardening gloves.

"So Willow's young man has finally arrived."

"Looks like." Huck reached for the second sandwich.

"She'll want to take him for a ride. Willow was always happiest on her horse. But I wish she'd put her young man to work. We have a lot of planting to do still."

"I'll do that with you." Huck rose, jamming the rest of the sandwich in his mouth. He had no desire to see Jake again and hear his opinion about anything or watch him and Willow ride off in a quest for privacy and a romantic reunion.

The sandwich felt like a stone in his stomach.

"The trellis you found is beautiful," Barb commented, as they walked down the stairs of the newly built back deck to the patio. "I think if we buy some silk flowers and vines to weave in through the leaves, that will look pretty, and one of the few things I brought with me when I sold off my home out near Flat Head Lake were some glass hummingbirds. We can hang them off the trellis for a touch of whimsy. I'll meet Jake, then we can do some planting before I head into town. We're having a family dinner tonight to welcome Jake, and I do hope you'll come. Roasted chicken, potatoes and vegetables. I'm thinking six."

"A pre-wedding family dinner to welcome Jake sounds like just the thing," Huck said, keeping his voice neutral. "But I'm going to meet up with my friend Jim, who's staying with his friend Ben Ballantyne at his ranch. Thought I'd treat him to dinner," Huck improvised.

Not only did he have no desire to see Willow playing happy lovers with Jake, he also wasn't sure if he could keep his distaste off his face long enough to choke down any food.

He breathed in deeply and headed over to the area where Barb and her sister had been planting arrangements of plants and flowers. He might need a plan B. Tonight he'd hoped to finish his surprise for Willow in the barn's loft—that would be hard to do if he was kicked off the property now that Jake was here, though he couldn't imagine the cowboy getting his hands dirty and working sixteen-hour days spiffing up a garden and barn for his wedding.

He hadn't given much thought to where he should park his rig and stable his horse once Jake arrived. Hopefully the rodeo committee would let him move Midnight and himself over to the fairgrounds today instead of Thursday.

"I hope you reconsider, Huck," Barb said. "Perhaps invite Jim to dinner as well. There's plenty and Mandy and I don't often get a chance to entertain."

That hit home. They were isolated way out here, and he knew that Barb had only moved back to Marietta after her nephew and brother-in-law's deaths.

"It would ease the strain of Jake being the only guest."

Jake definitely wouldn't welcome him, and that settled it for Huck. Served the idiot right for being MIA. And he'd be able to finish his project in the barn for Willow.

"Thank you. That's kind of you," Huck said, thinking

that Jim would enjoy a home-cooked meal and the company of Barb and her sister. He'd like Barb's no-nonsense approach, and Mandy's eccentricities were amusing. And who knew, maybe Ben Ballantyne would like to come.

Barb smiled. "Another cowboy around the table is always welcome. Who knows, maybe having more people sitting down and breaking bread with us will help Mandy focus on the people who are actually there."

Huck swore he saw her wink before she walked toward Willow and Jake, peeling off her gloves. Huck continued toward the gardening station. His pots wouldn't be as beautiful as the ones Barb and Mandy had done, but he had eyes and strong hands and could follow directions.

Chapter Ten

WILLOW NUZZLED BIG Blue Sky, taking comfort in her silky warmth, strength and love. Montana Wind stomped a hoof as if annoyed at being neglected and Willow could relate.

She'd spent the last nearly forty-five minutes with Jake and the film crew stalking about the property, framing shots, discussing possibilities, answering personal and emotional questions posed by a man she'd just met while Lucy stood 'out of the frame,' prompting her like she knew anything about her life.

While Willow had entertained the film crew, Huck and her aunt had strung lights, silk flowers and vines and ornaments through the rusted trellis that was now nailed into the ground. Jake had adjusted her clothing and fussed with her hair like he was some personal assistant. It had been annoying to feel so useless, and her slow burn of irritation at Jake's behavior threatened to boil over. Jake hadn't helped at all with their wedding, whereas Huck's T-shirt was sweat-painted on his body.

Was it wrong that she was not only relieved that the film crew had left to visit other ranches but even happier that Jake had offered to help them? He'd driven off with only a cheery wave out the window with Lucy riding shotgun? Willow needed to calm down and think. Lucy, had one-arm hugged her and whispered, 'wedding nerves,' though Willow didn't see a ring on her finger.

"Not one on mine either." She looked at her bare hands, dirt under her fingernails.

There was still work to do, but for a moment she just closed her eyes and breathed in the familiar, comforting scent of horse, sawdust, barn and leather. She really needed to ride. Montana Wind needed to run. And Huck's Midnight too had been stinted on exercise. It had been three days of working to get the garden, porch and deck fixed up, and while Willow was grateful for Colt's crew, she was worried about the bill.

She heard the glide of the barn door opening.

"Thought I'd find you in here," Huck said.

"Almost always," she admitted.

Effortlessly his presence comforted her. He didn't make her feel wanting or embarrassed that her fiancé had ditched the family dinner meant to celebrate their wedding. But was it worse that she was happy Jake had left? She didn't feel like she had the emotional energy to argue.

Didn't that make her a coward? Should the idea of marriage fill her with such conflict?

"You okay?"

No.

"Thank you for helping me set out the tables and chairs for tomorrow."

"Thank you. Watching Jim and Ben argue over table seating arrangements was eye-opening and hellish."

She stroked Montana Wind and tried to dredge up a smile.

"Decaf coffee and some kind of homemade wine is on the table, and I believe your mom is giving Jim a reading before they set up for a round of gin rummy. That's before she told him he had pink and green streaking through his gray aura—the gray means he's skeptical and the pink and green mean that he's loving."

"And he didn't speed off in his truck?"

Huck laughed. "No. He's having a blast. Holding court. He and Ben are regaling them with stories of their antics when they were young men and rodeoing together."

Huck walked all the way into the barn.

"Jim was more lonely than I realized," he said soberly. "He's been slowing down on his ranch as his two great-nephews are taking over more. I thought having family close would ease his mind, but I think stepping back makes him feel useless. Thank you."

"For what?" Why was it so hard to breathe when Huck was here?

"For inviting him to share in a family meal. For encouraging him to bring Ben."

"Of course." Willow frowned. She wanted to ask Huck

what he thought about Jake. If it was as weird to him that Jake hadn't been at the dinner as she thought it was, and if he thought wanting to cancel everything was wedding nerves or smart.

If she hadn't been expecting Jake's baby, she'd have no doubts about kicking him to the curb, but she couldn't just think about herself anymore.

She opened her mouth, but then closed it. Dragging Huck into her emotional drama wasn't fair. Her baby deserved to have a chance at a mother and father. And her mom was happier and more engaged than she'd ever seen her. She'd talked to Jim and Ben about goats and the two men—cattle men to their bones and souls—had offered to send a crew to fix the homestead's fences and Ben said one of his daughters was running some sort of ranch staycation in the summers and that they'd buy some of their goat cheese.

"Dinner with neighbors was good for all of us. I wish—" She broke off.

She wished Jake had been there, but did she really? Tonight's conversation was fun and free-flowing. Jake had an ability to turn conversations more toward himself.

"My mom's worried about Jim," she said softly, admitting something she hadn't thought she'd share.

"He was…sick a few years back. Cancer. Melanoma, but also some cheek or throat cancer—probably from chew. I came home, got him treated, but I…" He gulped in a deep breath. "I worry that it's back, and he won't do anything about it this time. Maybe he thinks it's too late or that there's no point because he's got family running his ranch. His great-nephews have finished college. One's married with a baby on the way. Next generation." Huck jammed his thumbs in his front pocket and blew out a breath.

"But he's still got a lot of life in him. Seeing him on the rodeo circuit with me, he has a spark, and then tonight…"

Montana Wind leaned into Huck, nuzzling, but not stomping or snuffling in demand. And Blue tucked her head in the crook of her neck, but for once didn't try to chew on her hair. Midnight tossed his head as if too cool to want love.

"I loved my brother," she admitted to herself as much as Huck. "I felt the sun rose and set with him. My parents did too—well, my dad. They spent a lot of time together. When he left, I felt so abandoned," she admitted. "Resentful. And then when he died, I felt…" She broke off.

She wasn't used to sharing. And Huck listened. He listened with his whole body, silently urging her to continue. No judgment.

"Angry. I know Anger is a stage of grief, but I just felt consumed by it, but I don't anymore. You did that, Huck. You helped me remember how my brother was always kind and giving to people. I know people said he had a wild streak. And maybe he did, but hearing the way you talk about him, hearing what Cross thought about him…my brother was amazing."

"He was."

"Let's take a ride," she invited.

The sky was purpling.

"It will be dark within an hour."

"We'll just ride on the homestead land—and explore some of what's left of the McBride ranch. When I was little. I used to be embarrassed by my mom. She'd talk to spirits. She'd wander around the ranch barefoot, smudging with sage and apologizing to a spirit that she said the McBrides had done wrong."

She looked to see how Huck took that. He met her gaze, his expression open, curious, welcoming more.

"My mom thinks part of the McBride land is cursed. I don't think she was really sorry to see the bulk of the ranch go. She always wanted to come back here to the original Boylen house that's only two hundred fifty acres. My dad got that when he married her."

She couldn't believe she was telling Huck this. She hadn't told Jake.

"Was the land cursed?"

She blinked at him in surprise. "You don't seem like the type of man who would believe in that."

"What type of man am I?"

WHY HAD HE asked that question?

Willow smiled. "Saddle up, Cowboy. Maybe I'll tell

you."

The ride was just what he needed. He gave Midnight more lead so he broke into a canter, and Huck's head calmed and his body relaxed.

They didn't speak. He'd followed Willow as they rode across the empty, mostly flat land—no trees—the Absaroka Range muscling up in the distance.

The ride felt meditative, and if there were any restless spirits chanting curses or haunting, Huck felt none of it. The air was just starting to crisp and carry the scent of pine, and the twilight deepened to charcoal when they turned around and rode back to the barn.

They decided to deliver the horses to the fairgrounds tonight, using Willow's rig so they could settle in before the chaos of the wedding. Huck promised to care for the horses in the morning so that she could pamper herself and have plenty of time to get ready.

"The dress." She said the word like a curse, and he laughed.

He and Willow unloaded and settled the horses like they'd been teaming up for years. He admired how she moved so efficiently, and yet found moments to stroke each of the horses, compliment and soothe them and sneak them a treat or two.

Another woman was also there when they arrived. She had deep auburn hair, an air of competence and the face and body of a beauty queen. Huck noted the small baby bump.

Willow obviously knew her as she ran over, hugged her tightly. The woman talked a mile a minute to Willow, occasionally interrupting herself to call out directions to the teen who was working with her.

Huck raked the sawdust more evenly around the side-by-side corrals and tried not to eavesdrop, but Willow looked so serious as she talked to her friend, who at one point hugged her and made a motion of zipping her lips. She continued to nod her head and say "of course," and "anything," and "always," to Willow.

The teen approached each of the horses, talking quietly and loving on them a little, while he loosened the flakes of orchard grass and placed them in the feeders. Willow's friend watched the boy, her expression approving.

"Did you weigh each one?" she asked quietly. The kid nodded.

"Don't get cocky, mister. Stay in school." She smiled. "Water next and then a treat for each of these beauties."

"Hey, Parker, trying to work me out of a job?" Willow asked.

"You heard the boss, I gotta stay in school—eighth grade. Such drama," he stated.

Willow's friend laughed at him. "If you weren't so pretty and smart and sweet maybe a few girls would give you some peace, Mr. Parker. Don't let those cowgirls distract you from your studies."

"I won't." He smiled a little shyly. "I'm still gunning for

vet school like my mom."

"How about enjoying high school starting next year first?" Willow teased.

He grinned cheekily. "Who says I can't do both?"

He looked curiously at Huck, who was returning with feed for Montana and Midnight.

"Is that him?" Parker whispered.

"Him who?" Willow looked around and smiled at Huck as he weighed each flake of hay.

"The guy you're marrying. My mom's making me wear a blazer to your wedding. Can you believe it?"

"You're coming?"

"We all are." Willow's friend finished her careful examination of one of the horse's hooves and sauntered over. "My favorite champion protégé getting married and then kicking butt at the Copper Mountain Rodeo before finishing the year in first place and then slumming back to the barn to work with me."

"Yeah slumming, that's right," Willow said.

"I'm glad you're not heading to Hollywood with Mr. Hollywood."

"I'm not sure what we're doing," Willow said so quietly that Huck couldn't hear, but he shouldn't be trying to, he reminded himself again. It was just that Willow had an almost furtive look about her. "I just wanted to…you know."

"I got you, girl," the other woman said, and then she

raised her voice so that Huck assumed she was talking to him. "Hey, Cowboy."

"Yes, ma'am."

Willow laughed. "Huck Jones, this is Tucker Wilder. She's my mentor, and I work at her stables on the off-season."

There was a tone in Willow's voice he didn't quite understand.

"Hey, Huck." Tucker smiled and shook his hand. "Take this girl out to Grey's. Give her a two-step dance—her last as a single lady—to remember since I got kid duty."

"I am not a kid," the kid objected.

"It's her last night of freedom—go wild." Tucker winked. "Do something that I would have done."

Willow laughed, her cheeks going rosy and her eyes sparkling like amber marbles in the barn's yellow lighting.

"As if. No one can keep up with you now, Tucker." Willow hip-checked her friend, and Huck relaxed, happy to see her enjoying herself and that she had the support of at least one girlfriend. It had pissed him off that Jake had taken off with the film crew, but it had been bewildering that the tone of the dinner had been so relaxed and upbeat.

He'd also wondered why Willow didn't have any girlfriends taking her out for her 'last night of freedom.'

"What do you say?" he asked as they said good night, checked on the horses one last time and headed to her truck. He'd already unhitched her trailer.

"To what?"

"A drink and a dance." He braced himself for a no. He wasn't Jake or one of her friends, but he found himself hoping for a yes.

"You serious?"

Huck felt like he was standing on the edge of a sheer side of Copper Mountain with only one toe hold and a couple of finger holds.

"We've been working all week. Let's have some fun."

"Cowboy bar before the rodeo? You missing the battlefield, Soldier?"

"Cowboy now. Dancing with you is that hazardous?" Even as he teased her, he knew dancing with Willow McBride was fraught with peril. "I'm done with danger," he promised.

"Yeah 'cuz bucking broncs and steer wrestling is so safe." She laughed. "Okay, Cowboy, take me to Grey's. I want a game of pool, a game of darts and more than one dance."

She issued it like a dare, and excitement surged even as he tried to tamp it down. If he could have met her before…no, no use thinking like that.

"Yes, ma'am." He tipped his hat and earned a boot slapped against his butt.

He caught her leg and held her in place. Her eyes flared. "Now what?" she asked innocently.

"Behave."

"Tucker told me not to, and she's my boss."

So that was what that was about. Willow was asking for her old job back. His heart sank. She wasn't going to go into business for herself, at least not yet. He wondered why, but it wasn't his place to ask. But that answered one question. Willow was staying in Marietta. It made sense. Her mom and aunt were here. But would Marietta be big enough for Mr. Hollywood?

And if she stayed, he should probably go. If he'd learned anything this week, it was that Willow McBride was his Kryptonite.

"You gonna dance with all of me, Cowboy or just my left leg?"

He released her. Her smile warmed him in all the places he'd been cold for so long.

They walked across the quiet field, crossed a bridge, cut through a park and then walked down Main Street to the double doors of Grey's Saloon.

"Last chance," she said, as his hand reached out to open the door for her.

He cocked his head. "Worried I'll step on your toes?"

She sighed. "I know you're only doing this for Jace, but…"

"No, Willow." He'd stopped lying to himself about that at the barn sale. "I'm doing this for you." He opened the door to the famous cowboy bar he'd heard stories about even in Wyoming while he was on the circuit and followed Willow inside.

She paused. "In the barn you asked what kind of man you were, Huck."

He braced himself.

"You're absolutely the best," she told him, and then walked past him and into Grey's Saloon.

Chapter Eleven

THE EVENING OUT was more enjoyable than she'd imagined. Instead of dwelling on her hesitations about Jake, Willow ended up having fun. She and Huck teamed up and played two rounds of darts against his friend from the service and a woman he was obviously interested in. And then Tucker and her husband, Laird Wilder, showed up buying rounds of drinks and getting everyone to toast the bride and bet on darts and their pool games.

"I did not know you were a pool shark." Huck had switched to water after one beer and Willow's club sodas and limes hadn't sparked the questions she feared they would.

"There's a lot you don't know about me," she teased, but there was even more she didn't know about Huck.

And a big part of her regretted that. After tomorrow Huck would be staying in his trailer at the fairgrounds. Other than seeing him in passing or competing, they wouldn't get a chance to talk again. Laugh. Or talk about Jace.

Tomorrow her life would be totally different.

As if reading her mind, Huck seemed determined she have her night out. He and others ordered appetizers. They ate, talked, joked, played games and then after she'd blissfully chewed and swallowed and savored her last jalapeño popper, he stood, held his hand out and guided her onto the small and crowded dance floor.

They started with a closed position, two-stepped, and then Huck moved her around the floor working in a variety of spins and turns. When the music switched to a more upbeat song, Huck faced her palms up.

"Swing?"

"Why not."

Heart thumping with pleasure, Willow gave herself up to the music, the moves and the feel of Huck's hands and his body guiding and brushing against hers.

Willow lost track of time. The bar didn't slow down, and more couples hit the dance floor, forcing her and Huck closer. She felt like she was in a dream. The night was perfect. She wanted to close Grey's down, even as she wanted to head home because tonight was her last opportunity to spend time with Huck and talk—maybe they could sit on the deck with the new gas fireplace that had been delivered today as an 'anonymous wedding present.' Huck could share more stories about Jace. She would have those to share with her child about his or her uncle.

"I better get this cowgirl princess home before her coach turns into a pumpkin," Huck murmured when yet another song ended. "Big day tomorrow."

And just like that, Willow bumped back down to earth.

Her life was no longer her own. She was going to have a baby. She was getting married. She needed to make sure her mom and her aunt had a safe home and economic support.

And yet she didn't regret letting go of all that responsibility for a couple of hours.

"Thank you, Huck. I had fun."

Her hands still held on to his. She should let go. She knew it, but he felt like a lifeline.

"My pleasure." His low voice was a growl, cutting through the next song.

They stood in the middle of the dance floor, and she felt like steam might start wafting off her.

"Tonight felt magical," she told him. "But you made this whole week magic. I was dreading going home," she confessed, and it felt safe. "I'm still conflicted about getting married, but you've made the wedding and me and my mom and aunt feel special. Thank you."

She stood on her tiptoes to kiss his cheek. Just a brush of her lips. Surely they were friends, but his scent, his essence drew her in deeper, and she paused, angling toward his lips.

"I'll take you home, Cowgirl." He broke the spell.

She pulled her truck key out of her back pocket. "I'll take *you* home, Cowboy."

HE WAS ACCUSTOMED to working in the dark. Usually

stealth and secrecy meant that he'd live another day. This mission was not so dangerous, but he did want to surprise Willow tomorrow after her wedding, but even as he put the finishing touches on the loft bedroom he'd created in secret over the past few nights, he wondered if he'd gone too far.

He'd seen the small bedroom that was more of an alcove where Willow had been sleeping. There was barely room for her, much less her new husband. And one bathroom for all four family members. Creating a romantic space for the newlyweds' wedding night had seemed practical. But now seeing it all come together—the antique wrought-iron queen bed, special-ordered purple mattresses that had been delivered in a box and the pretty, high-thread-count sheets, comforter and quilt, he wondered if he'd hopped the line, landing in Creepville.

And that was before the strings of twinkle lights, diaphanous fabric hung from the beam to drape around the bed, and the antique bridge lamp and throw pillows. Nervously he ran a hand through his hair. If there was a heaven, Jace was definitely up there laughing his ass off.

And what had Willow meant—she was conflicted about getting married—not just the wedding?

Should he do anything about that? Talk to her? Help her make an escape plan?

"Whoa, Cowboy," he muttered. "Way out in front of your horse."

That was wishful thinking, and he needed to keep his

focus on creating the romantic space—and who would have ever guessed he could think those words, much less carry the concept out?

Just to make sure he'd finished all the details, Huck turned on the bedside lamp. The golden glow was inviting. He'd filled rustic aluminum milk pails from the barn sale with sunflowers. It looked like something out of a magazine, and he felt exposed. What kind of idiot who'd often not had a bed growing up and had spent years sleeping outdoors or on a narrow bunk in the service, attempted to create a bridal suite in a barn?

Cursing himself, he switched off the light. Maybe he wouldn't show her. She'd see right through him. And Jake would want to take a swing, and even though he deserved it, he wouldn't be able to let that fly.

Just as he was about to climb back down the ladder, Huck saw a light turn on in the distance. They'd ridden by that small building earlier. Retrieving his Glock from his duffel bag, he tucked it at the small of his back and headed out into the night silently walking across the pasture toward the ancient oak that seemed to be protecting what looked like a ramshackle shed. The front door was ajar. The golden light beckoned.

"Hello, Huck. It's just me," Mandy called out even though his ascent to the small porch had been silent.

He tucked his gun back, lowered his shirt over it and pushed open the front door that definitely needed to be sanded and rehung. This ranch was one project after another.

"You're up late."

A faint smell of paint lingered as he walked into the room. Mandy smiled, and it hit him again how young she appeared for a woman who'd had two children, the oldest had been in his mid-thirties.

"I didn't know you painted."

"I have since I was a child. I'm not an artist though, of course."

He stared at the canvases lined up against the wall—some five to ten deep. He didn't know anything about art—hadn't attempted anything with crayons or colored pencils except at the odd diner he'd been taken to as a kid.

"Why not?"

She smiled. "That's an interesting way of asking," she said, while he continued to look around what he now realized was a studio—she had shelves of art supplies, two aisles, and then some sort of machine that he thought might do something like stretch canvases, maybe.

"My husband used to build the frames for my canvases. It's so expensive otherwise."

"Are these landscapes from different areas in the ranch?"

"I wanted the memories for when Willow has a family of her own."

Of course she'd be thinking of grandchildren. Normal. And yet tragic as Jace could not add to the McBride legacy.

"Probably won't have too long to wait now." He tried to

keep his voice neutral since Willow's future family plans had nothing to do with him.

"Much sooner than you think," Mandy said. She sounded so complacent that he shot her a look. Maybe the woman could tell the future, and he wondered if she'd known the moment Jace had passed.

"May I?" he asked, his curiosity growing.

"I have some of Willow riding and growing up in that pile," she said tilting her head. "I was wondering about giving her one for her wedding—of the ranch, where she used to ride and play, but I thought that might upset her."

"I'm sure she'd love to have a painting from her mom." No-brainer in his opinion.

"I don't know," Mandy said as Huck looked through the stacked canvases, each one more evocative than the last. "I'm a disappointment to Willow. She's grounded. Practical. Jace was more like me."

Surprised by that statement, Huck stopped his art perusal. Mandy was small, feminine and looked like she'd materialized from another world. Jace had been tall, large, loud and in charge. You'd never had to wonder where you stood with Jace.

"Really?"

She laughed. "He knew things," she said. "Felt them. There was a…" she paused and waved her hand "…a knowing about him."

Huck didn't want to think about that.

"It's not your fault, Huck."

He'd gone back to looking at Willow on Montana Wind rounding a barrel in the heat of competition.

"What?"

"You need to forgive yourself," Mandy said placidly. "Why do you think Jace chose you to walk Willow down the aisle?"

"Ahhh…" Did he really want to tell her it was all random? No. But he didn't want to lie. "There were five things Jace needed done. And five of us mustering out within the next year. We each drew a task for Jace."

And that was all the detail he was giving.

"Nothing happens randomly," Mandy said in a firm voice.

"This is extraordinary," he said, choosing to focus on the artworks rather than on how unsettling her words were. Montana Wind and Willow seemed in motion. He could practically hear the hooves, the snort, the jingle of the metal of the bridal. He could feel the determination of Willow, the life energy.

"Then that's the one you should take."

"Ma'am, I can't take something so valuable."

"Value is in the eye and heart of the beholder," she said. "And take one for Willow for whatever secret you've been keeping in the barn."

"Ma'am." He felt himself flush.

Mandy reached for the light and turned it off. They were

shrouded in dark, his fingers on two canvases. Moonlight spilled through the door, brighter than it would be in any city, and Huck knew then, that he would only accept a job on a ranch. He needed nature. Space.

"Jace chose you, Huck. He knew what he was doing."

For a moment he couldn't breathe. Her hand was like a whisper on his skin. He shifted the paintings to one hand and pulled out his Maglite. He always had it. It would light their way back to the house.

Mandy moved across the floor silent as a specter.

"Huck, you need to let that moment go so you can hold on to something else."

Her words hit hard. He had to come clean.

"Ma'am, Mandy," he said before he turned his back on her to close the door and make sure it was shut tightly so no critters could get in. He shook the knob a little and silently promised he'd install a lock on her studio.

He gulped in a deep breath of night air and confessed, not quite having the balls to face her yet, "I was there," he told the closed door. "I was with Jace when he died."

He turned around waiting for her condemnation, but the porch was empty. In the distance, halfway to the house already, he could dimly see Mandy making her way back home alone without his guilt, his protection or the Maglite that could bring the sun.

Chapter Twelve

"YOU LOOK BEAUTIFUL," Huck said the next morning when he joined Willow in the kitchen.

She stared at the worn, wide-plank oak and tried not to hyperventilate. Her mom and aunt were out in the garden greeting the guests.

"You're stunning. I can barely breathe looking at you."

"Huck."

He couldn't say such nice things to her. She'd cry. Or freak out when she wanted to be cowgirl tough.

"Wow." Instead of the suit he'd bought, Huck wore his dress uniform, and he looked so handsome her mouth dried. "You clean up good."

"Just needed a hose and a bar of soap."

She winced. It was true. They'd been so busy this morning that Huck hadn't been able to use the small bathroom in the house. Instead he'd washed up in the barn after he'd hit the fairgrounds at dawn to care for Midnight and Montana Wind. "Sorry about the lack of bathrooms."

He shrugged it off. "Still better than what I'm used to."

She glanced out of the kitchen window again. More people kept arriving—the Wilders were there in force. The

Telfords. Even the Ballantynes. She saw Jim and Ben Ballantyne pouring coffee from the large silver carafe and talking to her mom.

She didn't see Jake yet, but he always ran a few minutes late. She bit back questioning Huck if he'd seen Jake. It seemed disloyal. Jake was the one who'd suggested marriage and hadn't wavered over the summer, whereas her feelings had bounced around, especially lately. She needed to stay calm, but she couldn't grab a deep breath in this dress. How could it be tighter in just four days?

A text flooped in on her phone.

"What?" She stared at the words as if they were in a foreign language. Huck leaned forward to see, but she turned the phone away and called Jake.

"Sorry, babe," he said. "I got a phone call like forty-five minutes ago from my agent. Total hassle as the doc film crew texted they've arrived. You'll have to explain. I have a callback today in LA. I have to grab it. This could be my big break."

The words wouldn't organize properly.

"What? We're getting married this morning." She could hear wind and an engine and a country song by Luke Combs, she thought. "Where are you?"

"Nearly to Bozeman."

"Bozeman." Why did she keep repeating everything like an idiot?

"It's not that big of a deal," Jake said, soothingly. "The

audition is for a Netflix show with a recurring role. They liked me in a previous audition and requested me, and I have a callback and scene reading with another actor so it's a much bigger deal than that rodeo documentary thing."

Her lips moved but she had no words. She turned her back on Huck who vibrated at attention like a guard dog.

"Let me talk to him," Huck said, behind her his voice low and dark with intent and sending shivers of something down her spine.

She clutched the phone and stared out of the window at all the people milling about. Oh. My. Even Ginny and her father, Mr. Lane, her high school guidance counselor, had shown up. And yes, there was the film crew.

"We're getting married," she repeated as if that would make it true. "Couldn't you have caught a later flight?"

"Babe, I'm sorry," Jake said, contrition easing in his tone. "It's LA. I'm nobody yet, but I got a callback. I'll be in Marietta by the weekend. I still want to make the rodeo. We can marry on Monday at the courthouse. You didn't want the whole wedding fuss anyway."

Like he was doing her a favor by jilting her after putting them all through this expense and the frickin' dress.

"No."

"No? No, what?" Jake's voice changed, and the wind lessened as if he'd slowed or rolled up the window. "Babe, I'm sorry. I am. I want to marry you. I don't want to be like my dad."

"Deadbeat? Running away?"

"Willow." Jake's voice rose. "I'm not running. I'm not like him. I'm just…this is important for my future."

"I'm sure your dad thought he had more important things to do than parent you," Willow said, her voice as icy cold as her body, but just as her mind had been chaos earlier, everything stilled. Her body, her mind, the kitchen, the garden, her future.

Frozen in time. And she knew what she wanted.

"I'm not my dad, Willow. I'm not. I'm going to the audition, not jilting you. I'm nailing it. Getting the part. I'll be able to support us and…"

"Super. Break a leg."

She disconnected the call. "Literally." She stared at the dark screen.

She'd just done that. Freed herself. Doomed herself to being a single mom. But who was she kidding? Jake would have just been one more person to take care of.

Her face felt like it was on fire, and she looked around for someplace to sit because her legs felt wobbly, and she was incredibly dizzy and if she had anything in her stomach, she would have thrown up.

"What the hell? He legged it?" Huck took her hands in his and led her to the scarred farm table that gleamed with polish.

"I can't sit." She swayed. "I'll bust a seam."

"I'm a good tailor," he said. "I've stitched men up while

being shot at, myself included. A seam will be nothing."

She stared at him feeling an inappropriate urge to laugh, which is probably what Huck intended. But no. He looked dead serious and ready to murder.

Anger and humiliation hit at the same time. "I was an idiot to ever say yes," she condemned herself. "I had doubts from the beginning. Huge ones. But I was dumber to get manipulated into making the whole fiasco that much more public and expensive."

The time. The money wasted. Her mom's happiness. Her baby daddy. All of it gone.

He crouched down next to her, his hands rubbing hers to warm them.

"I'll chase him down. I'll bring him back."

"I don't want him back." She was clear about that even though the awkwardness and embarrassment felt catastrophic.

It was salt on her gaping wound when she heard her friend from high school, Riley Telford, who had agreed to play music at her wedding that wasn't, swing into one of her favorite Lumineers' songs, 'Brightside.'

"I'm just furious at the waste of time and money," she told him, pressing her hands to her flaming cheeks, hoping to cool herself enough so she'd only be bright pink, not boiled lobster red when she faced the guests.

"I'm humiliated to be stood up and to have made such a production that dragged so many people into my drama. I should have had the courage to call it off long ago." And now she was going to have to go out there and tell everyone that yes, the McBrides were still cursed and bringing more melodrama. Let the film crew document that.

Huck rocked back on his heels. "Don't you love him?"

"No," she finally admitted it, shame washing through her.

"Then why the hell…excuse me. Why the heck did you agree to marry him?"

She flushed some more. "Dumbest reason."

"The sex was that good?"

Willow choked. "No sex could be that good," she said bitterly. "Even dumber. I'm pregnant."

Huck fell on his ass and then popped to his feet. He swiped his truck keys off the counter. "I'll get him back."

"No." She caught his arm. "No. I don't want him."

"You're pregnant with his child."

"No." She felt something quiver deep inside her, and she brushed her hand low over her abdomen. "I am pregnant with my child."

HUCK DREW IN a deep breath, his ears ringing. He couldn't stop staring. Willow had never looked more beautiful, more determined. But this was beyond a disaster.

What would Jace do?

Jace would never leave his sister to raise her child alone on a struggling ranch. He opened his mouth.

"Here's what we're going to do." Willow stood up and squared her shoulders. "You're going to walk me down the aisle and then I'm…"

"Marry me." He said the words he never thought he'd utter.

Willow looked up at him, pale, eyes gleaming like agates on a beach. He had no idea what she'd been about to say, but he wasn't leaving her alone to raise a child or humiliated on her wedding day.

"Wwwwhat?"

Okay, so her mind hadn't drawn the same conclusion his had. "You will need help and a father for your child."

"So you're just sticking your hand up in the air like a good soldier reporting to duty? One more Jace task to check off your list?"

Her fists balled and she marched toward the door that led from the kitchen's small breakfast nook out to the new deck and the garden and her guests.

"If I marry, and that's a huge if, I will only marry for love, so there's no need for you, Huck Jones, to fall on your proverbial sword."

He kept pace with her and held the door shut.

"Marry me." The repeated words rang in the small space. He'd never meant anything more, and he'd examine his rising desperation that played tug-of-war with his determination later. "It makes sense. You can't deny the pull we've both been fighting."

"You're as full of yourself as Jake," she said, but her voice held no heat, and she didn't make eye contact.

"You can rely on me, Willow. I'll never let you down."

She opened her mouth, then closed it. She took a deep breath. Wet a paper towel and briefly held it to her rosy cheeks. Her eyes glittered with fire.

"I know, Huck. But you'd be doing it for Jace and because you're a good man. I want to be loved. I'm just realizing that I should have held out for that, but I got caught up in Jake's wants and my mom's happiness. But I want to be loved for me, not because I'm pregnant. I won't ever settle for less. I don't need to be taken care of as part of one more duty heaped on you. I'm going to raise my baby alone and rely only on myself."

Her smile was sad, then she reached out and brushed her icy cold knuckles along his cheek and then trailed them down his scar. He held his breath thinking he'd combust. But no. He was still in one piece, barely able to breathe after he'd all but begged her to marry him.

She was free of Jake.

But it killed him that she'd been hurt and intended to go it alone.

"So, Mr. Responsible, you going to walk me down the aisle so I can tell my guests that while they came for a wedding, all they're getting is me and some really delicious sandwiches from the Java Café?"

"They can still have a wedding," he said. "There's cake."

"No means no."

"I'm just going to have to change your mind about that, Cowgirl."

"As if." She regally turned around, and he swung open the door and then side by side, her arm through his and her trembling fingers resting loosely on the sleeve of his stiff, itchy dress uniform, they descended the stairs together.

The hush was instantaneous. Even the guitarist stopped playing. The guests looked up at the preacher standing alone in the arbor Huck had created yesterday, the water feature splashing happily, and then, almost as one, their attention swung back to Willow and Huck.

Willow looked like a goddess. She glowed with health and determination. She carried life inside of her, and Huck had to fight the urge to pick her up and make a mad dash to his truck and drive and drive until he could change her mind.

Jim's usually shuttered features were alive with curiosity, but Huck let nothing show. This was Willow's rodeo. He was just going to have to work behind the scenes to create a different outcome from the one she thought she was getting. He'd run harder missions with less chance for a positive outcome. But none had felt so personal.

They walked to the preacher and then turned around. Willow waved him away toward the empty seat near Jim. He stayed.

"I know y'all thought you were coming to a wedding." Willow smiled brightly. "But there's a slight change in plans."

The crowd was still silent, but Huck felt the energy shift. The sun that had been playing peek-a-boo with a few puffy white clouds partially ducked out between two clouds playing tag and shafted Willow in light so that her hair glowed gold and pink, and she looked like a shimmering flame.

"I know you know there have been two deaths in our family recently, but today, I want to celebrate life—my brother Jace and my father." Her hand tellingly brushed her abdomen. "And the future of the McBrides."

The dismay was palpable. No one knew what to do, including Huck. But he was not going to let her go through any more of life's trials or joys alone. Then he spotted the ice buckets with several bottles of champagne. The woman with the vibrant red hair he'd met last night—Tucker—half rose out of her seat, and he nodded toward the buckets with champagne chilling. Holding a toddler, she practically sprinted to the bucket and hoisted a bottle and brought it to him.

"To the future," he called out and popped the first cork.

Chapter Thirteen

MONTANA WIND SHOT out of the alley, rounded the first barrel and rocketed off toward the second. Willow kept her body slightly planed forward, toes angled down to get closer to the barrel but not too close. They rounded that one and headed back to complete the clover leaf pattern around the last barrel and race back down the alley. Willow subtly shifted in the saddle, anticipation zinging through her. She felt as if time slowed so she could analyze her form along with Montana Wind's. What were the micro adjustments she needed to make to shave off a tenth of a second here and then another tenth as she lightly tapped Montana Wind's flank—a signal to fly back down the alley, even though Montana Wind didn't need the reminder.

Willow lightly reined her horse and stroked her neck. She could feel the heat from her horse and see the sheen of sweat. Adrenaline poured through her veins like fire. Finally, something had gone right today. She'd been doing her best to ignore her overly public rejection this morning. She was still angry with herself for letting things with Jake go this far. She'd seen all the warning signs—she'd even felt them, but no, she'd passively drifted in the current, not wanting one more fight. Playing martyr for her baby.

Totally unlike her.

The party at the homestead house this morning had gone surprisingly well—a celebration of life. Huck had spoken movingly about Jace, as had Remy Cross. Mr. Lane too remembered Jace. And other reticent ranchers and locals had spoken of Jace as a child, her father and even her grandfather. Even Carol Bingley had had something nice to say.

Then they'd eaten and enjoyed the cake.

Closure.

If only.

Now that she was at the fairgrounds taking her practice slot, she could no longer ignore the looks as more of the rodeo crowd poured in—the looks and the questions.

She urged Montana Wind back out at a slow trot to walk the course before running it one final practice time this afternoon. She leaned forward to soothe her competitive horse, and spotted Ruby Lancaster standing with Huck, heads together as they looked at something on Ruby's phone.

They looked beautiful together. Ruby had talent and drive and a sweetness Willow had never had. Good. He'd stop being ridiculous.

"Hey, Willow," Ruby called out.

Montana Wind jerked her head up and down as if greeting Ruby, who almost always handed out peppermints.

Even though they were always neck and neck in the stats,

Willow liked the much younger woman. She felt protective and yeah, if she were having a self-reflective moment, she was envious. Ruby's parents often traveled with her, smoothing her way, providing moral and financial support, and steering the more undesirable elements of the rodeo circuit far away from their cherished child.

No sleeping in second-hand trailers or crappy motels with questionable, lumpy mattresses for Ruby or fending off handsy B- or C-level sponsors or drunk cowboys.

"Looking good." Ruby held up her phone, but the screen had gone black. "Your last two times were under fifteen, and you were holding Montana Wind back. Still." Ruby shimmied a little, her voice going cocky. "Only one of your times was under my two best runs at practice today."

"You were timing me?"

"Of course. So was Huck." She smiled blindingly up at the cowboy, who hadn't once taken his dark, brooding gaze off of Willow.

Willow's nipples pebbled even though she internally yelled at her dumb hormones to knock it off. They'd already gotten her in trouble, with one cowboy. Huck was as dark and inscrutable and intense as Jake had been golden, charming and sunny. Jake was cheerfully self-serving, but Huck was fiercely dedicated to Jace.

Not me.

What would it be like to have all that attention fixed on her?

She couldn't afford to think like that.

"I'm heading over to Tucker Wilder's tomorrow for a private assessment and tune-up," Ruby burbled happily, dragging Willow away from her dark musings. "Tucker was one of the best in her day."

"She's in her early thirties, not an AARP member," Willow said.

She'd also been considering taking Montana Wind and Blue over to Tucker's tomorrow. Not just for practice but to steer clear of the rodeo crowds and locals as well as escape her house and the mockingly beautiful new garden, patio and back deck that were all a riot of artfully arranged color.

"Huh?" Ruby crinkled her nose adoringly and gazed up at Huck, looking as if she wanted an explanation.

Huck barely glanced down at his adoring fan. Instead, his gaze was honed on Willow as if he was calculating a higher-level math problem. Willow could practically feel his gaze on her skin like a drip of candle wax. He looked predatory. Huck might be hunting, but she was not prey. And definitely not a sacrifice.

"You auditioning for some *Jane Eyre* or *Wuthering Heights* remake?" She stared right back at him.

"Oh, is that where Jake went today, an audition?" Ruby sounded impressed. "That's so exciting. Did he get the role?"

"No idea. Jake and I are done." There—she'd said the words. They felt good. She'd probably have to say them another fifty times before anyone on the rodeo circuit would believe her. Jake was a favorite.

"What?" Ruby nearly dropped her phone.

"Time me again," Willow said imperiously, spinning around on her boot heel. "I'm going to do three more runs."

She swung herself up onto Montana Wind, who tossed her head as if offended Willow had kept her waiting. Her horse trotted to the backstage area, clearly in the mood to impress.

"You and me both, girl." She ran her hand along Montana Wind's strong, elegant neck. Up here she reigned. Up here all was right with her world.

"We have a tenth of a second to shave," she whispered to the twitching ears as she lined them up. "And my ego to boost."

"YOU MADE YOUR point." Huck approached Willow as she groomed Montana Wind. Her strokes were methodical, firm yet loving, and she hummed some song with a familiar tune, but he couldn't remember the title.

"Being?" She didn't look at him.

"You're at the top of your game."

By the slight relaxing of her shoulders, that had surprised her. Good. Because he was out of his depth. He had no idea how to woo a woman.

"Doesn't feel like it," she said.

"Why not?"

The prickly Willow was back. He looked at Midnight, who snorted his disapproval most likely that Montana had had a run, but he hadn't.

"You shaved two-tenths off your time with your second series of runs."

She huffed out a breath.

"Huck, you don't need to follow me around. I'm fine." She stopped grooming her horse and instead turned to face him, dumping the currycomb in a green bucket hanging outside the stall, along with a hoof-pick and medical wrap tape and chemical ice packs.

"Okay, I'm not fine. I'm pissed at myself for just going along with Jake's proposal. And I have no idea how to be a good mother. Ugh." She dropped the currycomb in the bucket and then exited the stall and fast-walked down the long aisle reserved for horses.

He could help her there. He hadn't had a storybook childhood and had no examples to draw from. But she and her child would have a comfortable, stable life. He would treat her with respect, her child with kindness and care.

Midnight stuck his head out, clearly wanting some love. He liked that his horse already liked her. She passed the horse, paused and then backtracked. She reached in her pocket, retrieved a sugar cube and offered it to the horse along with a few finger-combs of his mane. If only he could get her attention that easily.

He followed her. "Have you heard from Jake?"

"He texted a couple times and called."

He wondered if the fact that she was still talking to him was progress. She leaned against the gate, crossed her arms and kicked at the dirt.

"It's okay to grieve," Huck said.

"Grieve?" She looked up at him. "I feel like my life has been one long lesson in grieving," she said, her voice low and angry. "I'm angry."

"Of course you are," he said, relieved. "Jake's a selfish, starstruck idiot."

She waved the concept of Jake away.

"I'm mad at myself. Jake and I had a thing last year. I thought it was over and was fine with that, then at an exhibition rodeo, he showed up at my trailer ready to resume, and it just was easy…nice to be wanted."

She closed her eyes as if that part of the explanation was the hardest.

"So, you're not heartbroken?"

She winced. "Not about Jake. About my own stupidity, definitely."

"So, you're not going to marry him, even if he returns with a smile, large bouquet of wildflowers and a big ole sparkler and a fat advance because he landed the role?"

"God, no." She bounced a little against the wooden railing. "You have a vivid imagination, Huck Jones. You must watch a lot of Hallmark movies."

Said no one ever.

"No. Jake and I are done. We want different things. I don't want to live in LA or raise my child there. It's going to be complicated." She nibbled on her thumbnail. "Jake may keep saying he doesn't want to be a deadbeat dad like his was, but…" She shrugged impatiently. "That sounds awful. I only considered marrying him because of the baby. I got caught up in the whole American dream, and then my mom snapping out of her fugue state."

"Nothing wrong with that."

Except Jake was the wrong guy.

She flitted a glance at him, and then her long, pale reddish-blonde eyelashes lowered and fanned along her cheeks.

He liked that she was natural. Real. Complicated. No longer another man's.

"You can stop worrying about me, Huck. I'll be fine. We'll be fine," she whispered. Her fluttering fingers skimmed over her still-flat abdomen before she jammed her hands in her pockets.

Briefly an image of Willow, swollen with child, tummy bare, her hands over her womb, and his hands covering hers branded his brain, and he couldn't shake it.

"I'm not going anywhere." He thought it only fair to warn her, though talking didn't seem to be advancing his agenda.

Her full lips tightened, and he wondered if now that he'd stated his intentions, drawn his line in the sand as Jace used to say, he could allow some of the sexual fantasies Willow had effortlessly kicked up in his head since he'd first seen her arguing with Jake play out.

Hell, yeah.

He took a step toward her. Her lips parted, but a thought stopped him. Would Jace want Huck to be the man to care for his sister and niece or nephew? His heart clenched, but then he shook off the hesitation. He couldn't let guilt control him any longer. As Willow had said, Jace was no longer here.

And I am.

Eyes on her, he walked toward her, determined to stake his claim. Action had always worked better for him than words.

"Huck, what are you doing?" She sounded breathless.

"What I should have done this morning."

"Which was?" She met his no doubt hungry gaze, trying to look tough, but he was affecting her as much as she was affecting him.

Huck might not believe in fate, but his body had definitely chosen this woman.

"Change your mind." He took that final step, caging her in and not bothering to look around to see if Ruby or any of the other nosy people who'd been dogging Willow and peppering her with questions all afternoon were *still* around.

Huck didn't listen to caution. He didn't acknowledge the bonds of control he always kept tightly wrapped around his actions and emotions. He let everything go—the past, his doubts, reason—and finally kissed her.

I'M KISSING HUCK.

It didn't seem real.

And yet, as his hand splayed across her lower back, pulling her snug into his body, and his other hand cupped her cheek and jaw before his fingers worked the elastic out of her ponytail and buried in her hair, the kiss seemed inevitable. Willow had a momentary flash of déjà vu that her mother would derive some mystical meaning from, but Willow shoved the thought away.

After so much doubt and stress and hurt, she didn't want to think. Thinking never made her feel this good. For once she just wanted to feel.

His lips teased hers apart and a stroke of his tongue had her clutching his shoulders to hold herself up.

Huck deepened the kiss, taking even more control.

Willow could feel her heart slam against his, and she whispered his name like a confession as she chased his lips and shared breath with him.

Kissing Huck was wrong.

It didn't mean anything. It couldn't. It was just hormones. Boosting her ego. Blowing off steam.

"We are creating a lot of steam," Huck murmured

against her lips.

"I didn't say that out loud," she objected, feeling too good to care. She wasn't using him to boost her ego was she?

"Happy to be of service." He kissed the corner of her mouth again, and stroked his tongue along her upper lip.

Shivers coursed through her body. "Stop pretending you're a mind reader."

"And you are not a quiet kisser," he murmured kissing his way along her jawline.

She sighed her pleasure. It felt so wonderful to be held, and to touch and be touched and the heat building rather than confusing her felt inevitable. But it wasn't fair to him. Or her. She shouldn't jump to another man just because her life had skidded into the weeds.

One hand stroked through the length of her hair, sending shivers through her body, while the other angled her mouth to once again be plundered by his. She could feel the hard length of him. So much power and pleasure to be had when she'd felt alone and lonely for so long.

Just one more minute, she promised, then she'd grab on to reason with both hands. Or maybe at least one.

"Huck," she breathed. Her hands pushed under his T-shirt, exploring his abs, smoothing the material up so she could feel his hot, tight skin and the hard flex of muscle. His back and shoulder muscles felt freaking amazing.

She kissed him again, needing the heat building to a fire, the connection, the momentary escape from the rough and tumble of her thoughts.

Just one more second.

She blew by her promise to herself and continued to lose herself in his kiss. For such a restrained, enigmatic man his kiss was pure fire, and the roughness of his calloused hands, combined with the reverent way he touched her, had her desperate with desire.

And then Montana Wind, tired of being ignored, nudged her head between them and snorted.

Willow stumbled back and would have plopped on her ass had Huck not kept hold of her.

"Well, that's one way to interrupt," she heard a laconic voice drawl behind her.

Willow whirled around. Huck's adopted grandfather, Jim, and Ben Ballantyne stood watching them along with one of Ben's grandsons—the pretty one, Bodhi, who'd always been full of flirt and tease and had driven every teen girl hormonally mad within a twenty-mile radius each summer he'd visited his granddad.

She hadn't seen him or his cousins in years except for Beck and Bowen this morning at her supposed wedding. She wished she weren't seeing him now. She must be tomato red, and she was still clutching a handful of Huck's shirt. She'd been about to marry another man this morning.

What must they think of her?

Bodhi's smile was megawatt wide, and if she'd known him better, she'd give him a quick kick in his shins. She'd heard he'd married and was now in med school at the University of Washington in Seattle.

"That's one way to complete a few practice patterns for your rodeo event," Bodhi said, sauntering forward to hold out his hand.

"Bodhi Ballantyne," he introduced himself to Huck.

They shook hands and Huck looked way more composed than she felt. Her heart felt like it was pounding in her throat, and she knew, just knew, her face and neck were bright red. Huck's hand splayed on her hip, and he pulled her into his body.

"Put up a sign, why don't you," she muttered.

"Good to see you again, Willow. Lil Strawberry and I go way back." Bodhi winked.

"You did not just call me that again." Willow narrowed her eyes, wishing she could kick him, but Huck was partially blocking him, and Jim and Ben were looking highly amused.

"Oops." Bodhi was unrepentant.

"I'm not ten anymore."

"I can see that. I wanted to apologize for missing your wedding but turns out I may still have a shot at attending after all."

His smile was full Bodhi—beautiful, sincere—and his dark blue eyes danced, enjoying himself at her expense way too much.

"I've always admired your grit and fire, Cowgirl, and the way you'd jump back on your horse after a tumble. Ouch!"

Bodhi laughed as did Ben and Jim. Huck stared at her, shocked.

Willow stared at the toe of her boot. She really had kicked Bodhi. Three times riling her must be the charm.

"Okay, Bodhi, you had your fun, son," Ben said. "Get to the point."

The point? Willow looked back at Bodhi, wishing perhaps that she hadn't kicked him quite so hard. The toes on her right foot throbbed.

"Sorry, Strawberry." Bodhi didn't look it. "But to your earlier statement, you did kick me more than a few times when you were ten."

"You deserved it then," she said loftily. "For teasing Lang and me. Dandelion." She rolled her eyes and crossed her arms, relieved that her nipples had finally flattened.

She was going to have to start wearing padded bras if Huck was going to stick around.

He's not.

And that should make her rejoice. He had some weird magnetic force that sucked her in and made her behave badly.

"What can I say?" He shrugged and spread his hands wide in appeal, looking so handsome Willow felt like that stupid documentary crew that Jake had been so thrilled by and had followed around like he was a golden retriever puppy, should be filming this very moment, giving Bodhi a close-up shot.

"I'm creative, and all the young ladies of Marietta loved me."

"Your point?"

"That was one."

She stared him down.

"Bodhi, you have the manners of a goat," Ben Ballantyne called out.

"You raised me, sir."

"I'll need a do-over on that."

Bodhi grinned his agreement. "First, Willow, I wanted to check if you were okay. Bowen told me what had happened, and I wanted to see if you needed anything."

His voice and expression shone with sincerity, and Willow found herself softening. She only remembered how all the girls had chased after Bodhi every summer making fools of themselves. She'd forgotten how he'd always been the first to help anyone up after a fall, render first aid, a shoulder to cry on and a kind word.

"But it looks like…" Again with that unholy light in his eyes.

"Quit while you're ahead." Huck finally spoke, his voice quiet, but it had a note in it that had Bodhi's attention snapping to him.

"Second, we wanted to invite you and your mom and aunt and…" he indicated Huck "…Huck Jones, if you like, to dinner tonight to celebrate the start of the rodeo, and also gift your mom and aunt a few goats if they're ready for them.

Beck and Ash took them in a couple of weeks ago from a rescue out of a place in Livingston. They're healthy now and Ash's been taking care of them, but with her kid and career and a baby on the way she doesn't need a herd. Granddad sent a crew over to fix the fencing on the two closest pastures to your barn."

"That was thoughtful of you, Bodhi." Willow was touched. It was the rancher code—help out neighbors—but this seemed above and beyond. It also made her determined to find a way to help others in Marietta as she raised her child.

Alone.

"And third—" Bodhi jerked his thumb at Huck "—concerns you."

Chapter Fourteen

"THAT WAS A lovely evening out," Mandy enthused as Huck pulled his truck up to the front porch of the homestead house. "I think even you enjoyed it, Barb, once you put the goat kids down and talked to the people."

"Even me," she said good-naturedly. "It's true I never really got along with Genevieve Ballantyne. She was always so competitive, but she seems to have mellowed."

"*She's* mellowed." Mandy's lips curved in a smile. She looked at Willow and raised her brows, welcoming her to be a part of the gentle teasing.

Barb was oblivious. "It's nice to remember we have neighbors."

Only in ranch country would someone who lived a twenty-five-minute drive away be considered a neighbor. He opened the door and helped first Mandy and then Barb out of the truck.

The motion-detector light he'd installed early this evening while he was waiting for them to get ready to go to the Ballantynes for dinner switched on.

"Huck." Mandy touched his arm. "You take such good care of us. You're taking the job at the Ballantynes' ranch aren't you?"

"Ma'am, couple hundred years ago you would have been burned at the stake," he teased, trying to side-step the question that still buzzed in his ears. Ben and Bowen Ballantyne's unexpected job offer had shocked him, and he hadn't begun to process it.

"I certainly hope not," she said. "I have never enjoyed sweating. All that salt is so itchy. And that wasn't something I divined from a spirit." A sly smile lit her expression. "I had to use the restroom, and I heard Ben talking in that serious voice he has—he was a good friend of our daddy's—and I wanted to know what he was saying so I just lingered a bit outside his study."

"You snooped?" Barb sounded outraged.

"I lingered and overheard a question. But I didn't hear your answer," she said to Huck.

Huck laughed. "The magic and smoke and mirrors are revealed."

Mandy waited, her expression expectant.

"I'm thinking on it," Huck repeated the answer he'd given the Ballantynes. Not because he didn't want or need a job. He would and this one came with a place to live—an old cabin that had recently been renovated on the property. "Going to spend the morning and afternoon on the Ballantyne spread tomorrow, and then we'll talk next week after the rodeo."

And after he had a hard conversation with Jim.

He watched Willow slip silently out of the truck and head to the barn. Dang. He'd hoped to take care of Big Blue so that she wouldn't see what a fool he'd made of himself trying to create a honeymoon suite in her barn.

Now she'd think he was going to try to seduce her. And why not—that kiss this afternoon had gone from a spark to a raging wildfire. He had meant to entice, not consume. He looked toward the barn wondering if he could head her off without being impolite to Mandy, then he winced because he saw that he'd left one of the small lamp lights on low. Dumb mistake. Out of character. He hadn't survived for years being a team member on dangerous missions by being careless.

Dragging in a deep breath of cool night air, he walked Mandy and Barb up to the front door, tipped his hat and wished them both a good night.

"We'll be cheering for you at the rodeo," Mandy said. "And hopefully you'll join us at the steak dinner."

"Wouldn't miss it, ma'am."

"Ma'am." Mandy rolled her eyes and laughed. "He makes me sound one hundred. I'm not even sixty yet. And sixty is the new forty."

Barb pushed open the front door. "I'm making chamomile tea, Mandy. Would you like some or do you want a Red Bull or whatever young almost forty-somethings drink?"

"Tea sounds lovely. Good night, Huck."

He closed the door behind them and turned to face the

barn.

WILLOW STROKED BIG Blue's neck and finger-combed his mane, but for once her attention wasn't completely on her horse. There was a light on in the loft of her barn. Had Huck been sleeping up there? Not that she would have minded. She would have offered him some quilts. Her paternal grandmother had been locally famous for her quilts. People had driven hundreds of miles to buy them. And the McBrides still had quite a few safely stored in zippered plastic in a cedar-lined chest that Jace and Mr. Lane had built for one of Jace's class projects when he'd been in high school.

Curiosity stirred, but Huck deserved his privacy. He was an honorable man. Jace's friend. He'd jumped in with both feet to help and was kind.

He kissed me.

Again she looked up at the loft. The glow was pinky gold and romantic. Totally unexpected for a man like Huck. What had he done—bought a lamp or… It was her barn.

Intrigued, she headed to the ladder rationalizing with each step and finishing that as a responsible owner, she should check for fire hazards.

Yup. Her halo was shiny.

She'd climbed this ladder many times as a child. But at

the top, she was so startled, she nearly let go.

She couldn't quite process what she was seeing. Huck had created a bedroom—a whimsical, romantic bedroom. A vintage, very rustic wrought-iron cushy canopy bed perched in the middle of the loft. Two pillows were on each side along with throw pillows that were color coordinated with the sage-colored quilt that had small squares of horses sewn into the pattern.

Almost in a daze Willow climbed all the way up. The floor was covered in straw, and there were several hay bales with slip covers over them, forming a colorful wall of intimacy. There were two antique nightstands, both with colorful bouquets of flowers and antique lights. There was also a winged-back chair with a bridge-style lamp over it.

The four tall bedposts were draped with fabric that looked like netting that would be used to create a tutu. The fabric extended above and across the bedposts, creating a canopy, and it looked like fairy lights had been added to some of the fabric.

"You found it." She knew he'd come, but she was too choked up to answer.

"Too much?"

She heard a hint of uncertainty in his voice and recognized it as she'd been feeling vulnerable since she'd seen the two pink lines in June.

"It's beautiful."

Huck had put himself out there with this gesture for her

and her supposed happy future with another man.

She tried not to read anything into the romantic honeymoon suite. It was for Jace's sister. Not her. But if she could have designed one, it would have looked just like this.

"No one has ever done anything so special for me, Huck," she admitted. "Never ever."

A hint of pink marred his deeply tanned face along his high cheekbones with the appealing hollow in them. Willow felt that his onyx gaze could see deeply into her soul—her loneliness as a child. Her pretended confidence and independence—it must have been a front for her to jump in with Jake's plans, so easily.

He looked as if he was searching for something easy to say. But she didn't want to hear what Jace would do because Jace hadn't.

"Thank you," she whispered, willing him to speak, but scared he'd ruin the moment by reminding her it was only because of Jace.

So many questions pounded on the door of her mind. Would he take the job at the Ballantyne ranch? Did she want him to? He would be so much easier to resist if he'd ride out of town Sunday evening like the rest of the cowboys.

"I wanted to do something special for you, Willow. You deserve special."

Did she?

"Because you think Jace would have made this sweet, tender, beautiful gesture for me?" she challenged, wanting to be angry, maybe even start a fight. But a bigger part of her wanted to hurtle into his arms. To feel safe and cared for.

"I wasn't thinking of Jace. I was thinking of you."

He stepped all the way into the loft, silently, his rangy body moving with enviable ease.

"You might as well see the rest," he said and hit a switch. Willow caught her breath as the fairy lights lit up, casting the loft in a golden glow. There was a pink tinge from a neon sign of a galloping horse and a heart of pink lights pinned on the wall.

"Wow," she breathed. "It's like out of a magazine."

He looked away from her, head tilted down. "I googled," he said, "and went back to the barn sale."

"Where did you get the paintings?" She walked to the back wall where the head of the bed was centered and looked at the four landscapes. They seemed familiar but were stylized enough that they didn't look like something someone would see when wandering into a small-town western art gallery. She stepped closer, her finger almost tracing a long oak branch with a dip in it where a young girl sat with a book. There was a gray shadow that almost looked vaguely like a figure far in the distance. Willow looked at each painting and came back to the one in the middle, trying to find the words to understand, to explain, to ask.

"It's me, I think," Willow said softly. "It's like I'm part of Montana Wind like that mythological creature, what was it called?"

"A Centaur," Huck said. "But those were men, and you are most definitely all woman. Your hair is like a banner pulling the sun through the end of a storm as you and Montana Wind scalpel it around that barrel."

"How…where did you…?"

"Your mother. She has hundreds."

Willow slowly sat on the edge of the bed.

"I was working up here late Wednesday night, stringing up the lights, and I saw a light out in the distance and went to investigate."

"Just like I did tonight."

"Your mother was looking for a wedding present for you. She wasn't sure you'd accept, but she offered me the one in the middle and then asked me to choose one for you. I chose four."

"She really was out there painting," Willow said softly, stunned. "She never let me see anything. She never shared. She never once sold…"

She looked at Huck helplessly, as if he'd have an explanation.

"Maybe she didn't feel safe."

Willow knew all about that. But instead of asking for help or hiding, she'd plowed her way through life. She'd been strong. And she needed to be even stronger.

"Marriage is a big step. I wasn't sure where you'd end up, so I wanted you to have pieces of home."

"I'm so tired," she admitted, overwhelmed and confused

by Huck's gesture. "I don't want to think any more tonight," she whispered, looking up at him. "I just want to feel."

As if pulled by a string, Willow stood up, and walked toward him, intent in every step. Desire raced through her blood like sparkling wine.

"It's so beautiful here," she tempted. "It would be a shame to let the room go to waste." She reached out and traced the silky black piping on his western-style shirt and then played with one of the black and silver snaps.

He caught her hand, his expression pained, and then he held her knuckles to his cheek.

"I told you my intentions this morning."

She could barely hear him through the roaring in her head and the hot blood zipping through her veins. And thinking? Her brain had hit pause long ago.

"I want to marry you. Take care of you and your baby. Nothing less."

And before she could begin to formulate an argument he was gone.

REJECTED BY TWO men in the same day. Willow finished her last practice run Friday morning at Tucker's. She was pleased with her times, but still unsettled by the events yesterday.

"I mean who does that?" she demanded of Tucker, who pocketed her phone she'd been using to time Willow's runs.

Last night she'd slept in the beautiful room—Huck had even whitewashed the ceiling of the loft—and she tried to sort through her feelings and the double rejection. Huck's stung far more than Jake bolting on their wedding day. And when Jake had awakened her in the middle of the night with a drunken phone call sharing that not only had he gotten the part, he was taking over for another actor who had family issues and had to bow out so the film company needed to reshoot several scenes starting next week.

Willow had said congrats and rolled over to go back to sleep. He was too drunk on whiskey and life for her to discuss the future.

"An honorable man," Tucker said. "Bastards." Then she laughed. "Cowboys. What's a cowgirl to do? Succumb?"

Willow popped off Montana Wind.

"But don't make it too easy on Huck." Tucker shook her finger at Willow and did a sexy dance move. "Make him work for it. Hard."

Willow had known Tucker since she'd been a young teen, and she still had the power to shock her. She was unfiltered, fearless and had epic experience with men, whereas Willow had a thimble full.

"Huck deserves a woman who is free and clear, not one who's pregnant, nearly married her baby daddy, got blessedly jilted at the altar, and kissed him stupid that afternoon and then propositioned him that night."

"Kiss?" Tucker's ears practically rotated toward her, and

her vivid green eyes shimmered with interest. "This is just about to get interesting, but here comes Ruby so gossip will have to wait. Hey, do you have something to do today, or can you help out? I've got several more appointments, and another group of horses to get to the fairgrounds, but Parker's got school and soccer practice."

"All yours," Willow said. She didn't want to be alone with her thoughts or wonder what was happening with Huck at the Ballantynes' ranch.

"Sweet."

Tucker gave her several tasks after she cooled Montana Wind down. It felt good to be useful and to belong.

She waited to call Jake until she was headed back to the fairgrounds with Montana Wind and also another horse that boarded with Tucker and belonged to a rodeo queen. The horse's name was Maple Bar because of her coloring and sweet nature, and Willow was trying to remember the last time she'd allowed herself a donut.

Maybe after the finals next month she'd loosen her restrictions—a little. After all she wouldn't be competing again except perhaps at a few local rodeos potentially next summer, if then. She didn't have to worry about Jake or any other man's opinion. The homestead house was safe and snug again. Her mom and aunt were happy and had an idea for a business and a beautiful garden. A weight fell off her shoulders.

Only one more thread to pull.

Her call went straight to voicemail, but he texted before she arrived at the fairgrounds.

In makeup. Shooting all afternoon. Not going to make CMR. My season's done. Talk tonight.

Was there more to say? Jake had spelled out his priorities. Talking in person would be the best, and phone a second choice. Willow, who'd always taken the hard way, copped out and sent a quick text just because she wanted closure, or as much closure as she could have until the baby was born.

Congratulations. Happy for you. Staying in MT. We can work out visitations if you want later.

She pushed send before she could second-guess herself. The backstage at the rodeo was humming by Friday afternoon. Staff circulated, sorting arrivals, livestock contractors and vendors. She wouldn't have had time for a call anyway.

Willow tucked her phone in her back pocket just as barrel racers Janice Brown and her sister Jessica barreled down on her.

"I can't believe it. I heard you and Jake didn't get married," Janice said. "What happened? Are you devastated? I'm so sorry." She gave Willow a hug. "You guys were so perfect together."

"Men are dogs," her younger sister Jessica said. "Did Jake cheat?"

"Nah. Jake did the right thing," Willow began.

"Wait, what, did he dump you?" Jessica nearly screeched. "Rude."

Willow tried to ignore that about fifteen people had

stopped what they were doing to swing around and look at her.

"Play it cool." Janice nudged her sister. "No woman wants everyone to know a famous, hot bull rider dumped them on their wedding day."

Willow smothered her sigh. She'd done the right thing avoiding the fairgrounds today until she couldn't. She wouldn't miss the gossip and drama, and her instinct to avoid tomorrow's morning parade was now a plan.

"We just reconsidered," Willow said. "We have different goals."

That sounded mature, but Jessica looked disappointed.

"But you're okay, Willow?" Janice asked, her brows scrunched in concern.

"I'm good, but just want…privacy. Time to process. After the finals I'm going to work on the Wild Wind Ranch again and figure out what comes next for me."

She smiled her fan smile. The sponsor smile.

No need to tell anyone about the baby or that she wouldn't be back next season. If she said those things, she'd be written off. That's all anyone would be talking about. This was her hometown. Copper Mountain Rodeo was her rodeo. And she was taking first place. No distraction of a broken engagement, jilted bride, bull rider turned actor or enigmatic sexy cowboy who had so much sweet he broke her heart was going to stand in her way.

Chapter Fifteen

SHE WAS A coward. Not proud to admit that she was hiding in her trailer, but if she heard one more person express 'sympathy' for her broken engagement and then eagerly dig for deets on the breakup or Jake's TV role, she was going to have to put the slap-down on some nosy person. Worse, everyone assumed she was heartbroken and putting on a brave front. Conversation stopped when she walked into the livestock barn. She saw the side-eyes, the sympathy. She heard the whispers in the bathroom or when she'd line up to get a breakfast taco without the tortilla.

She hated it. It reminded her of her childhood when she or her family had been the source of gossip. And now she was a topic of discussion again.

She sat at the small table, wishing Big Blue were in the trailer with her. At least she'd have company. She heard music, laughter, so much life outside, and the parade was gearing up, which she'd never missed, but she had to keep her head in the game. She was competing later this afternoon.

So, yeah, she was hiding. Determined to stay in here until it was time to watch Huck compete.

As if she'd summoned him by her thoughts, she heard a fist bang on her door. "Buck up, Cowgirl. Time to face the day."

Willow jumped and wondered if she stayed quiet whether he'd go away.

"Stop hiding."

If he hoped to goad her, he was out of luck.

"I heard the queens earlier."

Willow closed her eyes and covered her face, humiliation washing over her. They'd been particularly catty saying a combination of clever snark like: 'Willow knows how to keep her seat on a horse but not on a man.' And then there'd been the usual speculation of who Jake had been cheating with.

"Stop hiding."

He wasn't going away.

"I'm not hiding." She swung the door open with a flourish, and he jumped out of the way. He held a tray with two to-go cups from the Java Café and curiosity stirred.

His dark gaze walked over her, heating her, seeing too much. She held herself tall, swished her ponytail a little, but the longer he looked, the more she felt in danger of wilting. Huck was just so easy to let down her guard with.

"I hate being the subject of gossip," she admitted.

"Can't control that," he said. "But you can influence the narrative."

"Huh?"

"Come to the parade with me. I'll show you."

"That will give everyone even more to speculate about."

"Exactly."

His smile was wicked and heated her abdomen.

He held out his hand. She looked at it. Darkly tan, betraying years working outdoors and an ethnically ambiguous heritage. So strong and appealing. And it would be so easy to capitulate. Let him hold her. Take care of her for a moment. Let her get her bearings in this new world she was about to enter. But no. That wasn't fair to him or to her.

She wanted love. She was going to hold out for love even if she never got it.

"C'mon, Cowgirl. Flip some of that attitude that floored my attention the first moment I saw you."

"Is that tea?" She was so tired of tea.

He angled the tray a little farther away from her.

"You'll have to come out of your cave and find out."

"Funny."

"Been thinking of a few things to say to make you smile."

Willow took a deep breath and stepped down out of the trailer.

"That's better," he said softly.

He handed her a cup and she inhaled deeply.

"Oh, God," she breathed. "Coffee. I've missed this. So what if the baby has three arms. I need this."

"There's this thing called decaf," he said. "And there's a special drink this week called Copper Mountain Rodeo

Cowgirl. I got the Cowboy version. Thought we could do a taste test and see which one is more delicious—the cowboy or the cowgirl."

Was he trying to give her heatstroke? He hadn't backed off so she was pinned between his hard, rangy body and the side of her trailer. And now he was suggesting that they share drinks. Or was she reading him wrong? Last night he'd all but run away.

He sipped his coffee, pleasure on his face. "Okay, so that's the cowboy—take a sip, tell me what you taste."

Willow couldn't even swallow as all the blood from her brain raced south to peak her nipples and pool in her lower abdomen. She was taking back Huck's list of good traits. He was wicked. And a tease. And contrary. And Satan-hot.

He held his cup to her lips. "I dare you."

"What if I want a taste of something else cowboy that's not just coffee?" she pushed, just to see how far he'd take this.

His eyes lit—a silver star in all that midnight.

"I'm open to negotiation."

She sipped his coffee. "Mmmmm it's spicy, like a Mexican coffee," she said.

He sipped hers and then held it out to her. "And the cowgirl?"

Willow sipped, tasting caramel, but also a hint of salt and something mysterious.

"You tell me?"

He leaned down until his lips were nearly brushing hers, and it took all her willpower to not chase his mouth and demand a kiss. He'd rejected her, and now he was playing a game where she didn't know the rules. But she did want to play.

She just needed to be cautious—not her skill set.

"I'm thinking," she perseverated.

"You do you." He took a sip of his coffee. "I prefer the taste of the cowgirl…latte." He winked. "Let's head to the parade."

As they walked across the browned grass parking lot, Willow realized quite a few people had witnessed Huck's taste-testing game. Several groups of cowboys stood around, jawing, heating up eggs and bacon or coffee on their Coleman camp stoves, watching them walk by.

Her fighting spirit rose. She didn't have to pretend that she was okay. She was better than. And if Huck wanted to play games, she'd play and win.

She slipped her arm through his and beamed her fan smile at him before taking another sip of the delicious brew.

"I have a challenge for you, Cowboy."

"Name it."

"The person who scores the highest in their event today treats the other to the steak dinner tonight."

He looked a little staggered by that, and she was smiling for real, liking that she'd surprised him.

"I hope you've been saving your dollars, Huck."

Huck had been trained to withstand torture. He could compartmentalize pain to protect his mind and his men and the mission, but nothing had prepared him to resist a playful cowgirl. Willow flirted and teased and had him regretting his vow to keep their interactions G-rated. Dumb. Sex was practically his superpower, and he was sweeping it off the table in their battle.

Willow cheered on the parade, sharing kettle corn and brushing against his body at every opportunity while they stood on a crowded street corner watching what looked like half the town parade by on float, in costumes, on horses and in groups carrying signs, throwing candy and waving.

Her fingertips stroked his lips as she tempted him with kettle corn.

"You wanted it," she reminded him.

He let her feed him. She smiled, but there was a light in her eyes that shone full of wicked promise. She was pushing, trying to find his buttons and his limits, probably irritated with him for leaving her last night. But what else could he do? She didn't want him as a husband. He didn't blame her. But the thought of her trying to raise her baby alone hollowed him.

Jace wasn't here to help.

The only leverage he had was physical. He and Willow had connected on a chemical level since the beginning. Less of a slow burn than a barely avoided explosion. Only his honor and her loyalty to Jake had held them back. And now the fetters were cut.

But he needed more than sex to lure her.

He had to prove to Willow that her life and her child's life would be better with him in it.

But he'd never thought in terms like that before—being a partner.

How did other men do it? He looked at Jim. He'd been married. He'd lost his wife early to cancer. Had never remarried. He'd lost his son and grandson in a car accident and had kept going, keeping the ranch together, taking in a troubled teen boy for a few years and then helping to raise his two great-nephews, sending them to college and welcoming them back to the ranch to teach them the ropes so the family name and the ranch could endure.

Huck didn't have a name or a legacy.

But he could build one with Willow. And a family of his own—something he never imagined he'd have.

This morning he watched Bowen Ballantyne who had his wife tucked against his body and arms around her as they watched the parade. He'd be the one he'd be working with the most on the Three Tree Ranch if he took the job. Bowen was quiet. His wife, however, shone with excitement as she chatted with another woman with long, dark hair, who was just starting to swell with pregnancy—again, judging by the fact that her husband, Beck, had a toddler on his shoulders.

He too was laughing and talking a mile a minute to his two cousins and granddad and Jim.

Jim had purchased large pretzels and had handed them out with Mandy and Barb, splitting one, while he chomped on one with mustard.

Would rekindling his friendship with the Ballantynes be enough for Jim to get his health checked? Would he be willing to stay on in Marietta, which had a good hospital and a new cancer wing under construction?

Willow watched Beck and his wife with their little one, perhaps taking mental notes just like he was doing with the three Ballantyne men. They made being part of a couple look so easy.

But they were in love.

Love was what Willow wanted.

And he had no idea how to do that.

"I'm going to head back." She stood on her tiptoes and lightly nipped his ear.

He startled. "I'll walk with you."

She tucked her hand in his back pocket the minute they were out of sight from her family.

"How'd I do? Mission accomplished?" she asked.

"If you were trying to have me combust, and darn near get crippled from a permanent hard-on, then yeah. You slayed."

Willow laughed. "You started it, but we turned a few heads and maybe everyone will stop whispering about me being brokenhearted."

"Have you spoken to Jake?" he asked, feeling like he was holding his breath.

"Sort of. I had to resort to texting him as he's working. But he's done with the rodeo this season and probably forever. And I feel like something's wrong with me, because I only feel relieved."

"Nothing's wrong with you," he growled.

They still had at least an hour before the opening ceremonies started, but Huck was happy to get out of the crowds. He'd never liked them, and he was happy to get out of the sights of the documentary crew filming.

"You don't know that."

He hated the uncertainty in her voice, and the fact that she'd gone from tormenting him to worrying again.

He aimed for a distraction. "I've got two events today. I'll be working up an appetite for my steak dinner tonight that you're buying me."

They walked through the park by the courthouse and over the bridge and along the river path that led to the rodeo fairgrounds.

"You're buying *me* a steak dinner tonight—with the works. Baked potato, corn, salad," Willow corrected.

"You sure about that?"

"Definitely. I ride to win."

"I'm looking forward to watching you try, Cowgirl." He smoothed a few stray hairs that had escaped her ponytail.

"You mean succeed."

He wasn't sure who'd moved closer first, but her lips were temptingly close, and Huck was tired of trying to resist her pull.

"Willow," he whispered just as his lips sealed with hers.

"Willow McBride. Whatever are you doing?"

Huck was so caught up in the kiss that he could barely hear the voice. He'd reeled Willow in so that he could feel the press of her beautiful breasts and the restless shift of her lips and long, lean lines of her legs.

"Jilting a man one day and kissing another two days later in broad daylight near the courthouse in front of God and everyone."

Willow jumped. Huck felt as if he'd been doused with ice water as a matronly woman glared at them both.

"And you, young man, a soldier. You should know better. Willow is an engaged woman. Or she was. And now I think we will all know why her groom didn't show up on the big day."

There was so much to unpack in that diatribe that Huck had no idea where to start. Who was this judgmental witch? And why try to shame Willow?

"Mrs. Bingley," Willow said, her face flushed. Her breath was fetchingly quick, and it was hard not to stare at the quick movements of her chest in her tight shirt. "I appreciate you showing up at our house uninvited for the wedding, but it's not my fault Jake decided he wasn't ready. Huck is a friend and wishing me luck today."

"Uninvited," she huffed. "I was invited by your mother, but of course I took my gift back. And if that's what this young man claims will give you good luck then I truly fear for our youth."

Nose up in the air, she walked off.

"What's her problem?"

"That was actually pretty mild."

They walked to the fairgrounds. Most of the booths and food trucks were already set up. Some middle school kids had a lemonade stand for a 4-H club, and Huck bought a lemonade. He joined Willow who was writing something on a slip of paper. She stuffed it in a box.

"Raffle? What's the prize?" he asked, baffled as the booth looked rather patriotic and claimed that it represented Marietta City Government and Civic Organizations.

"Nominations for Marietta citizen of the year." Willow smirked. "I nominated Carol Bingley."

"Are you trying to torture us?"

"I am now. Carol's the anti-citizen. Taylor Swift should write a song. Carol involves herself in everyone and everything in the town—kind of a black cloud."

"Not very nice, Willow," a woman organizing the literature in the booth commented, smiling. "But unfortunately you are not the first to put in Carol's name sarcastically. I'm afraid she's been particularly trying the past few weeks. It's like she has something on her mind nibbling."

"Mayor, this is Huck Jones. He served with my brother. Our mayor, Chelsea Collier Flint."

Huck shook her hand.

"Thank you for your service." Then she winked at Willow. "Even for a barrel racer you move fast."

"As mayor you should be above gossip," Willow noted.

"I am," Chelsea said piously. "But I have eyes, and I saw you feeding this hungry cowboy popcorn during the parade."

"Oh," Willow said, blushing.

"I was hungry," Huck said, coming to the rescue.

"We've all been there. Montana cowboys are irresistible. I'll see you in the arena, and I'm rooting for our hometown girl to take first."

"You won't be disappointed."

Chapter Sixteen

WILLOW HAD WATCHED a few of the pre rodeo events sitting by his side. And she'd stayed in the stands next to Jim, her mom and aunt when he'd saddled up Midnight and earned one of his best times steer wrestling. Usually he'd stay backstage, relax, listen to music and think about his ride.

But the pull of Willow was stronger. He joined them, still in his chaps. Willow definitely noticed, but he played it cool.

When he left before the saddle bronc, Jim and Ben followed him.

He'd be lying to say he wasn't interested in the Three Trees Ranch job. He most definitely was. He felt like he'd be a part of something—an organization that was well run by people he could respect. But first he had an old man to persuade to see a doctor. And an independent cowgirl to woo.

He stood off on his own—pretty much how he'd lived his life, letting conversations roll over him. When the saddle bronc event began, he moved closer, waiting his turn, getting a feel of the competition and the stock.

Copper Mountain Rodeo was well run. The stock was top quality, and the talent pool was deep—competitive.

Didn't matter. He'd come to win. Only one local cowboy had bested him in steer wrestling today, and another cowboy—Rye Calhoun was hungry and hell-bent to win All-Around Cowboy judging from his events and stats. Huck had to watch out for him, but at least he was in the finals tomorrow for his first event. He'd gotten a solid draw on the bronc so now he just had to keep his seat and he'd be in the finals and the money tomorrow for both events.

But Huck watched cowboy after cowboy hit the dirt.

"Your boy up for this?" Ben Ballantyne asked Jim. "Our Montana cowboys are bred tough here."

"Wyoming-born cowboys are just as strong." Jim didn't look at him, but Huck could feel the old rancher's quiet affection. "Don't go trying to get in his head. None of your boys are still competing."

"You had a desk job in the service son?"

Now Ben was messing with him.

"You think that would help me stick the ride if I did?" Huck asked.

A smile played around Ben's mouth.

Huck's boots were tied on. Gloves too. His name was called, and he jammed in his mouth guard. Ben frowned at his hat—no helmet—but said nothing.

Maybe he should switch to a helmet. He had Willow and the baby to think about now, even though he was finishing out his season in a couple of weeks.

He clambered to the top of the chute and looked down on Jalapeño. He was a local bucking bronc from a stock contractor out past Livingston. Impressive stats. Huck watched, got a feel. Jim and Ben were up beside him conferring.

"Horse's hot," Jim said—no worry showed on his face, but he had a tone.

"Bring on the spice," Huck answered.

"See you after the bell." It was the same thing Jim always said.

Huck took a deep breath, absorbed the sounds of the crowd, the smells of the rodeo, the efficiency of the chute crew. The stock owner gave him a small salute and advice about the buck rein for this horse.

"Do your best, Soldier," Ben advised.

"Cowboy now," he answered, but his attention was on the bronc—the head, the shoulders, the energy.

He timed his drop, anticipating the shift and even though he'd lightly skimmed his boot across the horse to let it know he was coming on board, the bronc didn't like it.

It thrashed and twisted as the chute crew got the horse once again situated, cursing a little. Huck adjusted his grip on the buck rein. Repositioned his pelvis, shifted his center of gravity angled back.

Deep breath in and out. Another in and as he let out his breath, he gave the nod, his entire attention centered on the bronc as he let his body jump into the churning rapids generated by a bronc at the peak of its athleticism. Both man and animal careened into the arena, and as Jalapeño leaped forward in his trademark near vertical front end drop, Huck angled up in the stirrups to ensure his spurs touched the horse's shoulder high enough so that he marked out.

Huck usually gave his mounts a little less rein, but he'd seen rider after rider get pulled over the head of the horses today, and he hoped that the small adjustment, also recommended by the stock contractor, would not only keep him seated but allow Jalapeño to do his moves and earn a high enough score to keep him in the game.

As he countered Jalapeño's choppy rhythm, he kept his feet firmly in the stirrups, his toes pointed, his left hand up high and fluid—he always imagined himself high-fiving God—and his right hand anchored on the buck rein. So much success found in life came by just holding on.

HUCK SAW THE light rather than heard the bell. Jalapeño did another spin, and Huck kicked out of the stirrups and released his grip on the buck rein and shot over the top of Jalapeño's head. He ran for the fence and clamored up, briefly tipping his hat to the roaring crowd. Adrenaline still jacked through his system, making him feel like a god. More rides like that, and he'd be tempted—almost—to sign on for another year, but as he looked for his score, his gaze lit on Willow, standing behind the fence near the chute with Jim and Ben.

He dropped down. As soon as he straightened taking one step toward them, Willow hugged him hard.

"That was incredible." Her face shone with enthusiasm.

What felt better than incredible was the way her body molded against his but, too soon, she stepped back, tucking her hands in her back pockets.

"Huck Jones came to win," Willow noted.

"I always do."

She smiled, but he'd never felt more serious.

Like always, the current pulsed between them, ebbed and flowed and built. He'd fought it all week, but now he let the energy have its way with him. It was all he had to work with so he could reel her in to come around to his way of thinking.

She felt it too. Jim watched him. Ben stirred restlessly.

"You have the top score so far. Helps that you stuck your ride when so many others hit the dirt," Willow said cheekily, "but don't think that will get you out of buying me the steak dinner."

"I'll be there." He didn't break eye contact or fight the pull between them. "I'll watch your ride."

She nodded and then spun around and strode off to prepare.

Huck felt like she took all the warmth and life with her.

"That was quite a ride," Jim said, bumping Huck back to reality as he watched Willow walk away. Several people tried to talk to her, but she kept her gaze forward and held up a 'don't mess with me' hand.

"You look more like a man gearing up for more competition than a career change," Ben noted.

"No. This was a summer bucket list for me and Jim," Huck said. Determination stamped each word. "I do need a job, sir, after we talk." He pointed at Jim, expecting him to grouch. Instead he just looked away, a deep scowl settling in his features.

"Sounds good," Ben said. "We'll double-team him. I got Bodhi on our side. He's up at the medical school at the University of Washington, and there's a big-name cancer center there if we need the big guns."

We. The word rushed relief through him. He wasn't alone in this fight.

"Between the two of us, we should be able to strong-arm him into the truck to get him to a doctor," Huck ventured.

"I reckon we can."

"You reckon wrong," Jim said. "I'm not a child who needs my decisions made for me."

"Then don't act like one," Ben said mildly.

"And I can wrestle you into my truck." Huck tried to lighten the moment, savoring how he finally felt he could breathe properly without so much unspoken worry choking him. "I wrestled a steer this morning in under five seconds and didn't break a sweat."

Yeah, he was bragging. Jim grunted. Ben smiled, clapped his arm around Huck's shoulders. "You and I and the boys are going to get along just fine. Go get out of your cowboy duds—" he nodded toward the chaps, gloves, protective vest and likely the spurs "—and come join us in the stands to watch your girl ride."

His girl. He was still working on that.

Huck complied quickly, feeling for the first time in a long time that the future was something to embrace, not just face.

WILLOW SAT ATOP Montana Wind. She could feel her horse's anticipation matching hers. Barrel racing was always a big draw, just like bull riding, and the Copper Mountain Rodeo attracted top talent.

Willow wanted to savor every moment. This could be one of her last professional rides. She wasn't trying to be dramatic, but she wanted to be available to her child in a way she hadn't felt her parents were to her. And she'd be doing double duty, both mom and dad.

Unless you take Huck up on his offer.

Shshshsh, she shushed her conscience. Or was it her libido? The heat they'd generated with just a few kisses still scorched.

But it was more. She felt like Huck got her. Didn't judge. And as a man who'd grown up without the love, comfort and support of a traditional family, she felt he could relate.

And maybe he too wanted something he hadn't had.

Willow worried her bottom lip. Maybe there wasn't a normal. Maybe everyone did the best they could. Maybe she needed to trust herself more, open up her heart in a way she never had with Jake or anyone else.

Huck was someone she could lose her heart to. But could he love her back?

Had Huck been serious with his offer? Did it have anything to do with her—loving her and building a life with her and her child—or was it all about his duty and loyalty to Jace?

Could that loyalty turn to love?

How would I know?

Willow had never felt loved, but maybe that was on her—perception, not reality.

Ruby angled her horse into the alleyway.

"Wish me luck." Her eyes shone with excitement, and her mount danced sideways.

"You don't need luck, Ruby. You've got skills. Trust yourself, your training and your horse," she said to the younger girl, already slipping back into coach mode. "You have the competitive heart of a champion."

Ruby looked a little surprised and then she reached out,

brushing Willow's fingers. "Thanks, Willow."

Ruby's name was announced, and she moved into starting position. Willow was next. She knew Huck was watching, and happiness zinged through her blood more than it had when Jake had watched her rides.

She knew luck existed. She wasn't in denial. But she'd felt so out of control growing up that she could only trust her work ethic and drive.

Willow closed her eyes and breathed in slowly through her nose and out again. She centered herself, translating her calm and certainty to Montana Wind.

"This is our time to shine," she said.

Willow could tell by the crowd that Ruby had had an exceptional ride.

Good for her.

Didn't matter. She and Montana Wind were going to place first. Today and tomorrow. It was destiny. She felt it. A smile touched her lips. Perhaps she was more her mother's daughter than she admitted.

The applause was as thunderous as Ruby's horse as it galloped back up the alleyway. Ruby drew her horse up midway and her face shone with happiness.

"My best run this season," Ruby sang out.

"Congrats," Willow whispered moving into position and waiting for her name to be called. Anticipation zinged through her blood.

She was a champion, and she rode a champion. She drew

in a deep breath scented with dirt, feed, sawdust, horse, popcorn and grilling meat. This was where she felt at home. Where she and Montana Wind excelled, and she was going to give the gossips something other than her being jilted, flirting with a new cowboy and single motherhood to talk about.

Every nerve stretched with anticipation when she heard her name, and when she received the go signal, she was all instinct, muscle memory, confidence and a burgeoning feeling of joy.

WILLOW BARELY HAD time to swing off Montana Wind and accept a few congratulations before Huck was there.

"Those were the most beautiful rides I've ever seen." Huck's hug was sure and strong. He picked her up off her feet and spun them in a circle, holding her tightly. "Your top score ever. You and Montana Wind were one. You rode like the goddess of the wind."

Pleasure flushed through her. There were other people waiting to congratulate her, but she was only aware of Huck. He still held her, his hands warm and sure on her arms.

"Fast enough to get a free steak dinner?" She tried to keep the question light, flirty, but the way he was looking at her felt intense and strangled her breathing.

"And more."

Her heart was pounding, and it had nothing to do with her ride. No, it was this man and how he made her feel. But did he feel the same? Was it enough to build on?

Take a chance.

She wanted to. She was tired of always playing a lone hand and playing it safe. But she couldn't quite let go. She rocked forward on her tiptoes to whisper in his ear.

"Is this for real or are you still pretending, to help me save face?" She had to ask, though she sounded screamingly insecure, and maybe a bit too invested.

She leaned away from him, but he reeled her even closer. His lips touched hers, teasing them apart, and his tongue traced the seam of her lower lip. Willow gasped a little, shocked at his boldness and her own immediate and heated response. She deepened the kiss and was disappointed when he pulled away slightly to rest his forehead against hers.

"Does that answer your question?"

Her adrenaline began to ebb, even as her heart kicked up again after the kiss.

"I never do or say anything I don't mean, Willow McBride."

"Okay."

She had to let it go. She had to take care of her horse. She had to get herself back under control. But Huck continued to look at her like she was something special, and she was starting to believe it.

"Let's first get one beautiful champion settled." He took

Montana Wind's reins from her and began to walk down the aisle toward her stall.

"And then?" she asked, smiling and waving at a few people, but wishing she and Huck could have one moment of privacy. They'd hardly ever had that.

"The other champion's choice," he said, and the dark intent in his voice made her feel liquid. "Be creative," he urged banishing even the most cynical of her doubts and fears.

"DANCING UNDER THE stars is one of my favorite things in the world," Willow admitted dreamily. She looked up at him, a warm glow from the strings of party lights woven through the giant oaks in the park bathed her features in a golden glow.

She seemed more relaxed tonight following the steak dinner. Not holding so many pieces of herself back, and he dared himself to hope, but at the same time reminded himself not to push too hard too fast. Like many rodeo events, timing was key. Huck wondered if she'd finally come to an understanding with Jake, if that was why her guard was down, but he didn't want to bring up the other man's name. The other cowboy—now actor—had already sucked too much air out of Huck's week.

Willow sighed and hummed along with the band that

had finally swung into a slow ballad. Not that he minded country dancing. It was fun. Got his blood pumping and allowed for some old-fashioned flirting and showing off his physical skills, but he'd wanted to be alone with Willow. Make love to her. Finally have a moment for themselves.

He couldn't remember feeling so content. He and Willow had watched the bull riding part of the rodeo with the Ballantynes and her family. And then they'd later met up at the steak dinner. He'd allowed himself one beer to relax after a busy week and had enjoyed the conversation and the banter at their table. He'd never been comfortable in crowds or socially—always feeling on the outside. But tonight, seeing Jim and Ben tease each other about old times and being drawn into conversation with Ben's grandsons and their wives, and seeing Willow talk horses with Lang, Bowen's wife, he'd felt for the first time that maybe he could fit into a place, let his guard down, have a home.

He wanted to take the job offered on the Ballantynes' ranch, as long as Jim too intended to get any medical treatment he needed. And then there was the thorny problem of a stubborn cowgirl, and yet tonight, sitting next to her had felt right, almost like being part of a couple. And now dancing…maybe he wasn't that far away from winning her heart.

Heart?

His thudded. Marriage to Willow was a practical option, right? She'd have a steady man she could rely on. A reliable father for her child. Enough income. He'd have…a family.

The hope nearly paralyzed him. It was too big a risk, and yet he had to take it, right? For Jace?

Liar.

The accusation burned, but helping Willow, courting Willow had ceased to be anything about duty, honor and Jace for a long time, and he nearly choked on his terror. He couldn't love her. He had no idea how.

"I like your moves, Cowboy."

She kept her face tucked against his chest so he couldn't tell if she was fun flirting or once again giving him a green light. He swallowed his troubling fears that he was in too deep emotionally. That was dangerous.

"I got other moves too," he said, knowing it was safer to stick to the tools in his toolbox, and sex was a useful and enjoyable one.

"I bet you do." Her laughter was muffled by his shirt.

"I might even bust out one or two later tonight after dessert."

Some cowboys were swinging their partners in slow turns, but Huck didn't want to let Willow go. He hadn't held a lot of women—not like this. His interactions had been professional or short term—both of them looking for something quick, dirty, no strings.

Huck wanted to weave a net to hold on to Willow.

"What kind of dessert are you talking about?" Her eyes sparkling, she looked up at him, her face lit with longing and desire.

She was killing him. Seducing him when he was supposed to be seducing her. Being with Willow eased the sting out of his past and made him feel like the sun rose when she came into a room. With her, he felt he could live in the light. She was everything he would have wanted in a woman if he'd allowed himself to dream.

"They have pie." He pretended to think about it. "And ice cream."

"Perfect," she said as the song ended, and the lead singer began to talk. Seizing his hand, she marched to the dessert table.

Chapter Seventeen

"Oooooh God," Huck groaned through clenched teeth.

They were in Willow's trailer, and if he hadn't already been sprawled on her couch, boots, jeans, briefs off and his shirt undone and stripped by Willow's teeth minutes ago, he would have collapsed.

Willow's idea of dessert was going to destroy his ability to ever eat cherry or apple pie again without getting stiff and needing to rub one out.

"I can't decide what flavor I prefer." She was on her knees in front of him, fully dressed and her mouth, bright red with still-warm cherry pie filling, inches from his straining cock.

"Cherry is delicious," she breathed, sticking her finger in the pie and smearing it on her lips, while staring at him. Then she slowly sucked him deep into her mouth. "Sweet with a hint of savory. And then there's apple."

She took a small bite of the apple pie and then licked and sucked her way up and down his cock again.

The almost too hot pie filing combined with her mouth had him about to come and he wrestled for control, but she'd half-pulled his shirt off so that his arms were trapped, and he didn't want to ruin her fun, but if he couldn't touch her, taste her, he was going to lose it.

"Then there's ice cream." More cherry pie was swirled on his leaking tip. Then she spooned a scoop of ice cream in her mouth and went down on him again, slowly sucking in his length.

He bit back a groan and tried not to thrash. The hot and cold and suck of her lips was heaven and hell. Though most people were still at the steak dinner, trailers were not particularly private for horizontal antics. What he did with Willow was sacred. He didn't want an audience or to give anyone anything to talk about. Every cell in his body screamed at him to seize control and thrust in and out of her mouth, but he breathed through his need.

He dug his fingers into her couch.

"I love your control, Cowboy." She smiled up at him. "But I'm not stopping until you lose it."

"But I want…"

"Ladies first," she interrupted. "Then you'll get your turn."

Huck wanted to make this last, but his control was easily shredded by a gorgeous cowgirl who knew what she wanted and took it.

"Willow," he bit out, struggling free of his shirt. "You gotta stop. I'm gonna come."

Most women hated that.

"Mmmmmm," she murmured against his dick, jacking him up even more than he already was.

She eased off a little but continued with her long licks and playful nips at his tip, soothed by swirling her tongue on him. "We have all night," she promised.

She dipped once more into the ice cream, and he stared fascinated, his breathing ragged and his vision graying a little. What a way to die, but he wanted to live. He wanted… Willow kissed her way up his body, cutting off his last thought and then scooped up another bite of now melting ice cream, fed him, half kissed his lips and then put the rest of the ice cream in her mouth.

"Where was I?"

"Now you're just showing off," Willow said as Huck kissed his way up her spine.

His rumbled laugh made her smile. She stretched a little and turned toward him, a little shocked that she could feel him hardening against her thigh.

"Did you eat an energy bar and down an energy drink when I wasn't looking?"

"When did you stop looking?"

She laughed. "I'm a visual person and you have a lot to look at." She reached for him, palming his erection again. She loved the feel of him, his power and stamina and taste.

He was incredibly generous in bed and seemed fascinated by her body and intent on pleasing her.

"Hey, now." He nipped her shoulder and then licked what felt like a heart shape on her skin. "It's my turn," he prompted, rolling her over and levering himself over her.

"You just had your turn." Willow spread her legs so she could cradle his narrow hips between her thighs. She sighed, feeling so good and wanted.

"Is it a competition? Do we need to thumb wrestle for who gets to initiate first?"

"I'm not complaining," she said, smoothing her hands down his chest. He felt as good as he looked. "I just made a statement."

She kissed his chest, and then his neck, letting her tongue gently trace the scar. Her fingers followed.

"Does it still hurt?"

"Nah," he answered, but she wasn't sure if he was being honest about that. Huck didn't seem like a man who would complain.

She placed her palm over his neck. He'd been injured. Alone. Lucky to survive.

"It's a miracle you're alive," she breathed reverently.

He angled his head back, and she could practically hear his barriers snapping back into place. Dang it. Had she pushed him too far?

"You're the miracle." His voice was rougher, almost a growl.

He lodged his tip at her entrance, distracting her. "Mmmmmm," she moaned savoring his feel, but it wasn't enough. She wanted him to fill her. Over and over. She wanted his power and fire, but he waited, his dark gaze roving over her body with deep appreciation. Desire glittered in his eyes and in the harsh lines of his face.

She sucked in a breath. "Yes, yes."

"Where's my please?" He angled his cock between her seam back and forth, and she shivered underneath him, trying to get him to go faster.

But he smiled, the sweetest smile she'd ever seen. Then he stopped. She bit her lip to keep from screaming and slapped the bed with her palm.

"Huck, I need you to keep moving, now," she bossed.

"I can't hear you."

Who would have guessed Huck would be so playful? She chased his mouth with hers, opening to him, stroking her tongue along his. She could play too. He deepened the kiss and Willow sighed happily, moving against him, simulating what she wanted to do with him.

"Huck," she moaned trying to impale herself on his sheath, but he moved out of reach. "I need you."

"I want to make this last and I need to hear you beg."

She tangled her fingers in his silky dark hair and tugged.

He balanced on one arm and captured her hands, drawing her hands up above her head.

"Huck." She arched up into him. "Please, Huck. I need

you now."

He paused. His eyes were black windows, beautiful, mysterious, locking her out.

"What?" she whispered.

"Willow, I want…" He paused, his face tight with an emotion she didn't understand and, dizzy with desire, wasn't ready for.

She tugged one of her hands free and placed it on his lower back, angling her pelvis up so she could finally have him again.

They both moaned as he sheathed himself inside her and Willow started a slow grind meant to entice, only she quickly lost control as the beginning of another orgasm began to tingle in the pit of her tummy. Then Huck took over, strong and sure, and she hung on to him as bliss bathed her and she hoped she never had to let go.

THE NEXT MORNING, walking beside Huck toward Main Street, Willow felt like she was floating. She felt at one with her body after weeks of feeling alienated, a stranger, after learning about her pregnancy. She practically buzzed and shimmered.

Huck bumped lightly against her as they walked across the bridge.

"Why didn't you want to come to the pancake breakfast?"

She made a face. "I've been avoiding carbs. Pancakes are most definitely carb-loaded."

"Why would you avoid carbs?" he asked curiously.

She looked around, hoping no one was too close to overhear. "I'm trying to control my weight gain, especially until after the finals."

"Whose idea was that?" He sounded ominous.

"Mine," she stated. "I've been seeing a doctor regularly," she defended, seeing his frown, "and she gave me a nutrition list that I've been following."

He spread out his hands. "I know you're smart and responsible, Willow. It's your body and your baby, I just hope that you are…I don't know, enjoying this special, blessed moment in your life."

He led her out of the flow of pedestrian traffic on the other side of the bridge.

She looked at him. "A blessing?" she repeated, marveling at the way the word sounded in her mouth, how it opened something inside her heart that until now she'd kept locked up, unexamined.

"You're creating a life inside you," Huck said. "That's a miracle."

She was. Last night with Huck had been a revelation. He hadn't treated her like an unexploded bomb. Or something alien and a little scary—something to be avoided until she was 'her' again. Jake had been freaked out by the baby, and it was his. Huck treated her like a sexy, very desirable woman.

"I was upset at first," she confessed. "I didn't feel ready. I was focused on my career, and if I had been thinking about starting a family, I wouldn't have chosen Jake. He was fun, but not really…" She paused. Deep? Serious? "Grounded," she finished. "We always wanted different things."

As she spoke, it felt like the whole summer where the conflict that had roared through her causing her to feel angry and helpless had finally settled and clicked into place.

"It's strange," she mused. "I really didn't want to marry Jake, but it made sense for the baby. I wanted to be fair and give him or her the best chance at life. But I got so focused on the money and time we were all spending on the wedding, when there was so much that needed doing. I wasn't thinking of making the homestead house a home. But you and my mom and aunt were. We all pulled together like a family." She marveled as the pieces clicked into place. "Almost becoming whole again in a different way. You did that for us, Huck."

He opened his mouth to speak, but she lightly touched his lips, not wanting to hear about how he did it for Jace. She wanted him to do something for her that had nothing, absolutely nothing, to do with her brother.

Marathon sex wasn't for Jace.

She ignored her own snark. She had to reel herself back in. Huck was a good man. The best. She'd met no one as kind and generous. But she wanted love. And he deserved to find a woman he would love who had no ties to what might be a painful part of his past. Add in another man's baby, and Huck's sacrifice had the potential to be embarrassing in its scope.

She didn't want him to resent her later. She had to give him a graceful out, just as she'd done with Jake.

"But now, I'm looking forward to the baby. I was thinking about the tire swing you hung in the oak tree by the house. I'll be able to swing the baby in it. And the garden my mom and aunt are planting, he or she can help in it. And now that I have my job lined up at Tucker's stables, I don't have as many financial worries because the job comes with insurance."

She was rambling now and couldn't stop with her list proving that she was A-okay for him to leave.

"And Tucker's having a baby too, and she said I can bring my baby to work so I won't have the huge expense of childcare to deal with, at least not right away. I want to be a good mom. I want to be present."

"You're going to be a great mom, Willow."

He meant that. She could tell. His voice even hollowed out a little as if he was holding something in that hurt.

"But Willow…" He took both her hands, brought them to his lips. "You don't have to…"

"Huck, please." She pulled away. It hurt to put the distance between them. Physically and emotionally. She felt as if her blood cooled a few degrees so she was definitely doing the right thing creating distance between them.

"Please, let it be. Last night was wonderful. But that doesn't mean I'm ready to jump into anything with you. I jumped in with Jake for all the wrong reasons. I was thinking about the baby and my mom and family. I don't want to do the same thing with you."

"The reasons wouldn't be wrong."

How could he be so sure? "Huck, I have to consider the baby."

"This has everything to do with the baby," he said, his voice crackling with frustration. He ran a hand through his hair, looking for once slightly agitated.

Of course it did. Any hope she'd foolishly harbored died.

Huck was all about duty.

Not love.

And she wanted, no needed, love and she was very afraid that Huck would be so easy to fall in love with.

Who was she kidding? She'd fallen in love with him before she'd recognized the emotion. He was a good man. Kind. Generous. Reliable. Supportive. Easy to talk to. Easy to love. But she had to keep it together. She had finals to win. One more rodeo and then the finals. Then she had to build a life for herself and her child.

To Huck, she and her child would always be a responsibility.

"Let's just do today," she said carefully. "We've spent so much time together this week. It's been intense, but it's not real."

He stared at her like she'd started speaking French. He swallowed hard, ran his hand through his hair again.

"Feels real," he said softly.

"It's not," she said firmly, amazed her voice didn't shake. "But the pancakes are."

HUCK WOULD BE lying to say he wasn't devastated. No. He shoved that word out of his vocabulary. He'd lived through far worse. He was disappointed. He'd thought that action would work better than words to convince Willow that they'd be a good team. He wasn't good with words, but he'd been trying to ignore the pull between them for a week now and last night he'd deliberately slipped his leash.

Making love with her had been a revelation. For the first time he'd felt a connection to someone, yet Willow had just kicked him in the nuts saying it wasn't real.

He ached and felt as hollowed out as that damn bowl of ice cream Willow had eaten off his body last night. He sat next to her at one of the tables on Main Street with her mom and aunt and quite a few other people he couldn't keep straight. He choked down a couple of bites of a pancake, and then when that nosy, critical woman Carol Bingley won the prize of citizen of the year, Huck had had enough.

"I'm going to…" He didn't know what excuse to use—

take a run, throw a bucket of ice on his head, yell into a pillow? They all seemed absurdly melodramatic. "Later." He nodded and headed back toward the rodeo fairgrounds.

"Hey." Huck heard Cross's familiar voice cut over the happy conversations of families enjoying breakfast and catching up. "Leaving already?" Cross intercepted him. He was with a tall, blonde woman with spectacular eyes. A young teen girl with choppy black hair walked behind the woman. She peered at him suspiciously.

With the look Cross drilled, he might as well have been wearing a stethoscope around his neck and brandishing a handheld ultrasound.

"Shane, this is another Coyote Cowboy, Huck Jones. Huck this is Shane Knight and Arlo."

Cross's manner was easy. His body didn't hold the alert tension Huck was so familiar with. Cross had found a way to belong, a woman who wanted him.

He shook hands and quickly made an excuse.

"I'll walk with you a bit. Shane." He kissed her upturned mouth. "I'll catch you and Arlo up at the Wilder table in a few."

Shane nodded, and she and Arlo walked away down the street chatting.

"What's up?"

"Got two events later. Gonna get my head in the game." Huck kept walking, gaze straight ahead.

"You got hours still."

True. But Huck didn't want to talk. And he definitely didn't want to think. And he didn't want advice from anyone loved up.

"I wanted to do that too." Cross easily kept pace with him. "Run."

"I'm not running. I'm preparing to…"

"Run," Cross said. "You're running."

Huck stopped to save himself the indignity of Cross grabbing his arm, throwing a punch and having him retaliate.

"Ball up. You're a Coyote Cowboy. You stick your ride, and you do what you came to do."

"I did. I walked Willow down the aisle."

"And she got dumped."

"Good riddance." Huck couldn't hold that statement back. Not that it helped him one damn bit. "That was not my fault. The groom was a selfish idiot who would rather pretend to be a cowboy than actually be one, and only wanted to get married because he didn't want to be a deadbeat dad, but it looks to me like that's what he's going to be."

Cross held steady. "Willow's expecting? What you gonna do about that?"

Trust Cross to drill down to the core efficiently "Not my decision."

The look Cross gave him shriveled the hair off his balls.

"We made a vow."

Huck, who felt like punching something, squared off with Cross.

"We made a vow to Jace and each other." Cross was relentless. "But that's not what this is about."

"Yes it is."

"I saw the way you looked at Willow that first day. The way you're always aware of her. And at the steak dinner, everyone else saw it. You handed her your heart, and it's more terrifying than any of our missions that went south."

"You don't know how I feel," Huck seethed.

"You think I felt up to taking on a kid, a woman, learning about my family? Fuck no. But I manned up. I stuck it out. And after two days with Shane, I knew she was the one, and I didn't know what the hell had hit me and how I was going to hang on to her and not F it all up, but I found a way."

"I'll throw a party for you."

"I'll throw a fist through that pretty smile of yours," Cross said. And for a moment Huck wondered if he would. "What I didn't do was run."

Huck sucked in a deep breath. Steadied himself. Then stuck out his hand and Cross grabbed it and slammed him hard into his body and patted him on the back. They stared at each other, and the rest of the world disappeared. He'd been running. All his life.

That had to stop and no day better than today. He dragged in a deep breath. "I'm not running," Huck promised, knowing the words were true, "just regrouping."

"I'll hold you to that," Cross said. "And I expect to see you wearing at least one shiny new buckle tonight when we go for a drink."

"A drink, huh? Think you can pull yourself away from your woman long enough to catch a beer with me?"

"I don't have to. Shane's working tonight at the Graff. My treat. Two birds. Don't dog out."

"Hey, Willow." Lucy sat down beside her at the pancake breakfast.

Huck had just walked off after not talking much or eating anything, and Willow wanted to chase after him even though she knew she'd done the right thing. She needed the distance between them because after last night her barriers and guard were smashed on the ground.

"Good morning," she said. "Where's your crew?"

"Eating. And maybe a little hung over," Lucy said. "I tried to catch you last night, but you left early."

Willow took a sip of her water. "I was tired," she said. "And wanted to feel at the top of my game today."

It sounded better than 'I bounced all night,' although they had tried to keep their noise to a minimum for privacy, which had somehow made it hotter.

"I was so inspired by your story on Thursday about your

brother and his service. I got to thinking about all the men and women who've served our country and come home and struggle to reintegrate—they've changed and the families they've left are different. I stayed up most the night researching—your brother and his unit and programs for vets. There's two other men in Marietta who served with Jace—a Remington Cross and Huck Jones. I interviewed Huck about his transition from the service to the rodeo over at the Ballantyne ranch the other day. And there's a former soldier in town who's started a foundation that…"

Lucy continued to chat and Willow nodded, hopefully in the right places, and zoned out, wondering what Huck was doing.

"Was it hard to forgive him?"

"What?" Lucy was looking at her so intently that Willow realized she'd missed an important piece of the conversation.

"Huck. I mean I know it wasn't his fault exactly, but still. He came home and Jace didn't."

Willow stared at Lucy, willing her to make sense.

"And another weird thing I learned. I don't think Huck Jones is his real name. Well, it is now, but he doesn't seem to exist before he was fifteen. But I don't know if I need to pursue that angle. It's not like he's a criminal or a spy, although even with contacts it was hard to find out much about his service record—need to know, blah, blah, blah. Special Forces."

Lucy cut into her pancakes and took a bite, her expression thoughtful.

"But it's weird not to exist before fifteen and then to have ten years in the service all hush, hush."

"What?"

"The name change was legal—went through the courts in Cody. He's got a social too and a stellar military record though most of it is classified—I have connections, but not that good. But I'm more interested in how it felt to know that Huck was on a mission with your brother, and he came home but your brother didn't. That psychological angle would be interesting to…"

"You know what, Lucy." Willow stood up, her head spinning. "I don't know what you're talking about, and you have a right to film whatever story you want to, but that doesn't mean that the people you're covering have to cough up their lives for you and your crew."

"But it's history, and culture. Sociology. Psychology. Who we are. If we don't study and remember our past, who are we? How can we learn and grow?"

That's what Willow wanted to find out.

Chapter Eighteen

F INDING HUCK WAS not as easy as it seemed. First, she'd been waylaid by the local press, so of course she'd answered some questions and posed with a few local 4-H kids. Then a few fans approached, and Willow had chatted with them and their families. As she finally headed to the fairgrounds, she'd run into Ginny Lane, her friend from high school who now preferred to go by Gin, so she'd chatted with her, her father and her son, Lucas, promising to catch up for lunch after the finals in a few weeks if not before.

Gin was a single mom. Maybe she could get some tips. She could also turn to Tucker and her sisters-in-law who had children of various ages. Tucker had already promised that her twin sister and sisters-in-law could lend her clothes, books and a few loved toys so she wouldn't need to buy everything right away.

But she'd have to wait until she announced her pregnancy. She thought she'd tell her mom and aunt tonight as well as share her plans to move home. She didn't think they'd mind. The small bedroom would be tight when the baby came, but a baby wouldn't need its own room right away would it?

But by the time she finally got to the fairgrounds, people were arriving, grabbing snacks and merchandise and heading to find seats.

Did she really want to do this—chase after Huck, demand to know if he was with Jace when he died? What would that tell her? Did she think Jace had some prescient last words for her or their parents? Would it change anything if he had? She already knew whatever had happened to Jace had been catastrophic and had sent five men on a mission to accomplish things Jace had left undone.

Huck's past was his, yet she'd felt their connection. She'd been thinking they might have a chance…someday if he fell in love with her. She needed that. She also needed a man who was honest with her. Should she confront him before the rodeo events?

Probably not.

But who knew what the future would bring? Life was now or potentially never.

HUCK MOUNTED MIDNIGHT. He'd stuffed all the feelings Willow effortlessly evoked into a dark corner of his brain. Bowen Ballantyne was already mounted on his horse and in the box. He'd agreed to act as his hazer yesterday and today. It wasn't a position Bowen had regularly done for anyone since he'd been a teen, but Bowen seemed to do everything exquisitely well. He'd been fast off the mark, his horse running even with Midnight, and he'd kept the steer boxed in.

When Huck gave the nod, the gate was dropped, the steer ran out, and he and Bowen were fast on the mark. Huck leaned over, dropped, grabbed the horns and twisted. All four legs of the steer were up, and he released. The steer ran off shaking its head, and then ran back to the chute, eager for its treat.

"That's how it's done," Bowen said laconically looking at the score. Two-tenths faster than yesterday.

Somehow Bowen had even managed to snag Midnight, and Huck, pleased with his performance, led Midnight back to his corral, Bowen following.

Willow stood in the middle of the aisle. She looked a little pale but determined. He wasn't sure if he'd see her today except in competition.

"Can we talk?"

"Sure."

He continued to lead Midnight, and she fell in step.

"Thanks." He nodded to Bowen, who was returning his horse to a stall on another aisle. "Not sure if that will be good enough to buckle, but any prize money we can…"

"Keep it," Bowen said. "Helping was self-serving. Checking out your speed and skills since you're a new hire."

"Glad I didn't disgrace myself."

"I had the harder job. Hazers are notoriously underappreciated and blamed if the bulldogger F's up. Excuse my language," Bowen said to Willow as he walked off.

"Good ride," she said.

"What did you want to talk about?" He braced himself while trying to look unaffected.

She followed him to Midnight's stall, fidgeting with her ponytail.

"So you're taking the job at Three Trees Ranch?"

Her voice was neutral as was her expression, but he wished he knew what she was thinking—was she happy about that or wishing him back to Cody?

"Looks like," he admitted. "Jim's going to get some medical tests. He'll stay local for that, then I'll see what comes next. He's a priority for me, and the Ballantynes understand that. But you too, Willow, are…"

"Lucy approached me about some future documentary idea she had about soldiers coming home," Willow said quickly, interrupting as if she could no longer keep the words in. "She got it after talking to you and Colt and Remy at the wedding that wasn't."

He inwardly cursed. "She should have said she *tried* to talk to us about serving and mustering out." He bit out the qualifying word. "But why's that got you upset? She wants you to talk about Jace?"

Willow shrugged that off. "She said you changed your name."

Huck stilled. Even Midnight seemed to hold his breath.

"I know that's your business. It's just…" She broke off. "It's not my business…" She crossed her arms and stared at her toes. "We don't have a relationship. But…I think…I thought…" She sighed. "I thought maybe one day we might when it didn't look so impulsive, but I need you to be honest with me."

He unsaddled Midnight and rested the saddle on the top bar of the corral until he'd groomed Midnight and assessed him for any potential injuries from his sprint.

"It's not a secret," he said soothing himself more than Midnight by running his hands over Midnight's hocks. His horse nuzzled him.

"I told you I didn't have a stable childhood. I lived with different extended family as a little kid and then in and out of foster care. When I came to Jim it was a new start for me. He worked me hard. Made sure I got caught up in school and attended classes and learned how to run a ranch and care for the animals. I was…a pain in the ass. Angry. But I got on board quick. Saw that I had an opportunity. He said I could reframe my life, remake who I was and become the man I wanted to be."

He risked a look at her. As usual, she listened intently, with her whole body.

"He used to call me Huck Finn because I'd had so many adventures, like moving around and having such a flexible life was a good thing, and after a year, I liked it. Gave me power in a way. I chose Jones because there was a ranch hand with that last name who was kind when I first arrived. He treated me with respect instead of like a punk. Taught me how to whittle. Taught me how to cook over a campfire."

"That's a beautiful origin story," she said after a long while.

He stood up, still touching Midnight, the horse's calm contentment helping to ease his nerves. He felt on shaky ground with Willow, and while he'd told Cross he wasn't running, he definitely felt like he needed a new approach. But he hadn't had time to figure one out yet.

"Enough to give us a chance?"

"I don't know. I can't be lied to, Huck. I need honesty between us."

"Of course." He could definitely give her honesty. "I'll never lie to you."

"Really?"

Huck sensed a trap, and yet, he had been honest always with Jim once he'd settled into life on his ranch. Always with the Coyote Cowboys. Their lives depended on being able to trust each other.

"Were you with Jace when he died? Is that how you got that?" She touched her throat.

His stomach bottomed out. He nodded, not trusting his voice, which still was rough and cut out sometimes. The doctors had said he'd probably never sound like he used to, but it was a small price to pay considering he was alive and fairly healthy whereas Jace was dead.

"Tell me."

"We were together. Pinned down. I was trying to get a better position. I stepped on a rock that tumbled, giving away our position. Jace threw me down, covered me. He was hit more than me."

He waited for her condemnation.

"He protected you."

Huck nodded. "I couldn't stop the bleeding," he admitted. "I tried. I had my medical first aid kit with the pressure bandages we use in the field, but it was too much, too quickly, and I had to move him."

"Thank you for telling me. Thank you for trying to save his life. Thank you for caring enough that you came to Marietta to carry out his last wishes." Her voice was a somber ache.

"But, Willow, he's dead because of me."

"No, he's dead because he was killed by a sniper or shooter or whoever else was out there looking for you. You did your best and that's all anyone can ask, and I'm relieved he didn't die alone."

He sagged with relief.

"You don't owe Jace anything else."

"This isn't about Jace anymore," he said roughly.

"I need to be loved, Huck. I want to be loved like Tucker's husband loves her. And how your new boss Bowen loves Lang."

He nodded. "You deserve that, Willow." He dragged in a deep breath. She wanted honesty, and he intended to always give her that. "I can't do that." The words felt ripped out of his chest. "I don't know how to love. I don't know what love would look like. But I can give you my loyalty. My best effort every day. Honesty. Respect. I can be a friend. Companion. Lover. Father for your child and ours if we are blessed." He felt like lightning struck him, and he looked at his chest as if he'd see a smoking, blackened hole where his heart was.

She didn't immediately respond. And for a moment he hoped he would be enough. The silence was a cold wind between them, snatching away the dream he hadn't acknowledged he had.

She stepped forward, looking at him through the fencing of the corral.

"The thing is, Huck, you're selling yourself short. You deserve love too."

BRAVE WORDS SHE'D used pushing Huck away. Necessary ones. But instead of feeling righteous that she'd done the right thing and stood up for herself, she wanted to problem-solve, bargain, and maybe cry a little.

Instead, she and Montana Wind had their rounds to run and a final to win.

Huck had won the bucking-bronc final and placed second in steer wrestling. She'd watched both, silently cheering him on even though they were over.

Now barrels were beginning, and she dug deep for discipline. She was a cowgirl, and she knew how to work hard and win.

And win she did. Montana Wind did her job and Willow did hers.

When she made her final pass at the last barrel, she straightened out of the turn, giving her horse a light tap and loosening the reins so Montana Wind would race back down the alleyway. Willow felt like cheering herself.

Montana Wind was in peak condition, and if Willow had been thinking about possibly having this be her last race and not attend the finals, Montana Wind's performance this afternoon put that permanently to bed.

She popped off her horse and hugged Montana Wind, giving her a peppermint. The announcer talked over the cheering crowd. Willow made her way out to the arena to claim her prize and even though she'd felt she'd cut the last thread with Huck, she intended to savor this win and this moment.

Usually, she didn't like the often lame and repetitive interview questions, but today she listened, and focused on giving thoughtful answers. She saw Lucy and her crew working, and she wondered how she would decide what made the rodeo documentary cut and what didn't. Could life be so precise—cut what you didn't want out and keep what you did?

She had a momentary panic when the interviewer mentioned that this weekend had been a particularly important one for her.

"Yes, it was," she admitted. "We had a celebration at my mom and aunt's childhood home commemorating the life of my brother who died in service to our country this year and also my father who, in his grief, killed himself."

The crowd quieted, and that was the moment she spotted Huck sitting with his friend and the Wilders. She nearly lost her train of thought, but when Huck's dark gaze clashed with hers, she felt strength and a sense of belonging that had almost always been absent in her life.

The rest of what she said was unplanned, but it felt right.

"And I wanted to share with you all that I will be donating one-quarter of my winnings to Colt Wilder's foundation for veterans and also one-quarter to Harry's House and the newly planned Harry's House Annex that will serve the teens of Marietta. Marietta has always been a welcoming community, and I want to always remember my roots, but also to help others in our community dig strong roots here."

She would not look at Huck. She would not.

She did. His dark gaze and shuttered expression gave her nothing to work with, but she didn't need anything. She'd been alone for a long time, and she was fine on her own.

Chapter Nineteen

"Yes, the cancer's returned," the oncologist said. "We caught it early, and I'd like to discuss treatment options."

Huck had been bracing for a disaster, feeling a little dizzy as if he'd been holding his breath. "Okay," he said to the specialist, who didn't look much older than he was. "We want to hear all of the options."

"How long I got?" Jim asked, finally voicing a question after a week where Huck had driven him to several doctor's appointments for tests and consults.

"Depends," she said. "You planning on engaging in any TikTok challenges—Benadryl or Tide Pod, drinking a gallon of water at one time?"

"Huh?"

The specialist smiled.

"What's Tik-whatever, and who'd do a fool thing like that?" Jim demanded.

"Said the man who always had a wad of chew in his cheek for forty years."

"Thirty-eight, and I stopped because you kept on me like a rat terrier."

"A rat terrier." The specialist eyed Huck speculatively, amusement glimmering in her brown eyes. She was compassionate and attractive, but he felt nothing.

He wondered if he'd feel anything again, or if he even wanted to.

The last couple of weeks had felt long and lonely even though he'd been surrounded by people—Bowen and Beck Ballantyne and several ranch hands. He was starting to learn his way around the ranch—the skills came back, but his days had been broken up by taking Jim into Bozeman. Jim had been stoic and hadn't kicked up the fuss Huck had expected. He was still a guest at the Ballantyne ranch, and it was practically turning into an old folks' home, Huck had teased, because Ben was also hosting another rancher friend who was recovering from a fall off his horse. The three men stayed up late each night playing poker and streaming *Yellowstone*, opining on what the writers got wrong and sometimes right.

Seeing Jim with friends and having a good time had eased the sting of knowing that Willow was on the road, alone.

He'd settled into his cabin—not that he had much more than clothes. But he'd bought a bed—king size because he was an idiot and couldn't quite give up hope. He'd also purchased a cherry armoire that Willow had admired at the barn sale. And he'd ordered kitchen supplies—hadn't used them or put them away except his coffee maker and mugs.

He listened to the specialist, collected the literature she

had and scheduled a follow-up appointment for next week with the 'team.'

"We take a team approach here because cancer and the treatment impacts all of the body and the family. We want to have all of you covered," she said as if she were giving a public service announcement. "We also team up with Marietta General, so Jim will be able to have most of his appointments there as I think that will be more convenient for you, especially once the snow starts falling."

"That's good." Huck felt another weight lift.

As they drove home, he thought Jim would be quiet. But no, he'd wanted to stop at a Starbucks.

"Seriously?"

"Yeah, Ben's taken me and Sam Wilder out to that Java Café a couple of times. He has a Monday morning coffee group. We've been drinking fancy coffees."

Huck had never known Jim to drink fancy anything. His coffee looked like tar. "Aren't you supposed to limit your sugar intake?"

He'd read that in the literature that cancer could feed on sugar. Or maybe with all the fancy coffees, Jim would become diabetic. Jim was a meat and potatoes man—maybe a vegetable here or there.

"Why?" Jim looked at him. "Think I'll get cancer or something?"

"Funny. I'm more worried you might turn sweet."

"Nah that's you. I saw that flower website open on your

phone in the waiting room last week."

"Snoop."

"She come around yet?"

"No, and I don't need wooing advice from you."

"Good. I got none."

Huck pulled into the Starbucks parking lot. He intended to go through the drive-through, but Jim wanted to get out and see what they had on the menu.

"Here fall the last two people in America who haven't been in a Starbucks," Huck intoned.

"Sam Wilder hasn't," Jim said. "Ben said he'd drive me to one of my fool appointments and drag Sam with so we'd all go to a Starbucks, but I beat Sam to it."

Jim stared at the menu for a long time and asked a lot of questions. Huck expected the teenage barista in the green apron to roll her eyes, but she never did. She explained the drinks, told him how she made them and what was in them, and then he discussed some of the drinks he'd tried at the Java Café, and she suggested something that Jim agreed on.

"You should win employee of the month or maybe the year," Huck commented as he paid.

"Make him one of those too," Jim said. "He needs a little sweetness. And we'll take some of these cookies. They sound French."

The two of them probably looked like they'd just exited an underground bunker, and that was before Huck tried to swallow his shock that the two drinks and a package of madeleines cost nearly fifteen dollars.

"You gotta tip," Jim said taking the change from him and putting it in a square hard plastic tip jar. "Ben told me."

When they were back on the road, Jim contentedly sipping on his frozen whatever he'd ordered for them, he opened the cookie package and handed Huck one.

"What's the hang-up with Willow?"

"What?" he asked around a mouthful of cookie that was surprisingly good. He still hadn't worked up the courage to try the drink he couldn't pronounce.

"What's she want you don't got?"

It would be useless to evade the question. They still had thirty miles plus and Jim had become chattier over the summer.

"Love."

"Love," Jim ruminated taking another long sip. "Yeah. I can see it. Why's that a problem?"

He stared at Jim and then looked back to the road.

"Why you sending her flowers and a bunch of those rodeo cowboy boot chocolates from Copper Mountain Chocolates if you don't love her?"

"Do you know the passcode to my phone or something?" Huck had had the chocolates delivered to the house when he'd heard Willow had come home for the week before the finals. He'd also had a fruit basket and a collection of olive oil and spices delivered to the homestead house.

"The date you came to live with me," Jim said with satisfaction. "You were always a sentimental kid."

"I was not." Huck was outraged by that view of the past.

Jim continued to sip, and he even fished out some whipped cream with his straw and sucked on it.

"Do you love her?"

"You know what I came from. I don't know how to love." He was practically shouting now, and he made an effort to calm himself by reaching for his drink. He took an experimental sip. And then a longer one. Dang that was…so many flavors. Sweet but not cloying like he'd imagined.

"Is there coffee in this?"

"They say so. Why do you think you can't love? You were a very sensitive and loving kid."

"What? I was a sullen, mouthy, broody, angry kid, and I barely had two years of education combined before you got a hold of me."

"Your first week with me, you helped deliver a calf in the middle of the night. That was one of the most difficult births I'd seen. The vet arrived and told you to stick your arm up the birth canal, and you pulled and maneuvered and listened to the vet and helped no matter how bloody, and when the mama was too exhausted to nurse the calf, you cleaned it, wrapped it up, and slept with it in the warming barn, feeding the little rascal every couple of hours, and you kept trying to get the mama to nurse. You kept the stall clean, did your chores and completed your lessons in the barn. That ain't a kid who can't love. You named that calf and let it follow you around while you did your chores."

Jim lowered the truck seat and leaned back.

"You may guard your heart, but you got one. If you're too afraid to open up, that's on you, not wherever you were born or whatever happened to you when you were little. Love and happiness are a choice."

Jim closed his eyes, still holding his partially finished drink on his chest. After a few minutes, Huck moved the drink to the cup holder and finished his while thinking about Willow and how she had the finals coming up and would that be a good time for a grand gesture, or would it mean more if he waited until she came home for good?

WILLOW TURNED OFF the highway and took the back roads until she hit the gravel road that led to the long driveway to the homestead house.

"Home sweet home," her mother said from the back seat of the truck. "Although I enjoyed being away for the whole week much more than I thought I would, Willow. And seeing you win—it was so intense. I think Barb still has bruises from me clutching her arm so many times. Seeing you race around those barrels so fast and cutting it so tight is thrilling."

"Thank you," Willow said, putting the visor down on the truck as the sun lowered enough that it was right in her eyes.

"The road feels different," Barb said.

"I know. I don't feel like I'm bruising my kidneys," Willow marveled. She drove a little farther. "It is smoother." She rolled down her window to get a better look out the side of the truck. "The potholes are filled in and the road is regraded." Her voice rang with wonder. "I was going to wait until next spring to even attempt it but…did you two surprise me?"

"Sorry, no," Barb said. "We were hoping to get the small barn for the goats built before it got too late, but we haven't booked the workers yet. I didn't think we had the money yet to take the road on this year or next probably."

"We do now," Willow said thinking of her earnings. She'd treated all of them to a spa day while they were at the finals to celebrate themselves and also the baby.

Her mom hadn't acted surprised—she'd noticed the glow, but also something was 'different about Willow's eyes.' Willow let that late maternal pronouncement go. Her aunt was excited for her and to have a baby in the house next spring. She'd offered to switch bedrooms, but Willow had demurred.

"So we have a mystery on our hands," Willow said as she turned the final curve onto their land.

No. They had more than one mystery.

"What?" Willow got out of the truck slowly, staring at the house.

It had been repainted white and with the green tin roof it

looked cute rather than too far to the left of rustic. But there was more. The three women walked toward the garden in awe. Where last week there had been waving dead grass, there was now a fully fenced pasture, and a gate to another fully fenced pasture. In one of the pastures there was a sturdy-looking small barn painted to match the house and the horse barn, and what looked like a rustic children's play structure. Willow counted six goats playing on it while several more turned from their grazing to look at them. Bellowing loudly the goats ran to the fence, jumping up and sticking out their tongues.

"Goats. They're here. Willow you've surprised us." Barb hurried to the fence, already cooing. Willow blinked at the change in her usually serious aunt. Her mom walked more sedately, looking around, taking everything in.

There was now a covered picnic area behind the house and a picnic table was partially set. There was a pail with different drinks chilling in ice.

The back door of the house opened, and Huck walked out carrying a picnic basket. He stopped when he saw her.

"You're early."

"Maybe I'm late?"

He looked so beautiful. She hadn't seen him in seventeen days, and every one of those days had been long and while not dark, exactly, they'd felt pale and empty. She kept walking toward him. She wanted to run and throw her arms around him, but she was too afraid of never being able to let go.

But he was here, and Huck would never play with her. He didn't have a cruel or manipulative bone in his body.

"Did you do all this?"

"I did with some help."

"Why?" They were face-to-face now.

"Shane says doing things is my love language."

"The bartender at the Graff Hotel?"

"Yeah. She's a former army shrink it turns out and kind of a sister-in-law as she and Cross are getting married. And that got me thinking."

"It did?"

"I was wrong."

Her heart kicked up, but she didn't want to hope, not just yet, but how could she not? Huck had had their road regraded and graveled. He'd build a flipping goat enclosure, shelter and playhouse. He'd planned a picnic dinner for her family.

"It happens."

"Probably a lot to me, fair warning. But Jim reminded me that I do know how to love—something about a calf, which was rather a gruesome and gooey story that's not as romantic a story to tell you as I was hoping. Besides it's hard to be romantic with your mom and aunt here with us, but as a bonus, I never had a family and now I'm hoping that maybe I do."

"I love you," she said without hesitation. "From the beginning you made me feel special and seen and cherished, and I fell so hard, but I had the baby and Jake and a head full of doubt to sort through."

"And now?" He cupped her face, his face so serious she wanted to cry and laugh at the same time.

"No doubt. I love you, Huck. I want to be a family with you—me, the baby, my tarot-reading mom who actually made several hundred dollars at the finals reading for people randomly. I think she will need a booth at the market, and I'll also give you my goat-loving aunt."

He pulled her in to his body, and Willow felt that finally, finally she was home.

"I love you." He held her so tightly she could barely breathe, but she so didn't care.

"Will you marry me, Cowboy, please?"

"Absolutely. As many times as you wish. Will you marry me?"

"Yes, but not in that mermaid dress."

He trembled in her arms, and his heart pounded as hard as hers did, and it amazed her that this strong, generous, gorgeous man was hers.

"You can wear whatever you want as long as you say I do."

"I do." She smiled up at him and, not caring if her mom or aunt were watching, she stood on her tiptoes and kissed her cowboy.

The End

The Coyote Cowboys of Montana series

Book 1: *The Cowboy's Word*

Book 2: *Marry Me Please, Cowboy*

Book 3: *The Cowboy's Christmas Homecoming*

Book 4: *The Cowboy's Charm*

Book 5: *Coming soon*

Available now at your favorite online retailer!

The 85th Copper Mountain Rodeo Series

Book 1: *Take Me Please, Cowboy* by Jane Porter

Book 2: *Tempt Me Please, Cowboy* by Megan Crane

Book 3: *Marry Me Please, Cowboy* by Sinclair Jayne

Book 4: *Promise Me Please, Cowboy* by C.J. Carmichael

See Carol Bingley's story in....
The Untold Story of Carol Bingley by Jane Hartley

Available now at your favorite online retailer!

More Books by Sinclair Jayne

Montana Rodeo Brides series

Book 1: *The Cowboy Says I Do*

Book 2: *The Cowboy's Challenge*

Book 3: *Breaking the Cowboy's Rules*

The Texas Wolf Brothers series

Book 1: *A Son for the Texas Cowboy*

Book 2: *A Bride for the Texas Cowboy*

Book 3: *A Baby for the Texas Cowboy*

The Wilder Brothers series

Book 1: *Seducing the Bachelor*

Book 2: *Want Me, Cowboy*

Book 3: *The Christmas Challenge*

Book 4: *Cowboy Takes All*

The Misguided Masala Matchmaker series

Book 1: *A Hard Yes*

Book 2: *Swipe Right for Marriage*

Book 3: *An Unsuitable Boy*

Book 4: *Stealing Mr. Right*

Available now at your favorite online retailer!

About the Author

Sinclair Sawhney is a former journalist and middle school teacher who holds a BA in Political Science and K-8 teaching certificate from the University of California, Irvine and a MS in Education with an emphasis in teaching writing from the University of Washington. She has worked as Senior Editor with Tule Publishing for over seven years.

Writing as Sinclair Jayne she's published fifteen short contemporary romances with Tule Publishing with another four books being released in 2021. Married for over twenty-four years, she has two children, and when she isn't writing or editing, she and her husband, Deepak, are hosting wine tastings of their pinot noir and pinot noir rose at their vineyard Roshni, which is a Hindi word for light-filled, located in Oregon's Willamette Valley. Shaandaar!

Thank you for reading

Marry Me Please, Cowboy

If you enjoyed this book, you can find more from all our great authors at TulePublishing.com, or from your favorite online retailer.

Made in United States
Troutdale, OR
11/01/2023

14213164R00183